THE MARK OF SIX

S. Twaddell

D1304901

Facebook:
https://www.facebook.com/AuthorSTwaddell/

CHAPTER ONE

Amber drummed her fingers across the steering wheel while she watched Robert Kariot's front door from the driver seat of her car. If he stuck to his usual Sunday routine, and she had no reason to think he would change it, he would be going for his run in about five minutes. She turned the engine off. *Don't want to scare him off,* she thought.

The slow approach of a dark gray sedan reflected in her sideview mirror caught her attention. Her fingers stopping drumming when she saw the driver and when she caught sight of the old man in the backseat, she shed her impatience and replaced it with anger. Although anger was a mild term for what she was feeling. There was only one reason for them to be here and she would be damned if they were going to stop her now. The memory of her brother's words crept into her mind like a whisper, *Patience, little one.* She blew out of frustrated breath, she was tired of being patient.

The car pulled to a stop on the opposite side of the road and the driver immediately got out. He slithered to the rear of the car in his designer suit and opened the trunk. Amber's view of the other occupant was blocked but she did not mind, it provided an opportunity of its own for her.

"Sorry brother," she whispered as she pushed her door open and stepped out into the early morning.

The sun was barely over the rooftops and the air was already warm, promising it would be another hot Arizona day. She gently pushed her door closed and quickly scanned the area. There was no one else in sight and that

1

bothered her. *Where are the others?* she pondered. The old man should have had four guards with him, they always traveled with four. She crossed the street quickly, spinning a silencer onto her 9mm as she went. *Please God, let this be the beginning of the end,* she hoped and began praying to herself.

> *Our Father who art in heaven,*
> *Hallowed be thy name.*
> *Thy kingdom come. Thy will be done.*
> *On earth as it is in heaven.*
> *Give us our daily bread, And forgive us our*
> *trespasses.*

Before the driver could turn around and get a good look at who was coming she raised the gun and fired. The bullet caught him just behind the ear and other side of his head exploded outward covering the inside of the trunk in his blood. The force of the blow carried his upper body into the trunk and allowed her to scoop up his legs and toss the rest of him in. She could not afford Robert getting wind of any of this just yet.

> *As we forgive those who trespass against us.*
> *And lead us not into temptation,*
> *But deliver us from evil.*

She slammed the lid closed and saw the terrified look of the old man staring at her from the backseat. He lunged for the door and Amber darted around to the driver side of the car just as he pushed it open.

"For thine is the kingdom, and the power, and the glory, for ever and ever," she finished aloud with a joyless smile while pushing him back into the car so she could slide onto the seat next to him. "Hello Bishop Phillip."

"You," was all the old man could get out before Amber shot him in the chest.

"Amen," she whispered and looked out the back window as Robert opened his front door and started trotting down his walkway before breaking into a jog down the street. She was thankfully he was going in the other direction and did not have to see her fire three more rounds into the old man.

She thought about going after him but held herself in check. *There's three more of them around here somewhere,* she considered, *plus Justin.* She was not sure where they were, but she knew where they were going to be as she eyed Robert's home. She had always wanted to see the inside of his house and now seemed like a perfect time.

CHAPTER TWO

Even for Arizona it had been an unusually dry summer. People still flooded their yards from the river valves on their appointed day with the nectar of life in an attempt to appease the lawn gods. It was a feeble attempt at best and when the heat of the day hit its highest point some people would say that they swore they could hear the sun laughing at them. Inevitably, the grass was slowly turning to brown and the roads were slowly cracking under the strain of the scorching days and hot nights, but in the early morning magic hour Robert still found the road calling to him and he always answered its summons.

Normally, he would have turned on the morning news before heading out, but today he was tired of hearing the same depressing headlines over and over. Killings here. Murders over there. It never seemed to end. Lately it was the environment that had been taking center stage. Recent earthquakes had hit the Pacific Ocean near Hawaii which caused Tsunami warnings to be issued all along the west coast, but nothing had come of it. Except now the over the top environmentalists and the fear mongers were out in droves. Not that he was opposed to being environmentally conscious. He had after all spent the last eight years of life working to make energy resourcing more efficient but holding up a sign was not going to stop the Earth's tectonic plates from shifting.

He thought about the last news reports he had listened to and realized there did seem to be an increase in the number of earthquakes reported around the world in the last month. Two in Japan had made the headlines just before the one near Hawaii. There was one at the beginning of last week in the Middle East and a week before that there was a minor one off the east coast, somewhere by Maryland. Robert shrugged his shoulders. Even if it was the end of the world it was not like he could do anything about it.

He gave up thinking about the environment. He had been thinking about it all week at work. It was time to turn that part of his mind off, at least for a little while. He concentrated on his breathing instead until the rhythm became second nature. Eventually, Kate drifted into the forefront of his thoughts, along with the good and bad memories that came with her. *When was the last time I saw her?* he wondered. *Six weeks, give or take a few days.*

He still could not understand how one woman could have such an effect on him, but Kate was not just any woman. She was like heroin, only more addictive, and the two of them had been each other's puppet for the past five years in an on-again, off-again relationship. There was an old saying about opposites attracting one another and the two of them had certainly been that. Fire and ice, yin and yang, day and night. Mixed up in a reality where they both had been tied so close to each other that they should have seen that it was only a matter of time before their strings got all tangled and knotted. Maybe they had seen it and just did not care.

There was something different about Kate when they broke up this last time. There was a look in her eyes and tiredness in her voice that told him their relationship was finally over for good. He guessed that sometimes, when the knots finally got bad enough, the only way to get a string untangled was to cut it and make a fresh start. Truth be told, a part of him was glad that it was over. When things were good between them, they were really good, but when things were bad and it turned ugly, neither one of them knew how to back down. It could be days, weeks, even a couple of months, but eventually one of them would apologize and they would find themselves together once more.

After so many years in a chaotic relationship it was hard to remember what a normal life felt like. But out here in the rising heat there was only the road and the rhythmic breathing accompanying putting one foot in front of the other. It was these Sunday morning jogs that offered Robert a time for self-reflection and why he gladly accepted the offer of freedom it provided.

The dry cracked asphalt sounded like sandpaper under his feet as Robert approached the half-way point in his run. His mind lost in a blissful void of nothingness. Usually this would have been a generally quiet time to go running, but the growing sound of a quiet-shattering siren had warned him of a police car's approach before it arrived. In only a matter of seconds the siren had grown from a distant reminder of all the things wrong with the faraway world to an ear-piercing shriek demanding to be heard as the first of three squad cars rocketed by. As each vehicle passed it was almost as if Robert could feel the energy of the world shifting, like some form of premonition, dark, chilling, and warning him to keep on running. He glanced at his wristwatch; 8:00am.

It had taken him thirty-three minutes to reach the usual spot he used as a half way point, an isolated street sign about four miles from his home, and another forty-two minutes to make the return trip. Less than an hour and a half had passed in total from the time he had left his house to the time he returned. He was drenched in sweat but felt refreshed, clear headed, and free from his earlier dark reflections as he jogged around the final corner towards home looking forward to a cup of ice coffee and a long lukewarm shower.

Unfortunately, it appeared a peaceful morning was still going to be elusive. Less than one hundred yards away from his house, the street was clogged with emergency vehicles and personnel. The vehicle emergency lights were still ablaze, piercing flashes of red and blue, but thankfully the sirens had been silenced. The three police cars that had raced past Robert almost a half hour ago had been joined by two other patrol cars, an ambulance, and a fire truck. Their occupants were swarming like ants next to a nondescript dark gray sedan that was parked along the opposite side of the road, only three houses away from his. As the first emergency cones began to block off the street Robert spotted his next-door neighbor at the corner of the white picket fence that divided their yards.

Justin Rury had moved into the house next to Robert about one month ago. It was a fast sale, all cash. Robert had not even known the cozy two-bedroom ranch had gone on the market before Justin was moving in. He had gone over that first weekend and introduced himself and found his new neighbor to be quite accommodating. In fact, the two men had spent several evenings getting to know one another over cups of coffee or imported Italian red wine.

"Morning Justin," Robert announced as he closed the remaining gap between the two of them. "What's going on?"

Startled, Justin spun to face Robert. He seemed at a loss for words when he saw Robert approaching him. "Robert. You're alive."

"I'm fine, just getting back from my run. What's going on over there?" Robert asked again coming to a stop just beyond Justin's reach. It almost seemed to Robert that his friend appeared to have grown a good deal older since yesterday.

"A bishop was murdered," Justin answered, all traces of his lingering confusion replaced with a quiet anger Robert had never witnessed before.

"A bishop? When was this?"

"An hour ago, maybe. It must have been right after you went on your run, or just before. Did you see anything?" But he continued before Robert could answer him. "He was shot. I didn't hear any gun shots, but someone shot him while he was sitting in his car. I was just coming out front when I heard Liz screaming. She found him when she was taking Jack for a walk."

Robert did not see Liz or her beloved black Labrador, Jack, anywhere although he suspected the police were questioning her somewhere. "Why would anyone kill a priest? Especially here? Actually, what was a priest doing here to begin with?" he puzzled aloud looking around as if he might actually spot the killer standing idly by as events unfolded, but he only spotted the neighbors emerging to peer down the road.

Part of the reason he had bought his home in this part of town was for its tranquility. People said hello to one another, even if they did not know each other. The world was changing and apparently not for the better, it seemed. He had been thinking about selling the house and now that his research was just about complete perhaps this was a sign to do just that. Robert turned his attention back to Justin just as the guilt caught up to him at feeling happy that he was not the victim. "What about the guy who did it, did they catch him?"

"I don't think so," Justin replied, staring intently at Robert. "They haven't done much beyond what you see. Maybe they'll find something."

"Hopefully, but it seems we better get back inside," Robert advised when he noticed for the second time how the two of them had gained the attention of a young officer. The man did not seem thrilled with the aspect of citizens hanging around outside while a killer was on the loose and Robert had to agree. "Lock your door and all that stuff. Better safe than sorry you know."

Justin gave him a nod and started back towards the wrought iron gate that led to his backyard.

Robert jogged to his house and down the walkway. From what he could tell, his front door still seemed intact and he did not notice anyone hiding out front. Not that there were many places a person could hide in his modest garden of weeds. Other than a two-foot Mexican Honeysuckle plant, he kept the front of his single story, beige, ranch open to let the morning light provide a warm glow behind his drawn shades. The door, electronically locked, gave a welcoming motorized hum when he keyed in his code and the dead bolt slid open allowing him to enter his sanctuary.

There was a small rectangular table made of mahogany that had been his parents sitting against the wall next in the entranceway. It was adorned with yesterday's mail and a small digital clock that changed to 9:00AM as he walked in and kicked the door closed behind him. He had only taken a few steps past the heirloom when he realized the door had only closed halfway and was going to go back and finish the job before the automatic lock activated again but froze midturn.

His living room opened to his left. It was a small, sparsely furnished room. Its only contents were a glass top mahogany television stand, a knee-high glass top coffee table, and a tan sofa that sat next to the windows where a young woman he did not know sat waiting. She was sitting very still, in an almost dignified pose, was petite with olive skin and casually held a glistening handgun in her lap. A similar gun lay on the coffee table in front of her, but it was not the guns that Robert noticed. At least not at first. The first thing he saw, the thing that froze him in his place, were her eyes. Everything else about her in that first moment was a haze.

Her eyes were the color of pale blue ice, like the color of a glacier, with edges that were frosted in white and gave the impression she was staring at nothing. There was a vacancy in them. A depiction of an emptiness which was interrupted only by a rare blink of dark lashed eyelids. It was as if she was lost in some sort of daydream and did not realize Robert was even there, but he knew all too well that she was acutely aware of his presence.

His father had had that same stare after having served too many tours in a war zone. A look born from seeing more misery and death than any one person should ever have to. From learning that, in order to survive, you needed to be able to see everything at once. Robert knew she saw him, was watching and gauging him.

The pistols were the second thing he noticed. First, the one on the table, then the one in her lap and he did not need anything else to make an immediate connection to the crime scene outside. It was in those few short seconds that he looked away from her face and back that he found she had rotated her head slightly, a mere inch, but that was all she needed to shift her lifeless stare and bring him into her full view. By the time he blinked again her lifeless stare was gone, replaced with a bitter gaze that was focused solely on him.

Robert Kariot had only been home for thirty seconds, but it felt like the morning had come and gone. The two of them remained unmoving, Robert standing, her seated, as the distant cry of more sirens approaching entered the silent house. Just as Robert began to think of his options, this small woman moved with a speed Robert did not think possible. She launched herself from the couch, twisting herself to level her gun at him.

"On your knees grandson of Carl and Kate Kariot." She ordered as she took a step toward him.

He was frozen, not sure what to do, when he caught sight of the movement of another person in his kitchen and glanced down the short hall to see Justin creeping in with a knife in hand. He was looking at Robert with the expression of someone that was ready to kill. Whatever his friend had in mind Robert was sure it was a horrible idea. He wanted to scream at Justin to get out. The police were just down the road and he should be getting them not trying to stalk his way through Robert's home.

His glance must have been too long or given too much away because abruptly she was next to him. The fraction of a second he had to react was not enough. She grabbed him with one arm and used his imbalance to throw him into the living room. Before he slid to a crashing stop on the tiled floor he heard the *phut* of the silencer as the handgun discharged. He scrambled to his feet. Anger, panic and adrenalin kicked in and he hurled himself at her.

What happened immediately after that Robert could not understand. He saw and felt the world blurring around him. All he had to do was strike her and run yet somehow in that brief moment after he hit her he somehow went from being the attacker to a dazed victim. A second later his head was slammed against the hallway wall, cracking the drywall but not the beam behind it which nearly knocked him out. He had no time to recover before the shockwave of pain lancing up and down his body was replaced by a more focused and intense pain of something being pushed very hard against his temple.

A new level of fear gripped Robert as his dazed thoughts cleared and he realized she was pinning him to the wall using the silencer of her pistol.

CHAPTER THREE

Robert tried to strike at her with a weak kick, but she easily out maneuvered him and in response she twisted her hips and drove her knee into the soft flesh of his inner thigh before he could get his leg back down. A guttural sound of pain leapt from Robert's lungs and he would have collapsed if she was not squeezing his head so hard to the wall.

"Don't!" She hissed into his ear. "I've waited too long for this day."

To emphasize the point, she pushed the silencer even harder against his skull. He involuntarily gasped for air, squeezed his eyes shut, and held his arms up in feign resignation. He was alive, at least for the moment, and that was what was important. She had not killed him yet and even in his confused, pain packed mind he believed there had to be a reason for that.

Justin lay still and sprawled in the hallway. His head was tilted to the side letting Robert see the jagged circular wound in his forehead and the blood pooling on the tile floor in a near perfect circle around his head. His hand was near his side and still curled loosely around an ornamental dagger he had purchased overseas. The jet-black handle of the blade, inlaid with silver and gold trim, held a depiction of Jesus on the cross. Robert had always thought it an odd religious symbol to possess, but Justin had told him to read Matthew, chapter 10, verses 32 through 38 and he would understand. Robert had looked the verses up on his computer but found Justin's interpretation troubling.

Whosoever therefore who shall confess me before men, him will I also confess before my Father which is in heaven. But whosoever shall deny me before men, him will I also deny before my Father which is in heaven. Think not that I come to send peace on earth; I came not to send peace, but a sword. For I came to set man at variance against his father, and the daughter against her mother, and the daughter in law against her mother in law. And a man's foes shall be they of his own household. He that loveth the father or mother more than me is not worthy of me; and he that loveth son or daughter more than me is not worthy of me. And he that doth not taketh his cross, and followeth after me, is not worthy of me.

"Robert Kariot, the sixth son of Paul and Vanessa," the woman with pale eyes stated. Her voice was cold, disconnected, and totally focused on Robert which he found even more frightening. She had murdered his friend, probably the priest as well, and here she stood over him reciting his family linage as though she had already forgotten about the body growing cold in the hallway.

Robert needed time, even seconds if that was all he was going to get, so he slowly nodded.

"Where's your car?" she demanded, releasing his head and moving a step back to grab his key ring off the mahogany table.

"Outside," he lied, pointing towards the door. All he had to do was get her outside and the police would bring this nightmare to a close. "At the curb."

She stepped up next to Robert just as he was getting to his feet and drove her knee into his stomach with enough force to double him over. He slumped back to the ground gasping for air. "You shouldn't lie Robert. Your motorcycle is in the garage, but lately you've been riding to work with a colleague," she stated matter-of-factly and threw his keys into his face. "Didn't you learn not to screw with me yet, or should I throw you around some more?"

"If...you're...so...smart...why ask?" Robert hissed between gasps of air.

"Because I want you and I to understand one another Robert," she explained in a calm, controlled, and unconcerned voice as she squatted down next to him.

Robert looked at the pistol she held loosely between her legs. Before he could even finish the thought of making a grab for it he pushed the idea aside. Instead he continued sucking in air, waiting for her to say more, but when she did not he raised his head and looked at her.

"Come on Robert. It's time to go," she said and stood back up.

Robert staggered to his feet and caught sight of the digital clock sitting on his parent's table, 9:06AM. *Six minutes*, he thought. Six minutes ago, he had had a fairly normal life until he came through his front door.

She tossed her pistol next to the clock and it landed with a loud bang. Robert jumped at the sound and stared at it.

"If you think I need a gun, I don't," she threatened and pushed him out the front door.

Each step outside brought an increase in Robert's panic. For the first time in his life he had skirted death by a hair's breadth and now he truly understood how much he wanted to live. His heart rate was increasing, his breathing was turning more ragged and quick, and his lungs were fighting for what felt like so little oxygen in the air. His skin began to feel clammy and in some small, remote section of his brain Robert knew he was starting to go into shock.

At the sidewalk, she gave a surprisingly gentle nudge guiding him to the right. "Just breathe normal Robert," she told him softly as if she really cared. "It's going to be alright."

The flashing lights of the emergency service vehicles were calling to Robert like an oasis after a long desert trek, but she stopped him just past a red pickup truck where the world took on an even more surreal atmosphere when he realized he was standing next to a high end European sport car. If she was trying to stay below anyone's radar, he knew she had definitely picked the wrong car to escape attention. She opened the passenger door, struck him in the back of knee, and pushed him inside when he legs gave out. He barely had a hand on the door handle before she was slipping in the driver side and the murderous look she gave him stopped him from doing anything else.

Within moments the sixteen-valve super sport was brought to life and they pulled into the street. Quickly spinning the wheel, she turned the car around, leaving the bodies of her victims behind and slowly advanced down the street like a large cat stalking its next meal. Robert saw a patrol car and a uniformed officer at the end of his street. The cop had someone stopped, probably checking ID's, and Robert saw another chance at freedom closing in.

"Robert," her surprisingly soft, non-threatening voice broke through his thoughts. "Remember I told you that I wanted us to understand each other?"

"Yea, I remember," he answered while keeping his eyes fixed on the officer ahead.

"I don't want to kill anyone if I don't have to, but I will do whatever is required to keep you safe."

Keep me safe? he could not fathom what she was talking about. She had just made it perfectly clear to him that she could, and would, kill anyone she wanted to without pause or remorse. If she believed beating him up and pressing a gun to his head was a means of keeping him safe, then she was truly unbalanced, but he kept that thought to himself.

"This officer up ahead," she flicked her chin toward the same cop Robert had been watching. "He's pretty young looking. Probably has a couple of kids and a wife, or maybe a girlfriend. Either way they worry he won't be coming home every time he leaves for work. He's just like everyone else Robert. He just wants to do his job, get paid, and go home. So, you just sit there quietly while I talk to him and that way he'll have at least one more day with his family, ok?"

Robert did not have time to reply or even think of a response as she lowered the window and they coasted to a controlled stop next to the officer.

"May I see your driver's license please?" the patrolman asked. He was young, mid-twenties probably, but he had the confident tone of a police academy graduate.

"Of course, I have it here in my cup holder. Was someone really killed earlier?" She had lost the sinister tone in her voice, replacing it with a concerned fear that she had

17

somehow unknowingly broken the automotive driving laws. She glared at Robert as she reached into the cup holder for the license and there was a silent promise that very bad things were going to happen if he opened his mouth.

"There was a shooting Miss. Have you seen or heard anything out of the ordinary this morning? Perhaps saw someone new to the neighborhood?" the patrolman asked as he reached for the ID, the gleam of a simple gold wedding band on his hand catching Robert's attention. "Are you alright sir?"

Robert's heart sank. Even if he successfully escaped right now, he knew the patrolman was dead. He could not be responsible for that so he just nodded his head and sat staring at the dashboard in front of him.

"We just got a call that his mother was taken to the hospital," she interrupted, using her hand to give Robert's knee a slight squeeze of reassurance. "There was a shooting? Here?"

Robert was amazed at how surprised she sounded. If he did not know the truth he would have bought it too.

"Yes Miss...Mrs. ...Kariot?"

"Yes sir. We live just up the street there, on the right. I'm sorry, but I didn't notice anything earlier. Robert, Hon, did you?"

Robert wanted to throw up. He could feel the bile building in the back of his throat. The shock from this whole situation was beginning to subside and a deep loathing for this woman was taking hold in his gut. She had a driver's license using his name and was successfully playing off the lie that they were married. Her voice was so loving when she spoke to him, so full of concern, and hearing the mockery

18

behind it made him want to grab her by the throat and keep squeezing, but instead he just shook his head. She rewarded him with another supportive pat on his knee.

"Alright Mrs. Kariot, I'm not going to keep you from getting to the hospital. An officer may check in at your house later to speak with you. Use an extra amount of caution in the meantime and if you recall anything please notify the department."

And just like that they were on their way. Where they were going, Robert could not imagine as the dashboard clock changed to 9:16am. Sixteen minutes. Sixteen minutes for Robert's life to be upended, slammed around like a rag doll, and driven through a police checkpoint that was, perhaps, his last chance of getting out of this alive.

"Well done Robert," she congratulated him as they drove off, the façade of the concerned wife gone. "We might just make it out of this alive after all. My name is Amber by the way."

That was all she said to him and then they drove in silence, heading for the nearby highway entrance where they accelerated southward. For a while Robert thought of grabbing the steering wheel at every approaching lamp post or overpass and ending this saga once and for all. He wanted to live though, so the furthest he got with the idea was playing the self-mutilating fantasy over and over in his head until he finally grew tired of it. He figured that even if he had done it, a crash like that in a million-dollar car like the one he was in would only result in the two of them having to walk. That was if she did not decide to shoot him on the spot, but since he was still alive he partially believed he might even survive doing that.

The lack of any conversation between the two of them was one thing that did not bother him. He did however find the absence of any sound, other than the well muffled road noise which he discounted, a little unnerving. With nothing else to do, not even the radio to listen to, he mulled over her earlier words. *"I will do whatever is required to keep you safe", "We might just make it out of this alive after all"*. What game was she playing at? If there even was a game being played, what part of it pertained to him? He wondered if any of this dealt with Harmony, but the how or why if that were the case he could not fathom.

Robert would have given it more consideration if, at that exact moment, the driver side window had not shattered into thousands of pieces. He heard Amber gasp, the car swerved slightly, and then they rocketed forward when she slammed on the gas pedal. Robert had never felt such acceleration before in his life as he was physically pushed back in his seat from the torque being generated. He heard the lion like roar of the engine through the broken window and yet he could feel only a subtle vibration in his seat as the car came alive.

"What the hell is going on?" Robert screamed as she began swerving the car through the light traffic.

"Your life's in danger Robert and the people who want you dead are coming for you right now!"

CHAPTER FOUR

"Who wants me dead?" Robert shouted, but Amber did not reply to his demand for answers. Her attention was being drawn to the side view mirror while she tried to keep their speeding car from slamming into another vehicle as they hurtled along.

Before his gaze even reached the passenger's side mirror, Robert heard the whine of the motorcycles. He quickly spotted them, foreign made, Japanese he thought. There were two of them closing in and both could maneuver more easily around the cars then they could. The solid white motorcycles, practically gleaming in the morning sun, were a stark contrast to the black pavement. Even the riders wore white as if they had some sort of fetish with the color which left only their impenetrable, black tinted helmet visors standing out. Robert barely caught a glimpse of the pistols being aimed at him when Amber swerved and sent him sliding sideways as far as the seat belt would allow, which was unpleasantly not very far at all.

She swerved again into the center lane. A black BMW was losing ground on their left and one of their pursuers tried to take the shoulder on the other side of the it when Amber quickly opened the center console, removed her own pistol, and with a momentary flick of a switch near the handle making the pistol fully automatic she emptied an entire clip into the BMW's hood. Robert did not know if the driver was scared, wounded, or dead, but the car took a dramatic swerve onto the shoulder and slammed into the concrete divider, taking the white motorcycle and its rider with it.

She dropped the empty pistol on the floor and grabbed the steering wheel with both hands again. She weaved through another group of cars as the second motorcycle narrowed the distance between them. Amber made the car dance through the pack of cars, but their pursuer was still able to easily maneuver behind them and Amber took the opening presented to her and slammed on the breaks. Robert heard the screech of tires and the crash of twisting metal as cars collided in an effort to get out of the way. He felt the shuddering impact of the motorcycle striking the rear of their car with just enough force to momentarily throw Robert forward in his seat.

He only caught a glimpse of the white jacketed arm of the rider as the body rolled off the roof and past the driver side window. Then the woman next to him brought the car screaming back to life and they catapulted forward once more. He managed to turn enough in his seat to the see the pile of cars left in their wake growing smaller and smaller. It was only a few miles further on that Amber slowed down. Reaching beneath her seat she withdrew a black, handheld radio. It looked sophisticated to Robert, probably military issue, which did not make him feel any better about his situation or his chances of escaping.

"Come in Damon," she called into the mic.

"Go ahead," was the crisp response of a deep male voice a moment later.

"ETA, less than five. He's been discovered so make sure we're ready to go."

"Understood." Damon replied. To Robert, it sounded like the man could care less about what was going on.

She placed the radio back onto the floor and spared Robert a lingering glance. "Almost there."

There turned out to be a highway rest stop a few miles ahead. As they departed the highway the exit ramp divided into two paths before them. The left lane was for cars only while the right lane curved behind the small building to a larger parking lot for trucks. Without pause they took the right lane toward the tractor trailer parking area. Only a few trucks were in the lot, a group of three and a couple of singles by themselves. They made a wide turn around the group of tractor trailers, two box trucks with a car carrier between them, and drove up the extended ramp of the car carrier into the only unoccupied spot at the end. Robert could only see high end sport cars onboard.

"Time to change rides Robert. Be careful getting out," Amber told him as she unhooked her seatbelt.

Robert quickly unbuckled himself and slid out of the car. He glanced towards her and saw that she had picked the gun up off the floor and was only just starting to open her own door. He shot a quick look towards the rest area, it was close, he could make it he thought. Robert bolted, not wanting to lose what might be the only chance of escape he was going to get. He heard her yell his name, but he ignored her and kept running. A few more strides and he would be out from between the rigs and into the open. Even if he did not make it to the rest area at the very least someone was bound to see him if he could just get into the open and start screaming his head off. He did not make it that far.

Just as he was clearing the truck cabs, filling his lungs to scream for help, a crowbar shot out in front of him and clipped his throat. The pain from being clothes lined by a crowbar was immense and two things happened almost immediately. The first, he saw the world spin as his feet went out from under him causing him to land painfully on the jagged asphalt. The second, and even more horrifying thing to occur, was his throat closed shut. His body automatically began to panic before he even fully realized his predicament. He grasped at his throat and started rolling back and forth on the ground. He needed air but could not get any.

"Damn it Damon," Amber's voice cut through the air like an ice storm. She grabbed Robert by his shoulders and forced him flat on his back.

"Robert," she whispered to him. Her face was close, her voice losing its hard edge, turning soft, and her breath smelled slightly of berries and mint. "Robert, I'm going to help you, but I need you to try to stay still."

There was a quick handoff between Amber and Damon and then she stabbed a needle into his arm. Robert barely registered the pin prick, but almost instantly he could feel himself beginning to relax while she continued to murmur words of encouragement to him. His throat opened again and he could finally breath as his eyes became heavy and his vision narrowed as Amber glared at the man next to her.

"I've warned you about these sorts of tactics Damon," He towered over her like a titan, tapping the crowbar lightly against his broad shoulder, but her challenge and underlying threat were clear. "He isn't one of them."

"He would have survived. Might have a raspy voice for a while is all," he replied watching the scene unfold before him with a look that bordered on boredom.

"That's not the point," she growled and stood up. Even in his drugged state, Robert was sure the man took a half step away from her. She looked down at Robert just as the drug finally took full effect and his head, obliviously, slumped to the side. "Revelation, chapter 1, verse 3."

Blessed is he that readeth, and they that hear the words of this prophecy, and keep those things which are written therein: for the time is at hand.

"Yea?" Damon asked taking a closer look at Robert's now limp body. "What makes him so important?"

"Robert Kariot is the key to everything."

CHAPTER FIVE

Robert's mind struggled against a thick, heavy darkness that refused to release him. It was as if he was wrapped in some sinister cocoon that he wanted to be free of, but he was unable to find the strength to escape. After a time, the darkness started to lighten, like a light had been turned on somewhere behind the veil and he felt a gentle vibration course through him as feeling started to return. He doubled his effort to open his eyes and at last the medicated darkness finally gave up its hold on him.

His first glimpse of the world was of a fuzzy setting sun that was not quite orange or red, but somewhere in between. He thought it was beautiful. The soft blurry colors reminded him of a peach at first until they deepened to a fiery red and the glowing orb was overrun by purple clouds as the day ended. He could not remember the last time he had watched a sun set and he felt a profound sense of loss accompanying that thought. *I've wasted so much time*, he thought.

His throat was dry and sore, but the pain and panic he associated with that had subsided. Now his body felt like it had been run over by a truck from the way it was aching all over. Or at least what he thought getting hit by a truck must feel like. The pain from the beating he had received during the day had subsided a little, but his muscles were slow to respond and a lingering lethargy was keeping his mind a little muddled.

"I'm sorry about what happened to you at the truck stop," a strange, but at the same time familiar, female voice told him from the driver side of the car.

With a great effort, Robert turned his head toward the woman who spoke. The face was familiar too. And terrifying. Bringing the reality of his situation back into full focus. He did not say anything, he had nothing to say, so instead he took in his surroundings and allowed his mind to fully clear during the silence. He discovered that while he was unconscious he had been moved from a luxury sports car to a run of the mill four-door sedan and like before, she was driving and he was an unwilling passenger.

"I've warned Damon about using too much force when it isn't required." Amber continued while he looked around. "There's a bottle of water in the glove box. I'm sure you're thirsty."

Opening the glove box, Robert removed the warm bottle of water, opened the cap, and drank greedily. Even warm, the water was refreshing. He glanced at the dashboard clock, if it was still the same day of his abduction, he had been out for about ten hours. If they had given him an even stronger sedative he could not even begin to guess at how long he had been unconscious, but he felt reasonably sure it was the same day.

"How are you feeling?" she asked sparing a sideways glance at him.

Robert did not reply.

"Look," she started, her voice taking on an edge again. "I know you don't realize it, but I'm on your side."

"Sure you are," Robert said as he watched the outside world rush past his window. They were on the

highway again, but they were heading in the opposite direction they had been going earlier.

"I am."

"That's why you broke into my house, killed my neighbor, and beat me up while holding a gun to my head. Usually that's what my friends do to me on Saturday nights, but since we just met..." He replied with heavy sarcasm and a slight shrug of his shoulder.

"I did it to save your life! But maybe you like your neighbors sticking a knife in your back? Maybe it gets you off, but I need you alive!"

He leaned closer to her and she took her eyes off the road ahead to stare right back at him.

"Go to Hell," he pronounced the words slowly and smoothly to make sure she understood them and then shifted back to his side of the car. He was sore, tired, and past the point of caring.

"I'm sure one day I will," she murmured and gave up talking to him.

She drove for another hour before exiting the highway and fifteen minutes later they reached one member of a chain of moderate motels. Nothing top notch, but a person would find clean sheets, a working bathroom, and an instant pack of coffee in the room. She drove the car past the front office to a section of rooms a little farther back where she pulled into an empty spot.

Robert was actually a little surprised at her choice of accommodations. After all, he had spent a portion of the morning on the passenger side of a multi-million-dollar sports car.

"Are you going to give me any more problems today?" she asked, but Robert did not offer up a response. "We're in room six."

She opened her door, got out, and took her time scanning their surroundings. The L shape of the motel sang a song reminiscing back to its heyday twenty or more years ago. She surveyed the parking lot, it was less than half full now, another sign that motels like these were an endangered species, and then she looked at the building itself. Standing two stories high, the structure was ringed with rooms marked with small, dull, brass numbers and had an enormous number of hiding places, but she didn't see any obvious threats. When she was reasonably comfortable that everything was alright she leaned back into the car and stared at Robert while he in return tried to ignore her from the passenger seat.

"We can do this the easy way or the hard way Robert. Whichever you prefer."

He sat stoically for another moment before throwing his door open with enough force he had to catch it before it slammed shut again. His sore muscles protested as he pulled himself from the car and he sucked in his breath to hold off the pain.

"Room six," she reminded him as she popped the trunk and quickly removed a backpack and a sports bag before following him to the door.

"Since we're on such good terms now Robert," Amber sarcastically announced after opening the door and shoving him into the room. "Into the far corner if you please."

Robert hesitated which earned him a quick jab in the kidneys that ignited a burning pain that encompassed his entire lower back. Without any further prompting he moved into the cramped room and over to where she directed. He had to side step the circular table that was right next to the door and snake his way around the end of the first twin bed so he could walk the narrow path between the room's two beds and the hutch with the flat screen tv on it. When he reached the corner, he turned back to face her and leaned against the off-white wall while she removed what looked like a black shoe box from the smaller sports bag she had brought in.

"Have a seat and get comfortable," she instructed. Robert did not see any point in arguing and, even though it was painful to sit down, he felt better once he was on the drab brown carpet. "I had hoped for a more cordial introduction, but today hasn't turned out like either one of us expected it to. Now, since we both know I can't trust you not to run, this," she said holding up the shoe box, "is going to keep you behaved while I'm getting cleaned up."

She stepped closer to him and placed the box on the floor about three feet in front of where he was sitting. Immediately he could tell it was not a shoe box. What it was he did not know, but he was absolutely certain he would not like it whatever it was. It was made from what looked like black plastic and had small steel rods protruding from the side facing him.

"This is called a proximity Taser," she told him as if reading his mind and she slid a small handheld remote from the top of the unit. The corners of her mouth pulled slightly upward into a sadistic sort of smile. "Should you feel the

need to stray out of that corner, fifty thousand volts of electricity is going to course through your body. Then, after you've soiled your pants, you're going to lie convulsing on the floor for a while. Hopefully I'll be able to get to you before you swallow your own tongue and suffocate to death."

Continuing to face him she took a few steps backwards and retrieved a thick, white binder from her backpack and tossed it to him. It landed heavily in his lap causing him to suck in his breath as the soreness he was already feeling from where she had kicked him earlier amplified to a sharp pain. She then stepped into the small hallway that led to the bathroom and a pale red light flickered to life on the black box in front of him. She leaned backwards into the room and waggled the remote to get his attention.

"As I'm sure you just figured out, this is a remote that I can trigger should I feel the need to," she smiled sweetly at him. "Don't give me a reason to, okay Robert."

With a final affirming glance at him she disappeared from his view and entered the bathroom. He could tell that she had not bothered to close the door and he listened as the faucets were turned on and the shower head made sputtering noises before it reached its pressure. Easing his sore legs closer to his body Robert leaned his head back against the wall and closed his eyes. Unfortunately, no relaxation or comfort waited for him in his thoughts so within a few brief moments he found himself looking at the binder Amber had given him. There was a reason she gave it to him and maybe what was inside would provide some answers as to what he was being dragged into. With a heavy sigh, he finally opened the nondescript, white cover to view what lay behind it.

On the inside cover, a wallet sized photo of a stoned faced young man with dark brown eyes stared into the camera from under the hat brim of a Marine's dress blue uniform. Below it on a bold typed p-touch label were the words: "Justin H. Rury, United States Marine Corp. Boot Camp". Robert glanced at the soldier's name again and immediately felt a chill sweep through him. On the opposite page was a black and white picture of his neighbor inserted in a news article that had been cut out from a newspaper and carefully placed in a protective laminate. Justin's face was fuller, his eyes were not as sunken in, and there were far less wrinkles on his face then what Robert remembered. The article itself was a fluff piece used to fill empty column space and was dated ten years ago according to the somewhat faded date on the upper corner. The familiar broad grin creased his face even back then and below that grin, along the neckline, a priest's collar clearly stood out.

Robert closed the binder's cover. He did not like where this was heading. He had never known Justin was in the military or the priesthood. He knew had been a religious man, but they'd never spoken about him being a member of the priesthood. He had told Robert he was a retired insurance adjuster. Then the last conversation they had earlier today floated back to Robert. He had just returned from his jog and Justin had told him someone had killed a bishop. Now a decade old newspaper clipping showed Robert that more than one man of the cloth had been killed today.

How did Justin know a bishop was murdered anyway? he wondered. Robert would not have been able to tell the difference between a typical priest and a bishop, but Justin had said Liz found the body. *Would she have known the man was a bishop? Was he even wearing robes or whatever bishops wore?* Robert had too many questions with no answers.

After quieting the growing unsettling feeling in his chest, Robert reopened the binder. Underneath the picture of Justin, the soldier, Robert skimmed through a snapshot of the details concerning Justin's time in the military. It was the typical name, rank, and serial number stuff that he expected to find. It gave a brief listing of units Justin was assigned to and the dates, none of which meant anything to Robert. The list ended with Justin's assignment to a numbered unit that was followed by the words *special forces* in parentheses. Robert flipped the photo back down and stared at the Marine staring back at him. Although he could not bring himself to fully believe it, he knew the young man in the photo was his neighbor and also a complete stranger.

He shifted his attention to the news article on the opposite page again. It was a community farewell to a well-liked, neighborhood priest who was being offered a minor position at the Vatican. It was filled with the usual brief background of Justin's church career and a few brief statements from parishioners. All of which was news to Robert.

On the following pages, he flipped through a few smaller articles. Some were written in foreign languages with translations accompanying them. Some contained more photos of Justin and some only mentioned his name in print. These were all filler articles as well containing nothing that warranted front page news, yet all the articles reflected some benefit the church was working on. Whether it was a good will trip, a relief effort, or some other mission of mercy, Justin was somehow involved in all of them.

As Robert leafed through the pages he continued to find more pictures of Justin, but they were beginning to look more like surveillance photos instead of newspaper cutouts. Justin at an airport. Justin standing on a hotel balcony while talking on a cell phone. Justin getting into a nondescript car. Along with the pictures were photocopies of travel documents, phone records, hotel reservations, as well as other various receipts and invoices. Each page Robert turned reinforced the fact that he knew nothing about the man who lived next door to him and it was just after he came to accept his own ignorance that Robert found the first murder headline.

Sitting behind a beige divider Robert was caught off guard by the sudden change in topics. The subject matter before him described the murder of a young couple and their child in their home nine years ago. He took a moment to quickly scan through the remaining headlines in the binder and they all appeared to revolve around murders, suicides, or tragic accidents. The foreign papers he saw had accompanying translations and some articles, the more recent ones at least, appeared to have been printed off the internet.

When he reached the end, a murder suicide piece that had happened only a few months ago, Robert went back to the beginning of the section and looked more closely at the young couple's murder. He wondered what pertinent information it was supposed to provide him and he thought of a possible answer starting to form in the back of his mind.

34

It was a dark thought, a puzzle, that brought him back into Justin's files. It took him a few minutes but he found what he wanted near the front of the papers that detailed Justin's church travels. It confirmed Robert's suspicions that Justin had, indeed, been in the area around the time the crime had happened. He then rifled back and forth through the documents. Everywhere there was evidence of Justin's travels was an article or report of someone dying.

"Makes for some interesting reading, doesn't it?"

Robert jumped at Amber's sudden appearance and almost forgot how much he hated her when he looked up. Almost. She was standing just inside the room, her pale eyes focused on him, wrapped in one of hotel's white towels. Her black hair fell over her shoulders, a few stray strands outlining her face, and she had a natural beauty to her that Robert was not expecting. Along with a number of distinct but aging scars over her shoulders that gave him pause. *What had she been through to get scars like that?* he wondered.

"I guess you could say that," he replied, as he closed the folder and placed it on the floor next to him. "But why show me? I don't see what I have to do with any of this. And if this," he indicated the binder next him, "was supposed to shed some light on why I've been kidnapped, it falls short of explaining."

"Go get cleaned up," she told him and used the remote control to switched off the Taser. "Then we can talk and clear some things up."

Robert stiffly got to his feet. He was not going to argue with her and he was not in any condition to make a fighting escape. He found the bathroom windowless and still

35

a little steamy from her shower. He glanced back into the bedroom as he closed the door. She had her back turned to him, her towel had slipped a little further down her back, and he got a glimpse of dozens of crisscrossing, jagged, white scars covering her shoulder blades. *What the hell?* he thought as the door closed.

CHAPTER SIX

Robert was letting the hot water rain down on his head and run down his shoulders when he heard the bathroom door open. It had taken him awhile, but he had achieved a comfortable mental state of numbness and he dreaded what might happen. A few seconds later he heard the door closed again and his whole body relaxed once he realized he was alone again. When he finally had enough he shut off the shower and emerged into a white steam that engulfed the entire bathroom. He reached for the exhaust fan switch and wondered if this was what a swamp felt like on a humid morning as the overhead fan sprang to life and began to nosily suck the white mist away. On the edge of the sink he found a brand-new pair of blue jeans and a light gray tee shirt waiting for him. Wrapping a towel around his waist he sat on the toilet seat and put his head in his hands. *What the hell happened today and how am I supposed to get out of this?* he thought. He stayed there as the steam drifted up around him and escaped to its own salvation somewhere beyond the vent above. He wished he could have escaped with it.

He shivered as the temperature in the room dropped which finally broke himself free of his reverie and he reached for the gift of clothes Amber had brought him. Considering they had never met, or so he believed because if nothing else he thought he would have remembered her eyes if they had, she had gotten fairly close to his size. The shirt was the easy part, a medium soft cotton blend, but he was more impressed with the choice of pants. The thirty-four-inch waist was dead on, but the legs were a little long by a couple of inches and had to be rolled up. Even so, as she had already proven, she had reliable information on his personal life.

When he reluctantly exited the bathroom, he found her dressed, standing between the beds, and watching television. She had pulled her hair back into a pony tail instead of a single braid which still allowed her cold eyes to sweep over him unimpeded. She gave him a quick glance and a nod of approval, more to herself than to him, that the clothes she had gotten him were a good fit and turned her attention back to the television screen. Robert trudged down the hall and looked at what she was watching.

A helicopter camera view of his neighborhood was currently being broadcasted. The camera zoomed in on the crime scene from earlier and then zoomed back out to a wide angle shot. It was obviously a prerecording considering the sun had already set and what was on the television looked to have been filmed around noon. Archaic footage by today's news media standards.

"If anyone has information on the whereabouts of Robert Kariot, please contact the authorities at the number displayed on the bottom of your screen," the anchor woman said into the camera. Her voice was a little too happy in Robert's opinion considering the circumstances. "Now to our own weatherman, David Coarsen, for what's expected this weekend. Dave."

Amber turned off the television and tossed the remote onto the bed's dull brown comforter. "Seems that you've gotten the police's attention Robert," she paused, considering something she did not seem willing to share.

"Actually, there seems to be some concern that you may have suffered some sort of foul play. I was hoping the investigation would have gone a different route. I left the pistols behind in hopes that you'd become a suspect."

"Why are you doing this to me? I haven't done anything to you. I don't even know you."

"That's true. You haven't done anything to me," she admitted and shrugged. "As for why I did it, Cortes."

"Cortes? What the hell does that mean?"

"Hernan Cortés reached Mexico in 1519 and began his conquest of the Aztecs by destroying his own ships. He did it to eliminate the possibility that his men would give up on his mission. There was no going back."

"This isn't 1519," Robert challenged. "There's modern science now. Forensics. The police would figure out I didn't do it."

Amber laughed. It was spontaneous and happily sincere. Hearing it made Robert want to punch her.

"I wouldn't be worried about the police Robert. It's the people who sent those motorcycles after us that you should be concerned about. If you're taken into custody it will be a beacon for them to home in on and you'll be dead in less than twenty-four hours."

Robert did not say anything.

"My name is Amber, in case you don't remember," she reminded him and extended her hand towards him. Robert did not accept it, but she did not seem surprised or insulted. "I realize you think I've kidnapped you."

"You *did* kidnap me," Robert interrupted keeping his voice calm although in reality he wanted to scream at her.

"Well, I did what I had to do. I told you before I would do anything I had too in order to keep you safe. If that means putting a gun to your head and beating some obedience into you, so be it. I didn't have the spare time to explain things to you earlier. As it stands now, time is a commodity we're running very low on so let's start by having a little chat about your neighbor, shall we?"

She motioned him to the chair at the small table near the door and took a seat on the corner of the bed as Robert made his way over. The table itself was empty except for the folder he had been looking through earlier.

"Justin was going to kill you," she told him matter-of-factly, as if he should just accept that people trying to kill him were a common occurrence.

"Why would he want to kill me? We've been," Robert paused. "We were, neighbors for several weeks now so he had plenty of time to kill me, but he never tried during all that time. And that still doesn't explain why you kidnapped me."

She decided not to answer right away. Instead she continued to sit quietly on the corner of the bed studying him. At least it felt to Robert that he was being studied. Maybe she was evaluating him, wondering what to say and what not to.

"You didn't look too closely at the end of the folder I gave you, did you?"

"No."

"Take another look."

"I can't read whatever language they're in."

"Just take another look Robert."

With a forceful huff, he reached out one hand and flipped the binder back open causing the cover to slap hard against the tabletop. Grabbing hold of the front contents he unceremoniously tossed the pages over the metallic rings so that they landed with a dull thud on top of the cover. He shot Amber a scorn filled glance before turning his attention back to the articles. He scanned the pages quickly, flipping each with a carefree disregard when he finished and moved onto the next page.

When he reached the last few pages, Amber's crooked smiled appeared as she watched Robert stiffen just before he was about to flip another page. He gently laid the page back down again and began taking a closer look. She could see his eyes scanning through the text, searching for something he recognized, but there was no translation accompanying it and she could see the frustration at that starting to show on his face in how he clinched his jaw.

Robert turned to the next page with more care then he was feeling inside. His eyes darted across the text until he found what he was looking for. At that point he did not bother to try and figure out what the words meant anymore, he knew this entire section of the folder was about dead people, and he just needed to find out who the victim was. He quickly turned, searched, and repeated his way through each of the last pages.

"I don't understand," he mumbled while still looking at the obituary picture of the deceased man on the final page.

"I think you understand enough Robert."

"They're all..."

"Kariots," she answered for him. "Yes, Robert. Kariots, just like you. "

"I don't..."

"Did you know the Vatican is its own sovereign state?"

"What?" Robert hated being blindsided. He always wanted to know what was coming so he could prepare for it, but this woman kept throwing him curve balls from out of nowhere.

"Did you know the Vatican is its own sovereign state?" she asked again.

"Yea, I've heard that, but what does..."

"Have you ever heard of the Palatine Guard?" she cut him off again as if he was not even speaking.

Robert just sat there and looked at the binder again. He also hated being cut off during a conversation, it was disrespectful, and he was not going to give this vile creature next to him the satisfaction of pushing his buttons any longer.

"In the mid 1800's the Palatine Guard were based at the Vatican. They were an honor guard for the Pope and performed ceremonial functions and such. If you wanted to follow their history, you'd need to start looking at their creation sometime during the sixth century, but for what you and I are discussing that part of their history is irrelevant. What you need to know Robert is that in the late 1970's they were disbanded by Pope Paul VI and a year later a new group was formed known as the Saint Peter and Paul Association. The members of this new group were also made up from some of the former members of the Palatine Guard. Today members of the association volunteer for various services and charity works. Understand so far?"

Robert nodded that he did. He did not see the point she was trying to make so far or what it had to do with him, the binder, or anything else of relevance for that matter.

"Your neighbor, Justin," she started to explain again. "After a successful military career, became a listed member of this Saint Peter and Paul Association. But you see there's a problem with that Robert. No one in the Peter and Paul Association seems to know who Justin is.

"Now, I believe, that even though the Palatine Guard was disbanded, a part of it was also transformed or rearranged into a new department which you would consider to be equivalent to the United States' CIA or NSA, but for political reasons all of its members are listed as being part of the Peter and Paul Association. I also believe that Justin is a member of this nameless clandestine group and his membership in the Association is just a front."

"Okay. And the point you're supposed to be getting at?" Robert asked.

"I'm getting there," Amber replied in a tone which Robert thought sounded like a bit of a warning as well. "Justin was a member of this transformed guard. They call themselves the Knights of the Vatican. There are various levels within the organization, Squires, Knights, Inquisitors, and to be honest I'm not entirely sure how the hierarchy works, so let's just say Knight is the general term to use."

"Knights? You're saying Justin's a knight? Like some sort of Templar?"

"You do know a little church history after all. But no, Justin was no Templar," she commented and appeared to drift off into a side thought before catching herself and continuing. "He was an assassin and all those people in that binder have been his victims."

"An assassin? Are you insa..." Robert let the word die off in his mouth. Now was not the time to start trouble again.

"Insane? That's what you were going to say, wasn't it? Isn't everyone to some degree?" she asked, but then pressed on as if he had not said anything at all. "You need to look at the church's organization as a chess board Robert because that's what it's like dealing with the church, moves and counter moves. The pawns are the face of the church and are also the vast majority of people associated with it. They're your town priests, the missionaries, volunteers. You get the point. Everyday people for an everyday world.

"The rooks are the security forces. Remember the Vatican is its own sovereign state. It needs its own protection. The bishops are the ruling class which includes the pope, and cardinals, and all the rest with authority. And as I said before the knights are the secret police or special forces. After all what would the faithful followers of the world think if they knew the Christian church had a small army at its disposal?"

"What about the king and queen? What part do they play?" Robert mocked, his opinion of her insanity solidifying with each sentence she spoke.

"Who would be the royal family for the Christian church Robert?" she asked in the manner that said he should already know the answer.

"God maybe," he answered, not really caring.

"Close Robert, but not quite. Still a good guess considering you didn't put any thought into it. Jesus, Mary, and Joseph are considered the royal family in the church and it's God who watches over all of us. It's his board we're playing on and he can shake it anytime he wants to."

"Okay, so anyway what's any of this got to do with me?"

"Justin, the bishop I killed outside your house, the guys on the motorcycles, they were all after you Robert. You're the church's next target."

"You really are crazy," Robert verbally struck back and rose from his seat. "You think the church is after me just because my last name is Kariot!"

"It's not about your name Robert, it's about what you're going to do."

"Yea, well what the hell did I do to piss the church off to the point that they want to kill me?"

"It's not what you *did* Robert, it's about what you're *going* to do."

"And that would be?" he demanded, swirling his arm in front of himself as an invitation for her to explain.

"You're going to destroy the world," she told him and he probably would have laughed out loud if she had not looked so serious.

CHAPTER SEVEN

Pope John David Kase, Bishop of Rome, paused in his work at the sound of the approaching footfalls. It would still be a few minutes before the echoing feet reached him, but he appreciated having the advanced warning. It was one of the reasons he had the carpet removed from this hall shortly after he was named Pope. The carpet had covered up the beautiful tile work anyway so he did not consider it much of a loss, although he was sure a few of the lower ranked bishops disapproved.

But it was those same bishops that would have disapproved of the work he was doing presently, polishing that same tiled floor by hand. John David did not mind though. Although the work was taxing on his nearly eighty-year-old body, the experience kept him humble and a person in his position, with his authority, could easily lose his humbleness. He thought God would approve of his actions, of course he was not sure, but it felt right to him and God had always led him on a true and just course. Even if those journeys may have been trying at times, his faith had seen him through the darkness and to the better times beyond.

The footfalls were halfway to him now. The person was moving rapidly to cross the fifty-foot-long chamber as quickly as possible. One thing John David had been blessed with was good hearing and, thanks to God's will, he had never lost it. He often felt people to easily discounted what the ears heard. He believed that sound could tell a person a story of its own if one was really listening to the world around them. Like the sounds of the person approaching him, dragging one foot slightly over the tiles, told John David it was Bishop Thomas coming to see him.

John David liked Bishop Thomas immensely. He was a deeply faithful, true servant of the Lord, who did not partake in the trivial politics that many of the other bishops did. John David tried not to find fault in what he saw in the others, but saying it was difficult not to would be an understatement. Even on the rare occasions of such weakness when he very much wanted to stand before them and state his decree of damnation he refrained because he knew it was not his place, as stated in the book of Luke, chapter 6, verse 37 through 38:

> *Judge not, and ye shall not be judged: condemn not, and ye shall not be condemned: forgive and ye shall be forgiven:*
>
> *Give, and it shall be given unto you; good measure, pressed down, and shaken together, and running over, shall men give into your bosom. For with the same measure that ye mete withal it shall be measured to you again.*

John David had nearly finished cleaning the white marbled tile before him and expected he would be done by the time Bishop Thomas arrived. Normally, John David would have anyone approaching him during his cleaning penance assist him as they spoke, but there was something in the way that Bishop Thomas was moving, the unusual hurried steps and the sound of his haggard breathing as he neared, that gave the Pope pause. He believed his cleaning was going to end early today so he made a mental note of which tile he was on as he finished.

"Please forgive the interruption your Holiness," announced a winded and elderly bishop. "May I assist you?"

John David surveyed his work before turning to look at the man who had addressed him. Bishop Thomas was a few inches shorter than John David and even though he was fifteen years younger than the Pope his looks did not reflect such a large margin in their age. While the Pope was lanky, Thomas was slightly overweight, in part because his injured leg hindered his movements. John David's hair, although now white and thinned, was a contrast to Thomas's nearly bald head where only a well-kept ring of white hair around his ears remained.

"Not today Brother, I believe I am finished, but you have my thanks," John David told him as he placed his polishing rag in the nearby dull metal pail he used to do his work. "But if you would please help me up, I would greatly appreciate your assistance."

Without hesitating, Thomas took John David's elbow and steadied him as his rose.

"Thank you, Brother," John David told him once he had risen. He kept hold of Thomas's arm, even though he did not need too, and the two began to walk alongside the hall's mural walls. "I no longer have the agility I had once possessed in my youth. If only I had realized the truth of aging when I was young, I would have spent more time walking. But what has brought you here with such urgency?"

"He's been found your Holiness," Bishop Thomas told his Holiness with no other explanation, but the younger man's excitement was telling enough to the Pope.

Instead of replying John David turned his attention to the mural they were walking alongside of. It was a massive

48

depiction of the battle of Mont Gisard, where in 1177 King Balwin IV, a few hundred Templar knights, and several thousand-infantry defeated the much larger forces of Saladin. It was a stunning victory John David thought, but a shame that a decade later Saladin would finally capture Jerusalem.

For John David, the moral story behind the large painting was that victory could succumb to defeat if one was not always vigilant. He had personally seen the errors some of his predecessors had made when it came to the matter now before him and the blood that was on the church's hands because of it. Realizing he would have been quite content to spend his time as Pope without having to hear the news Thomas was bringing him, John David said a silent prayer to the Lord.

"Are you sure Thomas? *Absolutely* sure? I've heard this argument before and I've made it quite clear what I'll allow on this matter."

"No Holiness. I mean yes, Holiness," Thomas stammered as he tried to make his speech work as fast as his thoughts. "We have fully traced his lineage your Grace. We are certain beyond any doubt, but there have been complications."

John David stopped so suddenly it caused Thomas to stagger to a halt beside him.

"Complications? I have seen the ...*consequences* of *complications* Thomas. What sort of complications have you brought me now?"

"In order to insure we were correct Your Grace, Bishop Phillip was dispatched immediately along with four Knights," Thomas began to explain. He knew mistakes had been made in past. He had bared witness to many of them, had his hand in even less, but there was always a price that had to be paid and sometimes that price kept Thomas up at night. "They were to meet with Brother Justin, the Inquisitor we had placed as the man's neighbor, early this morning. American time that is."

"It didn't take place?" John David asked as he began walking again. If something had gone wrong then perhaps this really was the man they had been searching for. Already his mind was moving, plans would need to be initiated and people contacted.

"No Your Holiness," Thomas hesitated before continuing. "*She* was there."

John David stopped abruptly once again. He slowly turned, still holding Thomas's arm, which forced the younger bishop to face him. Brother Thomas cast his eyes downwards when he looked upon John David's face. Neither spoke for a moment, John David waiting for Thomas to elaborate, but at the same time not wanting him to.

"Amber. Your Holiness," Bishop Thomas whispered making the sign of the cross upon himself.

John David felt as though he had just aged another eighty years. Thomas had said there were complications, but that had been putting the situation mildly. The previous plans John David had been thinking of fell from his mind as if they were wisps of smoke in the breeze. This *complication* changed matters considerably.

John David realized the shock at hearing the news must have clearly shown on his face when he saw the look of concern Brother Thomas was showing on his own. Another sign John David was getting old. In his younger years, people often told him that he would have made an excellent card player instead of a priest. Sometimes he wished he had chosen that profession as well.

"Thomas," John David stated calmly. "Let's start at the point Bishop Phillip departed and proceed from there. What happened?"

"Your Holiness," Thomas began, clearly unsure how to proceed.

"I know we don't have all the details yet Brother," John David reassured him. "But we need a starting point."

"Very well Your Grace," Thomas replied and quickly cleared his throat before he began. "As I said before the scholars had discovered another lineage line that we were able to trace, with some difficulty, to a family in Arizona. The Kariot line is another forked lineage so we wanted to proceed with the utmost care considering, as you said, past occurrences. Initial contact was made and certain subtle inquires verified before Brother Phillip was dispatched to handle the final authorizations."

"How was Brother Phillip killed?" John David interrupted.

"He was shot Your Grace."

"What happened to the knights with him? They should have been guarding him."

"One was found with Brother Phillip. Two were killed while pursing Kariot. The fourth has so far remained unharmed and has been able to follow him. He's the only reason we know as much as we do. It seems Phillip was impatient which left him without protection..."

"Phillip has always been impatient Thomas and it is that impatience that killed him. He should never have been

51

sent in the first place," John David declared, clearly aggravated and not bothering to hide it. "This war has been going on for a long time Thomas and *impatience* has no part to play in it. Remind the others that if they are to travel then two knights must, *must,* remain with them at all times. This is the reason that rule was implemented to begin with. How many of our brother's must die for that to sink in? How many of the flock need to walk blindly to the slaughter before the rest finally understand?"

Thomas had no reply for the Pope and John David, lost in his own disgust, did not expect to hear one.

"Continue Thomas, continue," John David ordered with a wave of his hand. "What of the Inquisitor?"

"Justin Rury, Your Grace," Thomas stammered as he thoughts fell back into line. "He was also killed in the encounter."

Upon hearing this John David disengaged himself from Thomas and walked the perimeter of the room alone. He was sure events would move rapidly from this point forward. Amber must be feeling pressured if she had been forced to move and reveal herself this soon. Now John David needed to keep that pressure on her if he was going win this war. As he finished his first lap around the room the inkling of an idea began to form within his mind.

"Tell me about Robert Kariot," he instructed Brother Thomas.

"He's the youngest of six, Your Grace. Two brothers, three sisters," Thomas began, but the Pope waved him to silence.

"I want to know about Robert himself. His genealogy no longer matters at this point."

"We don't really know much Your Holiness," Thomas started. "He's a scientist and works at a local university. He performs research mainly, but occasionally stands in to teach classes. He lives alone. He was involved with a woman, but from what Justin had previously reported the relationship ended just after he moved in and Robert took it rather hard."

"You said he was a scientist. What did he specialize in?"

"Um... sound I believe."

"Sound?"

"Yes, Your Holiness," Thomas said then clarified. "I think acoustical science was what Justin had reported, but I'd have to locate the report to be certain."

John David was sure Thomas was correct. Thomas had a very good memory, another reason John David valued him. Although Thomas's memory was not at the level of a person with a photographic memory per say, but it was close and for John David close was good enough.

"Send someone to the American embassy Thomas. If the Americans haven't discovered who Brother Phillip is they soon will and we must have our position on the matter clear," John David instructed as he took the younger man's arm once more and began circling the room again. "Explain that just before he left for a scheduled trip to the States, he had asked permission to make a change in his itinerary for a personal matter. A former colleague, Justin Rury in this case, had reached out to Phillip regarding concerns he was having with his neighbor. If they ask, say that we do not know the name of his neighbor. Only that it seems a recent breakup had left his neighbor emotionally unstable and Justin wanted to hold an intervention out of concern for his new friend. Phillips who was going to be in Arizona anyway offered to come personally, but in the meantime, he had advised Justin to contact the authorities if his neighbor's condition deteriorated."

"I'll personally make the call your Holiness," Thomas assured him.

"Excellent. Now, who is this fourth knight you mentioned?" John David asked while his thoughts shifted to the next steps.

"Sebastian Wiles, Your Grace."

"I feel I should know that name."

"He took care of the Masterson incident."

"Ah yes," John David replied, patting Thomas's arm as the memory of the incident came back to him. Sebastian had been sent to correct that appalling matter and he had settled it quickly, neatly, and most importantly quietly. "I remember. He handled that problem very well. Good. Good."

"I want you to order Sebastian not to attempt a neutralizing before he's instructed to do so. There should be other Knights in the U.S., correct?"

"Ten missionaries I believe," Thomas answered.

"Instruct each of them to leave whatever they are doing and to join Sebastian. If the Americans have not taken Robert Kariot into custody before they arrive then we will take matters into our own hands."

After John David explained in further detail what he wanted Thomas to do, he saw him to the door and let out a shudder after it had closed. When he turned back towards the room his eyes fell onto his cleaning bucket and rags he had left in the middle of the hall. Although he suddenly felt very tired, John David had a strong inclination that he needed to continue his cleaning. How many years had it been since he had seen her he wondered. Six, six and half years. It had happened here, in this very same hall that he stood in now, and it was an encounter he could not forget.

CHAPTER EIGHT

John David had not slept much in the six weeks since being appointed Pope. Not that he slept much to begin with, but there was something in the air of late. An underlying feeling that plans were in motion that he was unaware of. He could see it in the unspoken conversations carried in people's glances to one another. He could hear it in the whispered conversations that fell silent when he drew near. He could feel it on his skin in the unexplainable goose bumps he felt that told him that whatever those plans were, they were reaching their apex. Much like the feeling of apprehension he felt now as he walked down the carpeted hall containing the mural of the battle at Mont Gisard in the early morning predawn hours. It was those goosebumps that were the only warning he had before the realization that he was not alone sunk in.

He glanced over his shoulder and turned around to find her less than twenty feet away and striding toward him. A young woman with long black hair, olive skin, and blue eyes like ice behind which churned the fury of a volcano. Neither of them spoke as she came to a stop only a few feet away. Neither of them moved as they stared at one another. John David would not be able to recall in the days and years that followed just how long they stood facing one another. It could have been a few seconds or a few minutes, he was never sure.

"I'll give you credit for keeping your head about you," she observed, breaking the silence with a hushed voice that carried easily in the hall and resonated her strength as well as her loathing. "Some of your predecessors were unable to do so much."

"And which predecessors do you speak of child?"

"John Paul the first," she answered as she began circling around him. Her predatory gaze measuring a potential prey. "Leo the eleventh. Pius the third. None of them had your...composure."

John David remembered each name as she spoke them. They had all been elected Popes in the past and none of their reigns had been for very long. John Paul the first was the most recent, and controversial, having only reigned for a little over a month before suffering a fatal heart attack. Leo the eleventh was risen to the position on the first of April in the first few years of the 1600's and was dead before the month ended. Pius the third had been elected to the position one hundred years earlier and had met a similar fate.

"They suffered from the sin of pride," she finished as she completed her circle around him and came to face him once more. "They thought that within these walls your position as head of the church somehow offered a degree of protection. They forgot that we are at war."

John David could feel the blood draining from his face. *It can't be.* He thought to himself. *It's impossible. It was written in the texts that the cult had been dealt with centuries ago. But if it wasn't? If it had survived in the shadows all this time...*He could not bring himself to finish the thought. The world became not only more dangerous, but more endangered.

"Mary," he whispered.

In two quick strides she closed the distance between them almost instantly. He could smell the slightest fragrance of mint and feel the heat of her breath as she spoke. "That is no longer my name John David."

"It will always be your name," he replied. He was the Pope. The elected leader of the Christian church and he was not going to let this creature standing before him cast a shadow over God's light. "No matter what you decide to call yourself now it is still the truth."

"Truth? Let us speak about *truth* Your Grace." Her lips curled into a smile that held no warmth and the disdain flowed freely from her mouth. "The only reason you still breathe is because I allow it and the only reason I allow it is because I want to hear the truth. Was it you who ordered the latest attempt on my life?"

"What? No!" he denied feeling betrayed as all the pieces fell into place. The whispers. The knowing glances. The hushed conversations. They had all been about her and no one had told him.

"You're shocked to see me. So the plan may have been put in motion by your predecessor before your rise to power. If nothing else it is your shock that proves your innocence."

"I've had no knowledge of any such plans Mary. I did not order..."

She answered his claim with a swift backhanded slap that staggered him. "I warned you that is no longer my name."

"And I told you, it will always be your name," he challenged, wiping a small trickle of blood from the corner of his mouth. "As for the attempt on your life, if you wish the truth, then if I had truly known of your existence I would have allowed it to proceed with my blessings."

58

"You are trying to play a dangerous game John David and I have had far more practice than you have. Remember that in the years to come. Stay out of my way and perhaps you will die peacefully in your bed." She spun on her heels, showing him her back, and began striding towards the door.

"I will follow the path God has set for me," he called after her. "Wherever it may lead."

She paused with her hand on the door handle as he finished and glanced over her shoulder at him. "It seems we have one thing in common then."

Then she was gone and John David found himself shaking in the silence that followed. Thomas found him sitting on the floor as the tall windows began to show the signs of dawn. He waved off the assistance that Thomas and the muscular man he had accompanying him offered and stood on his own. As he recanted his encounter to the two men John David could see a silent, but well controlled fury growing in the man and Thomas glanced at him several times through the brief recounting but said nothing.

"I will see your security is increased Your Grace," Thomas told him when he was finished. "It should have been done before hand."

"Nonsense," scoffed John David as he began circling the room. "I will not be shepherded in my own home."

"But Your Grace, please consider..."

"I said no Thomas and I mean exactly that. What is in place already is sufficient. Now, why have you brought this man to me?"

"It was to update Your Grace on the Amber situation." Thomas explained with a shake of his head. "A moot point now it seems."

"Yes, but it is a matter that should have been brought to my attention earlier," John David reprimanded. "Humor me though. What were you going to tell me?"

"That she's dead," the muscular man announced before Thomas could speak. "That I killed her."

"Your Grace," Thomas began and sighed. "This is Sebastian Wiles. A relatively new member to the order of knights and also the first person we've been able to get close to Amber. He infiltrated her group in Paris under a plan approved by your predecessor."

"I stood over her body," Sebastian continued his anger clearly showing now.

"You cannot kill a shadow Sebastian," John David announced. "That's all that Mary is."

With a sharp look and a hand upon his shoulder Thomas prevented Sebastian from saying anything else that would make the situation worse. He tilted his head in the direction of the door. Clearly not satisfied Sebastian trudged his way out while John David and Thomas silently watched.

"Your Grace," Thomas started and then paused when the door slammed closed. "I apologize. I know it doesn't make up for my failure, but still I am sorry."

"You are forgiven my friend," John David told him and attempted to hide his annoyance. "But is there anything else I haven't been told?"

"No, Your Grace. Although the Amber matter will have to be addressed I fear."

"As I said, she is a shadow and like all shadows once a light has been cast upon it, it flees."

"Yes, Your Grace, but our failure in dealing with her this time will certainly ensure some sort of retribution."

"Perhaps," John David whispered as he reconsidered his encounter. "Yes, I believe you are right. Inform the conclave I wish to speak to them this morning. We will have to make plans."

"Yes, Your Grace," Thomas complied, but remained where he stood.

"Is there another matter you wish to talk about?"

"There has been an incident involving Father Masterson, one of our missionaries, and a number of young girls, one of whom was found dead."

John David felt his own temper flare again. How many more scandals were his subordinates going to leave at his feet? "Murder?"

Thomas shook his head. "It is beginning to look like he accidentally killed her Your Grace. I don't have all the details yet, but from what I've heard Father Masterson had an appetite for young girls. For the moment it's a local matter, but news like this will spread quickly and saying that this will be a disaster for the church would be an understatement. Especially considering all the reforms we've been pushing to implement."

"And what course of action do you suggest I take?"

"It is a delicate matter Your Grace. We should proceed with the utmost care."

"Send Sebastian to deal with him." John David broke in.

"Your Grace?" Thomas exclaimed. "Sending a knight is ...is... well it lacks delicacy."

"Let it be Sebastian's atonement for his failure with Mary. Tell him to handle the matter *delicately*," John David ordered. He turned away and Thomas who, knowing he had been dismissed, began making his way from the hall. "And Thomas."

"Yes, Your Grace?" the younger man asked turning back towards his senior.

"Have this carpet removed from this room."

"As you wish Your Grace," Thomas answered, not voicing his confusion, and left to deliver Sebastian his new orders.

After Thomas left, John David slowly began circling the perimeter of the room. Eventually sunlight reached in with its light and warmth, but he paid it little attention as he continued to circle. Even the matter concerning Father Masterson was all but forgotten. Mary had placed herself solidly in his thoughts and it was his encounter with her that played itself over and over within his mind.

CHAPTER NINE

Sebastian Wiles sat silently in an unlit motel room where he gazed out over the parking lot below him. His focus was directed toward the room on the lower level Amber had taken Kariot into. After he had secured this room he had completely drawn the shades closed out of necessity. Now he had them open a couple of inches on the one end which did not offer him much in the way of a field of view, but it was all that he needed.

He sat at a small table which was empty except for a pair of 9mm pistols with sound suppressors affixed to the barrels. He had chosen this room of the L-shaped motel primarily for the two advantages it gave him, height and view. Being in the last room of the second floor also afforded him a certain degree of privacy along with a quick exit strategy should he need it. The twelve foot drop over the outside railing would do little to prevent him from jumping it if he needed to make a quick escape.

Unfortunately, the room had been occupied by a middle age couple when he arrived. He had offered them money at first and threats when that did not work. He thought the wife saw the danger as the situation deteriorated, but she stood by her stubborn husband and paid the price along with him. Presently their bodies now laid atop one another in the bathtub. Though it would still be some time before the bodies began to decompose he had turned the air conditioning wall unit onto high to at least slow the spreading smell of their death.

He had said a silent prayer for them after he had deposited them in the tub. It was not something he wanted to do, he took no pleasure in ending their lives, but it had to be done to give him the best tactical advantage he could get. It was as simple as that.

Now the bodies were all but forgotten to him. He had been near the dead long enough now that their presence held little value to him. Their smell and the sight of the decaying, bloated flesh no longer bothered him. The body was only a shell really. Carcasses to hold the souls that had once lived within.

During his years in the service of the Foreign Legion he had learned the ability to overlook little distracters, like decaying bodies. Distracters were what could ultimately make the difference between whether a mission succeeded or failed. Whether a soldier lived or died. God may have given him the capacity to kill, but it was the Legion that had refined that capacity and had trained it into an art form.

Sebastian was no stranger to sin, but neither was the Legion, so they made a good team. He could not help but feel a certain sense of gratitude to them for that. Sadly, his service with the Legion ended when his superiors were unable to fully appreciate the things he could do and had discharged him from their ranks. He forgave them for their error in judgment, just as it was written in Matthew, chapter 6, verses 14 through 15:

For if you forgive men their trespasses against you,
your heavenly Father will also forgive you. But if
ye forgive not men their trespasses, neither will
your Father forgive your trespasses.

But that was a lifetime ago and only a passing thought as he sat staring out the window, his right arm across his chest while his left hand supported his rough, unshaven chin. Even his normally bald and scarred head was starting to show signs of stubble and a lack of attention. He mentally took note of these things while he sat and stared out the window towards room six below, waiting for the door to open so he could get on with his work.

Amber was down there, along with the man that Bishop Phillip had been so interested in. Sebastian was tempted to go downstairs, kick their door in, shoot them both, and be done with the matter, but that was his emotions talking to him and emotions had a way of getting a person killed. He believed whole heartedly that knowledge was power and right now he lacked any useful information on what was behind their door. He would not have put it past Amber to put some sort of antipersonnel device on the door and he could not risk breaking the surveillance and costing the church another chance at ending this war. Whenever they decided to leave the room he would neutralize them then. He had already decided to kill the man quickly, but Amber was another matter entirely. The two of them had unfinished business that needed attending to and this time he was not going to be as nice as he was the last time.

His phone began vibrating in his chest pocket drawing him from his revere. He had been waiting for this call since the last time he had checked in to inform the Vatican of the events that had taken place. Without taking his eyes from the window he thumbed in his pass code on the touch screen and brought the phone to his ear.

"Wiles," his voice was deep, gravely, and emotionless.

He listened to the person on the other end.

"Yes, I understand."

He listened once more.

"I understand," he replied more forcefully than he intended.

A few minutes later he tapped the button to end the call and slid the phone back into his pocket with a heavy sigh. He had been given new orders, ones he did not like, but he knew how to follow orders. Another useful skill the Legion had taught him, don't ask, just do. Soldiers who took their own initiative, who did not know or understand the bigger picture, could jeopardize an entire operation. Sebastian had learned from their mistakes as well as his own. The order would come eventually and then he would take care of Amber once and for all.

He withdrew a small, plastic box from one of the many pockets that ran along his black pant legs. For the first time since he had begun his surveillance that evening he looked away from his prey and flipped the box open. Inside, surrounded by a dark grey foam lining, were small metallic squares about the size of a man's thumb. He removed one and pressed a small rubber button on top of it which caused a tiny red LED to blink three times and then go dark again. Sebastian had his orders.

While Amber and Robert were still tucked away in the hotel early the next morning, Sebastian was across the street, only thirty yards down the road, sitting inside a twenty-four-hour diner. A lukewarm cup of black coffee and a half-eaten donut occupied the tabletop in front of him.

"Can I get you anything else?" the waitress asked, pausing, on her way by his booth.

"Thank you, no," he replied turning his head from the window to give the older woman a warm smile. Her name tag read Jane. "Just the check please."

"Sure," she answered returning his smile. "I'll be right back with it."

Sebastian gave a brief nod and turned to look back out the window toward the hotel, but he found himself paying little attention to what he was looking at. His mind had wandered to the short, gray haired woman who went to get his check and how she reminded him of his own mother. She had been a waitress too and would probably have looked like Jane now, if she had lived that long.

He was fourteen years old when his mother died from the flu. It always struck him as odd that she would succumb to such a simple thing. With all the advances that medicine had made in the last century the flu was still a killer claiming the lives of thousands each year. His mother did not have any medical insurance and all her money went to paying bills so they could live in a lousy one-bedroom apartment in the armpit of the city. He figured her working two shifts, six days a week, for as long as he could remember had finally taken its toll on her. In the end, her body was just too tired to fight off the infection.

He never knew his father, at least not beyond a few fuzzy memories of the man. There were no pictures of him and his mother never talked about him, but Sebastian thought that she missed him. Usually around a holiday or his birthday he would catch her staring off through a window, not looking at anything in particular. He could tell she was remembering something good from a long time ago from the faint smile that tugged at her lips and the glow her eyes held.

Whoever his father was, Sebastian never thought poorly of him. There was a never-ending supply of dead beat dads where he had grown up. Many of his friends had to watch their moms getting abused. Others got cursed out daily, being blamed for all the trouble the family was in. Sebastian was considered one of the lucky ones. Maybe his life was hard, but he had a mother who loved him and made a point of telling him that every day in their brief moments together between her jobs. At some point, he had a father who he thought probably felt the same way too.

"Here you go Hun," Jane said, breaking through his thoughts, as she laid the check face down on the table.

"Thank you," he replied and she strode off with a fresh pot of coffee towards a nearby table. He glanced down at the bill and saw she had written the words *have a great day* with a smiley face on the back side. He could see his mother writing that too.

He looked at the screen on his smart phone within seconds of it turning itself on and saw a small blue dot beginning to move across a satellite image of the area. He looked out the window and began to count to himself. Six seconds later he saw them pull onto the road and accelerate away. He pulled a pen from the pocket of his jacket, quickly jotted a note next to the waitress's before pulling out his wallet, and tossed a couple of bills onto the table. He grabbed his jet-black motorcycle helmet from the bench seat and headed for the door, giving Jane a quick smile and a nod as he passed her while she was taking yet another order.

68

On her way to the kitchen with the new breakfast orders Jane stopped to pick up Sebastian's unfinished coffee and donut. When she saw the two, one hundred-dollar bills sitting there next to the note he had left she had to wipe a tear from her face. *I hope you do as well* was all he had written.

Outside Sebastian tightened the strap of his helmet as he straddled his motorcycle. It was not a road cruiser or a racing bike, but somewhere between. Custom built from the ground up. He had chosen every part right down to the nuts and bolts that held it together. Like any good weapon, the user had to know the machine like he knew himself. It was the perfect mixture of power and performance which could be heard in the low growl of its idling engine and seen in the curves of its charcoal black design.

He transported the bike everywhere the Vatican sent him. The other two knights who had traveled with him, Michael and Louis, had also been of a similar mindset. They had preferred white motorcycles though, saying it represented their purity in the eyes of the church and God. Sebastian had no such false preconceptions about himself as he turned on the display screen in his helmet that was linked to the tracking device on Amber's car. He was going to hell when the end came, but so long as Amber got there first, he was fine with that outcome.

CHAPTER TEN

Amber had been driving for an hour while Robert just sat staring out the window at the world speeding by. She had used the drive through at a fast food restaurant near the motel to get breakfast, but Robert ignored her when she asked him what he wanted. He had once again taken on the role of a silent objector. Now a breakfast sandwich and a cold cup of coffee she had chosen for him sat untouched between the two of them.

"We're almost there Robert," she told him indicating a sign showing a highway exit, two miles, ahead. "You really should eat you know."

"You said last night that we'd talk more today. That you'd explain things," he replied ignoring her concern about his eating habits or lack thereof.

"And I will, but I want to put more distance between your place and us."

"More distance?" Robert sounded incredulous. "We've been driving since yesterday."

"It's not far enough."

"Well exactly how far is *far enough*?"

"Let's just say once we're a few miles off this exit I'll feel a lot better," she answered. "The church has been around for quite a long time, they'll react faster than you realize."

That fact was not a comforting thought to Robert. He still could not bring himself to believe the accusations she was leveling against the Vatican. He could see the extremely unlikely possibility of a group composed of misguided, religious fanatics chasing him down, but not the organization at the heart of Christianity. Last night she had been adamant that the Vatican had been looking for him for a very long time and now that they had found him they were going to be relentless is their pursuit.

After they exited the highway they drove a few more miles before turning into the parking lot of a small airfield where they parked their sedan near the trailer style office that served also as an entrance to the tarmac beyond. Robert noted the airfield itself was not very secure. It was surrounded by a chain link fence topped with razor wire that anyone who was half asleep could get around. Then the perpetrator could walk right onto the field and choose from a handful of small planes that sat silently covered and lashed to the ground.

"I don't like flying," Robert told her as she turned off the engine and unbuckled her seat belt.

"Sorry Robert, but this is how it's going to be."

He looked back over the airfield, unbuckled his own seat belt, and then opened his door.

"Why don't you like flying?" she asked him while she retrieved her two small bags from the trunk.

"It's not the flying part that bothers me."

As they neared the entrance she moved in close behind him so she could lean closer to his ear. "There are probably only one or two people working. Should they have anything to worry about?"

Robert knew she was making a reference to her threat concerning the policeman at the checkpoint from the day before. She had not assaulted Robert since their initial meeting yesterday, but she was letting him know that she

71

still considered killing others as an acceptable form of controlling him.

"No," he snapped and then they were up the three wooden steps, through the door, and into the office. It was a cramped space. Not much better than their hotel room Robert thought as he looked around at the decade old, gray metal desks and half dozen, beat up, beige file cabinets. At least the air conditioning worked otherwise it would have been unbearable. He had already started to sweat on the walk from the car.

A balding, middle aged, man sat at one desk on the other side of a white, chipped, counter with a pair of glasses propped on top of his head. He was leaning back in his well-worn upholstered chair reading a magazine on remote control planes and wore faded forest green coveralls, complete with telltale oil and grease stains. Using his index finger as a bookmark, the man closed the magazine over and looked up just as Amber and Robert turned towards him.

"Hi folks," he greeted them, an easy smile forming on his lips as he looked them over. "What can I help you with?"

Robert thought he saw a brief look of recognition register on the man's face, Eric according to his nametag, when he looked at Robert. Robert on the other hand was unable to say the same about this fellow.

"We're picking up our flight here," Amber informed him. "L9-59-62."

"Ok, yea," Eric said looking over at a clipboard near a small radio set. "They radioed in not that long ago. They're coming in now. Should be down in a few minutes."

"Thank you," Amber replied and motioned for Robert to go out another door the led onto the airfield.

"Take care. Have a good flight," Eric called after them.

Once outside she directed him away from the trailer towards an open staging area where they would wait for the plane. Robert shielded his eyes so he could see it approaching. It was a white, small private jet with two engines mounted near the rear. He had seen the picture of that type of aircraft before, a countless number of times, but had never bothered trying to find out exactly what it was.

"So, what is it then?" Amber asked him as they waited.

"What's what?" he countered.

"You said it's not the flying that bothers you. So, what is it?"

Robert did not answer right away. Inside he cursed himself for saying anything. "It's the unexpected stops," he told her. Which was partly true since crashing could be considered an unexpected stop. In reality, he hated the lack of control that came with being a passenger on a plane. If something went wrong he had no control over his fate and could only sit in a cushioned seat going two or three hundred miles an hour and hope everything turned out alright. In a car, on a bike, even walking, if something happened, a person could react in some way, do something, but not on a plane.

"I think that guy recognized me," he told her in an attempt to draw the topic away from himself.

"He may have, but we'll be gone before anyone can do anything about it."

"And where are we going?" Robert asked.

73

"The east coast."

"What's on the east coast?"

"You'll see," she told him and gave him a crooked grin that he had to admit suited the shape of her face.

***

"It's the guy you guys have been looking for," Eric said hurriedly into the phone. "Robert Carrot. Chariot. Something like that."

He stopped talking to listen to the emergency operator on the other end of the line. He was feeling both excited and scared. He never had something of this magnitude happen to him. He was so excited that he barely gave the man entering the office a glance. "Yea, Kariot, that guy. He's here with a woman. Their jet is about to land."

He paused to listen to the operator again. "Yea, Wing Road. You better hurry though like I said..."

There was a thunderous boom from behind him and the tempered glass window Eric had been looking out of had cracked, creating a spider web design that spread out from the hole that had just been made in it. He could not figure how he wound up on the floor and unable to finish what he was saying. His throat burned and he knew that something was seriously wrong. He had dropped the phone receiver somewhere, he couldn't remember doing that, as he reached up to his neck and felt the blood. He realized it had to be his blood, but by then it was too late for him to do anything about it.

Sebastian lowered his pistol to his side so he could watch the man slowly die. He knew the emergency responder's computer system would still show the line being connected as he opened the small door in the counter and

74

stepped through. He could hear the operator's desperation as she tried to get Eric to answer her. Gingerly he picked up the receiver and placed it near Eric's blood-stained mouth so the operator could hear the man's dying gurgles. Death was all about the delivery, it was an artform after all, and even the dying could serve God. Or so Sebastian believed.

"Help," was the last word Eric could sputter as blood filled his mouth and Sebastian smiled down on him from above.

***

Robert and Amber both instinctively ducked at the sound of the pistol crack that came from the airport's office. Robert tucked his head to his chest and waited for the next round to be fired while Amber spun into a protective stance making her body a shield for him. Without looking she reached into one of the bags she was holding, withdraw a pistol, and trained it on the office. Once he got over the immediate shock Robert started back towards the office but Amber grabbed his upper arm in a vice like grip and began pushing him in the other direction.

"We need to do something!" he yelled while he struggled against her. *How could someone this small be so strong?* he thought as he fought to loosen her grip on his arm.

Amber ignored his protests and used her leverage to keep him off balance so she could keep pushing him away from the office. The chirping sounds of the approaching jet's tires touching down drew Robert's attention so he missed the momentary appearance of a man's face in the window.

"Sebastian," Amber whispered sounding shocked and then pulled the trigger a half second too late.

Her pistol did not have suppressor on it and the loud concussion brought Robert's struggles against her to a halt. The burst stole all the quiet nuances of the world that a man is unaware of until he has lost his hearing. The gentle rustle of bushes in the breeze mixed with the occasional song of a distant bird, the far away sound of the highway, and even the engines of the approaching jet were all lost in a flicker of a second as Robert's ears began ringing. Survival mode kicked in a moment later and he ceased his struggles and began to move with her. He saw the jet swinging towards them but it was still a hundred feet away which he knew was a long way off if a gun fight were to suddenly break out.

Amber kept hold of Robert and aimed her gun at the office door while she silently cursed herself for not acting faster. She knew she had not hit Sebastian and she was infuriated with herself for missing. The half-second she had paused from the shock of seeing him was all the time he needed to duck out of sight. He was still in there though, she was sure of that, but why did it appear like he was not doing anything was what she wanted to know. He knew where they were now, why was he not shooting back?

The jet engines whined louder as they began to throttle up once the pilot became aware his passengers were in trouble. He swung the plane into a wide arc to provide cover for Amber and Robert as they hurried onto the tarmac. The cabin door swung down just as the nose of the aircraft passed the two of them. The ladder was built into the door and could not be fully extended as the jet kept moving, but it still left the two of them enough room to climb aboard.

"Go!" Amber yelled over the jet noise and pushed Robert ahead of her.

He staggered towards the aircraft and took a running leap for the entrance where an old man with a head of thick white hair and holding a sub-machine gun was beckoning to him.

"Come on Robert!" hollered the gravelly voiced old man as he reached down and grabbed Robert's shoulder to help pull him onboard.

Robert used the last of his momentum to scramble to the other side of the small cabin as Amber bounded up behind him. Even before she was clear of the entrance, the old man had pressed a button next to the doorway which brought a hydraulic piston to life that began closing the door. With agile grace Amber was on her feet again in a blur and moving towards the nearby cockpit. She pushed open the folding door, leaned her back against the door frame, and, with pistol at the ready, gazed out the large front windshields.

"Get us out of here," she ordered the muscular African American sitting in the pilot seat, but it was an unnecessary order since the jet's engines where already gleefully rumbling with newly released power.

"It's never easy with you, is it?" the old man wanted to know while looking out the window port next to Robert. "Who's chasing you? Cops?"

"Knights," Amber answered as she leaned over the pilot for her own survey of the landscape outside.

"Will you get out of my way!" growled the pilot. The deepness of his voice made his complaint difficult to ignore as he pushed Amber away from the controls.

"Is that who that Sebastian guy is?" Robert asked, picking himself off the floor.

The old man stopped looking out the small window and turned to Amber. "Sebastian's chasing you?"

Instead of answering him Amber left the cockpit and walked further into the passenger area. She kept looking out the aircraft's windows toward the fading airport for as long as she could until the jet began its escape down the runway.

"Great! Just fucking great," the old man exclaimed and brushed past Robert to get to the cockpit where he threw himself into the copilot's seat. "Did you hear that Walt? Sebastian's after us."

"Yea I heard." Walt muttered in obvious displeasure. Robert wondered if that was how Walt's voice always sounded or if he only growled when he was angry.

Amber ignored the loud remarks from the two men in the front of the aircraft and continued her vigil until they were finally airborne. As the noise of the landing gear folding into the undercarriage vibrated through the cabin she turned away from the front of the plane without saying a word and stomped her way to a seat in last row. It was the first time in over a day Robert felt like no one was paying any attention to him and even though it should have given him a feeling of comfort it gave birth to a feeling of dread inside.

Back in the airport's small office Sebastian picked up the phone receiver from the floor, the dead man now silent, and hung up on the operator who was still trying to get a response. He watched the plane take off with a certain sense of satisfaction. The Vatican had told him not to engage them and he had not, at least not directly. Following orders was one thing, but conditions on the battlefield often dictated when those orders needed to be altered. The countdown for

Amber's ultimate plan had started. He could feel it in every fiber of his body. She needed to know, to feel, the presence of the hunters closing in so that was what he did. Behind him, he heard the jingle of the door knob beginning to turn and spun around bringing his pistol to bear.

He waited with practiced slow even breaths and his gun trained on where the chest of the person on the other side of the door would be. Someone had once told him to aim for the head, but the torso and chest area was a much bigger target and there was less of a chance of the shot missing. A man of fair, eastern European complexion with blonde hair poked his head around the door frame and fixed his eyes on Sebastian.

"Brother Sebastian," he announced with a heavy Nordic accent which made his S's sound more like Z's.

"Brother Hurst," Sebastian calmly replied and placed his gun back in its holster beneath his jacket. He afforded himself one more look at the shrinking plane before returning his attention back to his companion who had now fully entered the small office.

"It seems our little song bird has escaped," Hurst observed as he casually picked up the flight arrival and departure chart before giving the body on the other side of the counter a cursory glance.

"For now, Hurst, but not for long."

"What is this L9-59-62? For a flight number, it is very odd don't you think?" Hurst asked looking over the clipboard log.

"Amber," Sebastian replied as he glanced once more out the window, a very slight smile pulling at his lips. "Luke, chapter 9, verses 59 through 62:"

79

And he said unto another, Follow me. But he said,
Lord, suffer me first to go and bury my father.
Jesus said unto him, let the dead bury their dead:
but go thou and preach the kingdom of God. And
another also said, Lord, I will follow thee; but let
me bid them farewell, which are at home in my
house. And Jesus said unto him, No man, having
put his hand to the plough, and looking back, is fit
for the kingdom of God.

"Ah," Hurst said nodding his head in contemplation. "I suppose, in a way, that is fitting for any trip. Not to look back but focus on the destination before you."

"Perhaps," Sebastian grudgingly acknowledged. "We had better be on our way Brother. The police are on the way and we need to attend to some matters before flying to the coast."

"California?"

"The east coast."

"You believe they are heading for the east coast, why?"

"She's heading for Harmony."

"Harmony?" Hurst questioned as he opened the office door for Sebastian. A very gentle, and hot, breeze invited itself through the door and a very distant sound of a siren being carried on that wind could be heard if one stopped to listen.

"Yes Brother, but I'll explain what Harmony is later. Right now, we need to get out of here and I need to make a phone call. Then we need to look into getting some insurance," Sebastian told him as he withdrew his cell phone from his jacket pocket and they exited the office.

CHAPTER ELEVEN

Robert spent the first ten minutes of the flight sitting on the floor until the older man, who introduced himself as Jay, suggested a seat would be more comfortable. Wordlessly pulling himself off the plush carpet, he took the nearest seat next to a window and buckled himself in. Outside the sky was blue and the few clouds there were looked like white cotton balls. If it was any other day Robert would have appreciated the beauty of it more. The following half hour or so of the flight passed in silence, except for the muffled drone of the engines, until Jay extracted himself from the cockpit and came back to where Robert was sitting.

"Get you anything kid?" he asked. "You look like you could use a drink."

Robert shook his head and kept staring ahead towards an imaginary dot in the distance as the airplane bounced over a small pocket of turbulence.

"Not big on flying huh?"

"How'd you guess?" Robert asked sarcastically, but Jay seemed to pay little attention to the sarcasm and took a seat next to him.

"It'll pass you know," he told Robert reassuringly.

"What will?"

"The sensation that your life is spiraling out of control now that she's in it," he explained giving his head a tilt towards the rear of the plane where Amber had disappeared to.

"You mean after the bruises heal or after she decides to put a bullet in my head?"

"You got it all wrong kid," Jay replied sounding alarmed. "I don't know what you two have gone through, but believe me, you coming to harm is the *last* thing she wants. Unlike Sebastian back there who would rather see your head stuffed on his wall."

"So that's why she broke into my house, beat me up, murdered my neighbor, and kidnapped me?"

"Well," Jay started but stopped not sure what to say to that. "Guess you've had one hell of day then, haven't you?"

For some odd reason Robert found the absurdity of that statement humorous and began to laugh. It was not a happy laughter either, but a crazy, stress relieving laughter. The kind of laugh someone who is on the brink of mentally breaking down has.

"Do you believe in God kid?" Jay asked after Robert's laughing fit subsided.

"No," Robert answered.

"Me either. Until I met her that is. I've known Amber a long time and during that time I've come to realize that there really is a heaven and hell. It may not be exactly what they preach about in church. You know, angels singing on one hand, fire and brimstone on the other. But there is a war going on Robert. A war between those who believe in the word and those that don't and its outcome will be decided here on earth."

"So where do you fit into the war plans general?"

"General?" Jay replied seemingly amused. "No, I'm just a foot soldier."

Robert decided not to say anything else so they sat in silence for a while again. He was thankful the flight had been fairly smooth so far. If there had been bad turbulence he probably would have really started going crazy by now, but the small plane had only passed through light patches of it so far and the sky remained blue and the clouds were still a soft, fluffy white.

"Are you related to her? Like an uncle or grandfather? Or did she force you to come along too?" Robert asked trying to get his mind off thinking about what the next pocket of turbulence was going to feel like. Eventually they would hit something. No trip was ever without at least a few bumps.

"None of the above," Jay answered and glanced down the aisle in Amber's direction, but he was unable to see wherever she was hunched down at.

He reached into his back pocket, withdrew his battered black leather wallet, and started sifting through its contents. When he found what he was looking for, a black and white photo of years long gone, he paused to stare at it for a moment before giving it a quick dust off and handing it to Robert.

Robert in turn looked at the two figures posing in front of a neatly trimmed tall hedge. The faded, cracked picture was taken maybe forty or fifty years ago and the man was undoubtedly Jay in his younger years, still lean and full of health. The woman though was nearly Amber's twin. Her hair was a little different, shorter, but the two could have been sisters.

"She's your daughter," Robert said aloud as understanding came to mind. The man besides him, like so many others, had found God after becoming a father.

"Afraid not," Jay replied shaking his head. "Although, at times she feels like a daughter to me."

Jay leaned in a bit, closing the narrow gap between himself and Robert, and tapped the woman in the picture with his index finger.

"That," Jay explained holding his finger just above the woman's head. "*Is* Amber."

Robert eyed the old man next to him in disbelief. Perhaps Jay was going senile he thought because at least that was believable. There was no way that the woman in the picture was Amber. It was genetically impossible for someone to not age over the last four or more decades. Robert surmised that the man beside him probably often got confused about it considering how much Amber looked like the woman in the picture.

"You don't believe me," Jay stated as a matter of fact.

"Look," Robert started, but was quickly cut off when Jay put his hand in front of Robert's face.

"Doesn't matter kid," he clarified. "It is what it is. And don't ask how she does it because I don't know her secret."

"I age gracefully," Amber interrupted causing both men to jump in their seats.

"Another thing about her, in case you haven't figured it out, she's damn quiet too," Jay said before rising from the seat to face her. "Guess you want a word with the kid here. I'll go see how Walt's doing."

"Thanks Jay. Tell him we're changing course. I want to head to Denver," she instructed and gave him a genuinely warm smile.

"Expecting trouble?" he asked, his eyes narrowing in a scrutinizing manner.

"Come on Jay, it's me we're talking about."

"Yea, guess that's enough of an explanation," he remarked and gave Robert a nod of his head. "Hang in there kid."

Amber watched him slide into the copilot seat and pull the door closed before turning her attention to Robert. "How about we have that chat now."

Instead of sitting down she turned toward the rear of the plane and walked back down the aisle. With a sigh, Robert got up and followed her. He had not paid much attention to the plane until then, but it was definitely furnished with an eye for comfort. He was flanked by plush leather seats on each side of the aisle all the way to last row on the aircraft where Amber had gone. The last two rows had been set to face one another with a small square table separating them. Amber sat facing the rear of the aircraft and Robert took the seat across from her in the last row. The table between them was bare, but an identical one across the aisle had some books, binders, and a tablet computer sitting atop it.

"First off," Amber began, "I'm truly sorry you've had to get involved in this."

"Not like I had much of a choice in the matter," Robert muttered.

"No, you didn't. Life has a way of throwing the unexpected at us at the most inopportune times." She paused, thinking to herself, and looked out the small window before pushing an overturned business card across the table toward him. "I suppose a more formal introduction would be in order now."

Robert picked up the stiff white card and turned it over in his hand. It was relatively simple in design with no frills or flair, just clean and to the point. On the top left corner, a solid black image of a great bird, wings spread wide, appeared to be rising from a wall of flames and on the opposite corner in a plain bold black font was printed *Phoenix Industries.* On the bottom, right hand corner, was a single name: Amber Magdalene.

He raised an angry glare aimed at the woman across from him, but she only shrugged in response as if to ask him if knowing beforehand would have made a difference. After what she put him through, he supposed it probably would not have, but he still felt slighted. Research took time and money, and his research was generously funded by Phoenix Industries to ensure he had plenty of time to concentrate on nothing but that research.

"Maybe now you can explain what the hell is going on," Robert said with a heated voice and flipped the card back onto the table without a second glance.

"Do you believe in God Robert?"

"I just had this conversation with Jay," he answered, sensing a reoccurring theme with this group.

The corners of her mouth turned up in a slight grin.

"I believe in him," she whispered and Robert had to admit her eyes held some hypnotic quality to them when she was not being a bitch. "There's something I need from you Robert and I think we both know what that is."

"A working Harmony," he replied matter-of-factly.

"A working Harmony," she echoed. "Yes, but more specifically, I need a very complex harmonic equation to go along with it."

"That's what all that funding was for? Why? I thought you were looking at advances in deep sea drilling."

She did not answer. Instead she reached over to the neighboring table and grabbed a notepad and pen. Placing the pad on the table between them and with pen in hand she began to draw a simple picture on a blank page. In the center, she drew a large circle and inside it she drew a series of smaller circles all touching one another. She then surrounded that large circle with a bigger circle and placed a single circle on that line. She continued drawing larger circles with a single circle on each line three more times and pushed the paper toward Robert.

"What do you see?" she asked.

"A bunch of circles," he replied sarcastically and met her disapproving glare. He held up his hands as a sign of surrender and reexamined what she had drawn. "The structure of a simple atom. A core surrounded by four electron shells."

"That's right. A small building block, that when combined with others, makes something larger," she told him as she leaned over and wrote next to the large circle in the center of the page the word *Sun*. She then moved to the outer rings and continued by writing the words; *Mercury*, *Venus*, *Earth*, and *Mars*.

"You think our solar system is an atom?" Robert asked, clearly showing his disappointment in her thinking.

"Maybe, maybe not," she replied. "I don't know what our solar system is, but I do know it is part of something larger; the Milky Way Galaxy."

"What's your point?"

"Open up your mind Robert. You didn't theorize Harmony by sticking to conventional thought. You had to think outside the box, didn't you?"

"Look, I understand the whole molecule versus galaxy analogy. What I don't know is what that has to do with you and the other crazy people who are trying to kill us."

"Us?" Amber remarked as the left corner of her mouth curled into a lopsided grin.

"I don't know what to believe about any of this. Which includes you," Robert told her and pointed a finger at her to emphasize his point before he turned to look out the window. The puffy white clouds had become a blanket of white cotton sweeping past below them and he could see what looked like forever towards the horizon. "You helped me at the rest stop after your own guy nearly killed me. And you put yourself between me and that Sebastian guy back at the airport. Maybe they were after me at my house too. Maybe not. I don't know. But seeing as neither one of us is going anywhere I'm at least willing to listen."

"I'll take it," she said and a genuine warm smile spread across her face. Robert was shocked at how such a simple thing as a smile could change the whole dynamic of her face. It was the first time he had ever seen her smile so big and it lit up her face and her eyes sparkled in such a way that a person could get lost in them.

"Alright," he said mentally shaking himself free of her Siren's stare. "What does any of this got to do with me and Harmony?"

She reached across the aisle again grabbed one of her bags, removed something, and then slid a Lego piece across the table. It was a single red line brick, a four piece.

89

"Can you tell me what I'm going to build with this?" she asked.

Robert picked up the small brick and twirled the scarlet plastic casually in his fingers. It was smooth and cool to the touch, probably never even used, not that he could really tell one way or another. *What could you build with it?* he thought. An infinite number of possibilities stood before him. Although a gun of his own was his foremost thought, but he did not voice that idea.

"You can't, can you?" she asked. "It's only a single piece of something larger and not being able to see more really doesn't leave you much to go on. Life's like that too. There's only a finite amount of time everyone has to live. The earth is a fleck of dust in the universe and an individual's time spent on it really is insignificant in the grand scheme of things. So how is mankind supposed to understand God, the creator?"

"I think they call it the Bible," Robert answered, his sarcastic side showing itself which surprisingly earned him an approving smile from her. He had to admit she had a nice smile and she seemed to appreciate his sarcasm, at least some of the time. Kate never did.

"Do you know the gospels were written decades after Jesus died? In fact, there are dozens of gospels, but it was the church, at the council of Nicaea, who decided which of those would be combined into the bible." The scorn was evident as the venom passed through her lips.

"Then, you're saying the bible is a farce?"

"No. Not entirely anyway, but there's more to God than what the church preaches Robert. The bible is only a small... select portion," she tapped her drawing of the solar system. "Of something larger. Or if you prefer, the bible is like thinking the world is still flat."

"I understand what you're telling me, but I still don't see what this has to do with anything?"

"Think about the Lego piece again. It's a tiny and seemingly insignificant thing without being able to see the whole design. Religion is like that too. People think they understand what God wants, but they don't really, do they?"

Robert just stared at her and shrugged.

"It's an unfair comparison I know but think about it. How long can the average person live? Seventy, eighty, ninety years? What does the better part of a century mean compared to the eons God has witnessed? That's why I think the first couple of verses of Matthew's chapter seven are so important."

"Alright," Robert slowly replied, drawing out the L sound.

"Matthew, chapter seven, verses one and two," Amber announced and then began to recite it.

Judge not, that ye be not judged. For with what judgment ye judge, ye shall be judged: and with what measure ye mete, it shall be measured to you again.

She pulled out one of her pistols from the bag on her lap and held it up between them. Robert instinctively pushed himself back into his seat as if that was somehow going to lessen the blow should she decide to pull the trigger at that exact moment. She spun a suppressor onto the barrel, tossed the bag aside, and gave Robert one of her lopsided grins. He could not help but wonder how many people she had killed with that gun and if she smiled at them just before she pulled the trigger. She flipped the pistol in her hand, grasping the barrel, so the grip pointed towards the roof of the cabin.

"Jay showed you the picture of the two of us. Maybe he shouldn't have, but it doesn't really matter. That is me in the photo Robert and I'm very old. Older than even Jay realizes, but I need you to believe some things."

She lowered the gun so the handle faced Robert and the barrel aimed towards her chest. She inclined her head toward the pistol and Robert, hesitantly, took hold of it. The metal was still warm from her touch but Robert felt little comfort now that he had her at gunpoint. She continued to gently hold the barrel with one hand while using the other to place his finger on the trigger. He figured she was trying a new tactic to gain his trust. Robert thought about pulling the trigger, but he was pretty sure he was holding an empty gun or one that was using blanks.

"Does it feel ok?" she asked him, holding him in his seat with an intense stare.

"I guess so," he replied although in reality he was growing more uncomfortable with the whole exercise. "What do you need me to believe?"

"There are two things Robert. First, I need you to believe you can trust me."

"Ok," Robert responded unable to break away from her gaze. "What's the second?"

"I need you to believe that there really is a God," she said and then she forced his finger to pull the trigger.

The force of the bullet threw her body backwards into her seat and her blood splattered across the jet's windows, the table between them, the gun, and Robert's outstretched arm and face. The force of the unexpected kickback ripped the gun from Robert's hand and caused time to slow suddenly. His eyes followed the falling weapon. He saw it strike so clearly. It just kept falling, never getting any nearer to the table, for what seemed like hours, until it struck after being suspended in the air for an eternity. The back-left corner of the grip struck first. It did a little hop, with a miniscule twist as it climbed back into the air, before striking the tabletop once more. Little droplets of Amber's blood leapt from the black metal, showering the table beneath it in a surreal macabre dance. Then the gun pivoted on that precarious impact point, twirling just a few fractions of an inch to the left, before taking its final bow. Robert could not take his eyes off it as it landed.

The deep timber echo of the metallic casing reverberated in his ears and even that sound was slowed and drawn out in time. The whole process somehow seemed orchestrated in Robert's mind, in such a way that he would forever remember each, and every, detail as it occurred. In the recesses of his mind he registered the hollow drumming sound and the final metallic clang which summoned the specter of the grave to claim another victim. It was also the sound that burst the time bubble Robert was suspended in. The outside world mercilessly accelerated, slamming him back into reality as the final few metallic rattles ended and the chattering pistol fell silent.

His eyes darted between the gun now lying silently on the table and to Amber's lifeless body opposite him. Crimson rivers flowed down her chest. The blood, greedily, being soaked up in the cloth of her shirt like the first drink of a man who has not had a drop of water in days. Her head slumped over and her eyes, still bright and hypnotic, stared unseeingly at the blanket of clouds outside.

The blood flow quickly turned into a trickle. Her heart had stopped beating within seconds and the pressure forcing the blood through her veins was gone. Robert started panting for breath, he had never killed anyone before. Even if she forced him to pull the trigger, it was Robert that watched the story unfolding from the gunman's perspective and that vision kept replaying over and over in his mind. A never-ending nightmare giving birth to a scream only he could hear.

He was unsure when Jay got there. It was a sudden realization to him that the older man was standing next to him. Jay was as silent as Robert, neither of them said a word to the other, and a moment later Jay leaned over and closed Amber's eyes. He then murmured something in her ear that Robert was unable to make out and kissed her forehead before turning his attention to Robert.

"Jay, I...I..." Robert did not know what to say or where to begin. Every word that began forming in his mind just did not seem right and disappeared like a whisper in a storm.

"Don't worry about it kid," Jay replied softly. The grief etched on his face told Robert everything. "You better come up front though. We've got a problem."

Robert remained in his seat. He wanted to move. He wanted to run. He told his legs to stand him up, but the growing shock kept his body from responding. Understanding Robert's dilemma Jay hoisted him to his feet and helped him as he made him walk down the aisle towards the cockpit.

94

"It's going to be alright, but it seems like we're gonna' have to make a slight detour kid. And by detour, I mean forced landing."

"What?" Robert exclaimed.

"Couple of fighters just showed up and are directing us to an alternate airport. Bet you didn't realize just how important you are, huh?"

"Fighters? What? Why do we need to land?" Robert felt like only bits and pieces of what he was being told was registering and none of it was making any sense.

"Why? That may be our air force out there, but that doesn't mean they won't shoot us down if they suddenly feel the need to. This jet may be fast, but it's not fast enough to outrun air to air missiles."

"But how are we going to explain any of this?" Robert demanded. "Amber, the guns? How are you going to explain all the blood?"

"Don't worry kid, I got it covered."

Robert did not get the chance to ask how Jay was going to do it. His mind only registered the briefest pain on the back of his head before he blacked out. Even falling into the approaching void of nothingness seemed to take far longer than it should have and Amber's words echoed after him as he fell, "*Trust me. There is a God.*"

CHAPTER TWELVE

Robert had never been in a position before where he needed to sniff smelling salts. It was not what he would have called a pleasant experience, but it was brief because the throbbing pain in his head quickly forced the pungent fragrance aside and into the recesses of what was going to become a fuzzy memory. His vision focused, then blurred, and then focused again. He attempted to touch his head where it felt like a softball sized lump had formed but realized that his hands and feet were somehow bound behind his back. He was about to ask Jay what happened when he realized that the young EMT kneeling in front of him was not the old man.

It was obvious to Robert that he was still on the plane and lying just outside the cockpit. He could see out the open exit door, although his view was limited. A pleasantly warm breeze invited itself into the plane while he looked at the flashing lights of a police car and the occasional officer who walked by. He could see mountains in the distance, probably why it was some much cooler here, but he could not make out any specific details about them other than their shadowy profiles. He did not see Jay or Walt anywhere, but he could hear some low talking coming from the rear of the plane.

Barely a half step behind the EMT, a member of a special tactics team had his assault rifle trained on him and Robert almost immediately wrote off the officer as any real threat. Just by looking into the guy's adrenaline filled eyes he could tell the guy was on an invisible leash and was not going to do anything unless ordered to, or maybe provoked into it. Either one was fine by Robert, he figured the former would have happened already if it was going to and he was not planning on giving the guy the satisfaction of the latter.

Whoever this guy was, he would just have to go home and take it out on his wife. He seemed like a wife beater to Robert for some reason. A certain degree of smugness mixed in with the adrenaline junkie eyes gave it away. He enjoyed the job, got off on the rush, and Robert was not cooperating by giving him the satisfaction he craved. The fact that Robert had been unconscious until a few moments ago did not seem to make a difference. *Too bad Amber's dead*, he thought. He would have liked to have seen the fear on this guy's face when he came up against a real killer like her. Maybe that was why he discounted the officer so quickly. A couple of days ago Robert was certain looking down the barrel of an assault rifle would have terrified him, but that had been before he had met her.

Robert shifted his attention to the medic who had just asked him something, but he was not sure what. He wondered if the guy was an aspiring doctor and found it strange to give the matter any thought at all. He figured with Amber threatening everyone they had to talk to it was only natural he started to question the character behind the face. There did seem to be a certain amount of real concern on the young guy's face that reflected something more than just the circumstances of the situation. He appeared genuinely interested in Robert's wellbeing which, to Robert, meant that the guy either had a heart of gold or had not been on the job long enough for it to wear him down and turn him into some jaded shell of his former self.

"What's your name?" the EMT asked again.

"Robert," he answered. "What happened?"

"Welcome to Colorado, Robert," the EMT replied as he shown a flashlight in Robert's left eye and then his right. "My name's Doug. Follow my finger using just your eyes please."

Robert did as he was asked. He had been beaten up so many times in the last couple of days he felt relieved to see anyone employed in the medical field.

"Do you know how you got that bump on your head Robert?"

Forgetting that his hands were bound, Robert instinctively reached for his head again. His futile efforts were met by a quick kick to the shoulder from the wife beater's steel toed boot.

"Don't move asshole," his guard growled and lifted his assault rifle to look down the sites.

"If you need your sites at this distance, I'm the least of your problems officer." Robert blurted out the snide remark before he could prevent it. After everything he had been through these last couple of days he was getting pretty tired of other people trying to push him around. He felt a sense of satisfaction that the insult had the effect he wanted and, almost, regretted saying anything when the suppressed rage the officer was holding starting to show itself. The second, and much harder, kick he expected never came as another person entered the plane and interrupted the coming beating.

"Officer Simmens," a calm, even toned, and commanding voice interrupted just before the strike landed. "Find somewhere else to be."

"Sir, the detainee..." Simmens began to protest before being quickly cut off.

"Has his hands and feet bound officer, but if he tries to chew his way through either the medic's shoes or my own I'll expect your quick response. Now get off my plane."

Officer Simmens, rage in his eyes at this second insult, gave Robert one last glare before storming off the plane. There was a promise of bad things to come in the officer's face if Robert had the bad luck to wind up in detention with Simmens as his guard.

"How's he looking doc?" the man asked as he took the spot Officer Simmens had been occupying.

Robert could tell this new guy was important. Everything about him from his custom tailor-made clothes to his hair cut and clean-shaven face appeared crisp and well-kept. Where Officer Simmens came across as being arrogant and cocky, this middle-aged man looked confident to Robert. He was fairly certain he was looking at a government agent, but which agency he worked for was another mystery. There was something disconcerting about the lack of feelings that were reflected in the man's eyes. Robert felt like he was being viewed as a thing of little value, a simple object, instead of as a person.

"He doesn't appear to have suffered a concussion or broken bones. Vitals are good," Doug answered as he poked around Robert's chest and ribs. "There's some bruising and he's got a nice lump on the back of his head, but nothing life threatening. He should probably be taken to the hospital though just to be on the safe side."

"Alright, we'll send him over for a checkout after he and I have a little talk."

Doug knew when he was being dismissed and began packing up his bag. The agent took the lull to turn his attention towards the activity going on in the rear of the plane. He stepped aside to allow two men wearing white coveralls and carrying a black, vinyl, body bag to disembark. Doug shouldered his medical bag and followed the coroners off.

"I'm Agent Dublin, Mr. Kariot," the mystery agent in the black suit told Robert as he knelt down and withdrew a highly-polished pocket knife, flicked it open, and cut off the zip ties holding Robert's legs.

"Don't suppose you'd being willing to do the same for my hands?" Robert asked him while Dublin helped him up and onto a nearby seat.

"Sorry Mr. Kariot. Can't do that just yet."

"No harm in asking though," Robert said to give himself time to think.

"Not at all. But it seems the Arizona state police are interested in speaking with you in reference to a double murder at your home."

"I didn't kill anyone," Robert quickly denied and then paused as he thought about Amber forcing him to shot her.

Robert may not have thought anything about of his momentary lapse into silence, but Dublin eyed him with an apparent growing curiosity. "I didn't say you did Mr. Kariot, and quite frankly I'm more interested in how you ended up tied up on a plane flying over the continental United States. So how about you fill me in on that part first?"

"I went out running yesterday morning. When I got home there was a person in my house."

"A person?" Dublin interrupted.

"The woman that just got carried out of here."

Dublin nodded and indicated for him to continue.

"She took me to the airport where we got on this plane. I got knocked out and here you are." Robert was not keen on long stories to begin with and something was telling him to be careful about who to trust. He could not put his finger on why, but Agent Dublin fell into the category of people not to be trusted. The total truth of what he had been through was too unbelievable anyway.

"The woman, do you know who she is?"

"Her name's Amber." Robert replied, glancing towards the door. "That's all I know."

"Do you know how she was killed?"

Robert didn't answer.

Dublin waited a moment longer then continued as if nothing happened. "What about the other two men onboard? Do you know who they are? Ever meet them before today?"

"No. Today was the first day I ever saw them."

"Mr. Kariot, you said you were abducted yesterday morning. Do you have any idea where you were taken between the time that occurred and getting aboard this plane?"

"She took me to a motel last night, but that's it."

"The Super Six, off Highway Ten."

"Yea." Then Robert thought about what he had said and realized the innuendo gaffe he had made. "Nothing happened at the hotel. She just put me in a corner of the room and aimed a taser at me."

"Doesn't sound like a comfortable way to sleep."

"It wasn't," Robert truthfully answered. He had to take another hot shower in the morning just to work the cramps and kinks out of his muscles. "How'd you know where we stayed?"

"We've been following the trail of bodies Mr. Kariot. Thankfully, we finally caught you before anyone else was harmed."

"Bodies? We didn't kill anyone at the motel."

"Really? A couple was found slain there this morning by the cleaning staff."

Robert did not bothering saying anything else. He realized something was very wrong. He hardly slept last night and he did not think Amber did much either, but he knew she never left the room. *Could she have slipped out while I was in the shower*, he wondered. It was a possibility, but the way she had watched him like a hawk he highly doubted it. She was ruthless, yet he had not seen her kill indiscriminately. If she did kill people at the motel she must have had a reason.

"I suppose that's the nutshell version?" Dublin asked, clearly already knowing the answer.

"Yea, in a nutshell," Robert replied off-handedly while he thought about what Dublin had told him.

"Alright Mr. Kariot," Agent Dublin began as he pulled Robert to his feet and motioned him off the plane. "We'll get an official report on the details when we get to the local station and before you get transferred."

"Transferred? Where?" Robert demanded. "Am I under arrest?"

Instead of answering him, Dublin pushed him ahead and down the exit steps.

Finally outside, Robert could see that they had landed at another small airfield and it was quite far away from civilization, if the ghost image of a city towards the north was any indication of distance. The jet still sat where it had stopped, at the end of the runway, surrounded by special tactics vans and a dozen or so marked and unmarked police cars. Two ambulances and a fire truck rounded out the proceeding, but those sat quietly at a respectful distance with their crews just hanging around them.

"Initial inspection doesn't show any sign of explosives," another heavily armed officer told Dublin after they exited the plane.

"How long until the bomb squad gets here?"

"Forty-five minutes," the man answered while looking Robert over.

"Jesus Christ, forty-five minutes? Are you serious?" Dublin ridiculed while shaking his head in obvious disgust. "Fine. Just keep everyone back in the meantime. No one on or off until we get the all clear from them. Then I want this thing taken apart, down to the nuts and bolts holding it together."

Robert stood quietly taking in the surreal atmosphere that surrounded him and wondered once again how he managed to get dragged into this as a second, well dressed, man holding a cell phone next to his ear walked up.

"You got a call," he said to Dublin and handed him the cell phone.

"Thanks, keep an eye on him," Dublin instructed before taking the phone and walking away.

Neither Robert or his new bodyguard attempted to say anything to each other. From the general look of disdain

103

on his face, Robert got the impression that the man really did not like him all that much. Consequently, they just stood in silence glaring at each other while they waited for Dublin to return.

"Am I under arrest?" Robert demanded when he did.

"Being detained would be a better description Mr. Kariot," Dublin answered as he escorted Robert to an ordinary looking gray sedan.

"Shouldn't you read me my Miranda rights or something then? I have the right to remain silent and all that stuff."

"Seems like you already know it Mr. Kariot," Dublin said in a matter-of-fact way as he opened the car's rear door and helped Robert get in. He leaned on the car roof and looked Robert over again before he closed the door. Robert felt like it was the first time Dublin had really given him any serious consideration. "They say knowledge can be a dangerous thing in the wrong person's hand Mr. Kariot."

"Says who? You?" Robert scoffed as Dublin closed the door.

The nameless agent climbed in the driver's seat while Dublin made his way around the car and got in next to Robert. He buckled Robert's seatbelt and ignored his own as they waited for one of the ambulances to pass by and then followed it out onto the empty, two lane road. Free to press down on the accelerator now, they sped past the slower moving vehicle. From the way it suddenly swerved as they did, Robert was worried it might side swipe the car bringing this trip to a sudden conclusion. *What a perfect ending that would be*, Robert thought.

The whole situation felt wrong to him. Dublin knew too much about what had happened in the last twenty-four hours and why was he being so casual about it? It was something that Robert had to consider. If he was a murder suspect, he was certain he and Dublin would not be discussing the crime in such a casual manner. *Hell, he didn't even tell me my rights,* Robert thought. *He practically gave me a ticket out of jail for that.* Maybe Dublin was fishing for some detail and was hoping Robert would slipup, but there was nothing Robert could say that would incriminate himself.

"Why didn't you ask me if I knew anything about a bomb being onboard the plane?" Robert asked, but Dublin only shrugged his shoulders.

"A credible report has been issued concerning your involvement in a plot against this country and its government Mr. Kariot."

"A terrorist! You think I'm a terrorist!"

"No Mr. Kariot. I know you're not a terrorist, but that's going to be the story the news outlets get. All I know is that you are a very dangerous man and it'll be better for everyone when we bring your body back."

"You're a Knight," Robert accused him and caught the eye of the driver in the rear-view mirror. "Both of you."

"At one time," Dublin admitted. "I'm not sure how much Amber told you, but it probably would have been easier if she hadn't told you anything at all. I told you that knowledge could be dangerous in the wrong person's hands."

"Oh really, why's that?"

"At least then you wouldn't expect the bullet I'm going to put through the back of your head."

sent it spinning out of control. The rear of the car spun off the shoulder and onto the steep, rock strewn, embankment as the front of the sedan twisted helplessly into the path of the ambulance. Knowing the end had arrived the ambulance's engine howled as the driver slammed on the gas and delivered the finishing blow.

For a brief instance, Robert, and his two captors, experienced weightlessness as the car lifted off the ground to begin its death roll down the embankment, but the moment was a short and fleeting one. Robert was not sure how many times the car had rolled, three maybe four times, but at the end of the harrowing episode he found himself upside down, disorientated, and in a good deal of pain. The crushed ceiling, shattered glass, and Dublin's body lay below him. The driver was still strapped into the front seat, bloodied arms dangling above his head, but Robert could not be sure if he was dead or just unconscious. He believed Dublin's arms and legs had struck him a few, if not several, times as the tumbling car threw the unbuckled agent around like a rag doll. If he could have thought clearly enough, considering everything, Robert would have felt lucky he had not been killed.

He desperately wanted to get himself loose, but with his hands still secured behind his back there was little he could do to extricate himself. His head and neck were in agony and the blood rushing to his brain from being upside down was only amplifying the pain. Outside he heard the shifting of the embankment's rocks from somewhere above. Someone was coming to investigate the wreckage and whether or not they were friendly was another matter entirely.

While whoever was out there may have been trying to save him, Robert thought it was equally possible the person was taking the opportunity to make sure they had finished Robert off. Considering what he had been through in the last two days he surmised either outcome was a distinct possibility. With a sickening realization, he suddenly understood there was a likelihood that other factions were also after him. The person approaching from the outside came to a stop next to the driver's door, but all Robert could see was a pair of white sneakers and blue jeans. It was taking them some effort to pull the door open and the scraping metal cried out in its own sort of agony with each tug.

Once the door opened enough the person stepped closer and Robert saw the driver's dangling arms wobbling back and forth as he was being checked. The feet withdrew from the front and a moment later the loud *crack* of a pistol exploded the man's head. Deep red blood and pieces of bluish-green brain matter and bone splattered across the overturned ceiling.

Outside the feet began moving again and stopped outside Robert's door. Whoever was out there tried to pull open the door, but this time it refused to give and after several futile attempts they gave up and moved around the rear of the car and tried Dublin's door. This time the door barely made a sound as it opened with no remorse for what was about to happen to the occupants within.

Amber poked her head into the wreck and smiled at Robert. She ducked into the car and made her way over to him. Robert could see the bullet hole in her shirt and the dried blood from where he had shot her, but before he could say anything she released his seatbelt and he fell crashing to the floor where the impact delivered him to unconsciousness yet again.

CHAPTER THIRTEEN

As Robert dreamt his lucid self was unable to make any sense of the metallic *pinging* noises that kept interjecting themselves into his fantasy of a peaceful, grass covered mountainside and cool breeze that spoke of an approaching winter. There were also frequent firecracker *pop-pop* sounds and the *kish* of breaking glass and none of it really seemed to belong on his mountain escape. His mind tried to integrate the sounds into his dream, but the more it did, the more restless he grew. Something important was going on in the real world and he knew he needed wake up and he needed to do so right now.

His eyes fluttered opened, he drew a deep breath, and shuddered from the sudden cold that burned his lungs. He turned his head and saw he was alone, lying on a stretcher in the back of an ambulance, and covered by a paper-thin blanket. It did not feel like they were moving, but the idling engine was causing the whole vehicle to vibrate which made sense out of why there was a tabby cat in his dream that kept rubbing against him as it purred. The air conditioning had been set on high and the cold had gladly taken possession of the interior causing the rear window to become heavy with condensation.

Adrenaline began filling his veins as the memories of everything that had happened to him came back in a rush. He had been in the back of a car and Agent Dublin had told him he was a dead man. Then the crash happened, and Amber had come for him. Every bit of logic in his head told him she was dead, but he was certain that had been her

standing in the door of the car. Impossible as it seemed, she was alive.

He rubbed his wrists where the zip ties had been. There was an uncomfortable shadow feeling lingering in their absence and he hoped to never have to deal with that kind of experience again. His head was throbbing, but he pushed himself beyond the pain, grabbed onto the rear door handle, and shoved his way to freedom. Compared to the ambulance's air-conditioned interior, the outside summer air was hot, even at these high altitudes, and seared Robert's cold filled lungs when he emerged. His breathing seemed unnaturally loud to him in the utter stillness he found himself in. The empty roadway stretched out in front of him. The airport they had landed at was off to the right. He could see the small office building and even some of the runway, but there was no sign of any people. He did not see a single bird in the sky and there was not even the slightest breeze blowing to make the nearby tall grasses rustle. There were only the graceful curves from dozens of wings and propellers longing to return to the air.

Trying his best to stay hidden, he edged himself to the corner of the ambulance and peered around the side. The scene before him was surreal, horrifying, and told him why there was only silence now. Only a hundred feet away Amber stood reigning over a sea of bodies. Robert knew he should have been afraid. That he should be climbing into the ambulance and driving away, but he stood transfixed with awe. There had to have been three or four dozen well-armed police officers on the field when Dublin took him off the plane and now they were all dead. The magnitude of her lethal accomplishment was incomprehensible.

He watched the assault rifle she had been holding drop from her hand. Even at this distance he could hear the hollow clatter of it striking the ground but the sound was like a slap that broke him free of his shock and he started running towards her. She slumped against the side of the special tactic team's van and seemed oblivious of his approach until he was almost upon her and then she spun and aimed a pistol at his head.

Her blue eyes looked lifeless and unfocused and seeing her that way brought Robert to a sliding halt. Her skin looked so much paler to him now. Her ponytail, once neat, was disheveled and the way her black hair fell around her bloody face gave her a wild, untamed, look. She was wearing coveralls that were identical to the what the EMT, Doug, wore, only hers were torn and there was blood everywhere leaving Robert to wonder if all of it was hers or not.

It looked like a shotgun blast may have clipped her right arm where the top portion of her shoulder looked shredded. Blood ran down her dangling left arm in small crisscrossing and converging streams that were falling to the pavement in a growing pool of red and a bullet hole near her elbow told Robert all he needed. Other wounds dotted her body, but her head was surprisingly untouched except for a small gash that ran along the left side by her ear. The bullet had removed a small piece of her earlobe but if it had been another inch or two to the left it would have taken her face off instead.

How she was even standing Robert could not fathom. Even if it was sheer will power that was keeping her going it would not explain how she could do what she did. If it were anyone else standing before him, he would have

113

believed a zombie was returning from the grave. Yet she had proven to him that she was something else entirely now and he was not sure if he should feel in awe of her or be even more afraid.

"Amber, it's me. Robert," he said softly holding his hands up before him.

"Robert?" she murmured and the glare in her eyes softened as recognition of who she was facing began to register.

"Yea, that's right. So how about putting the gun down," he suggested and edged his way closer.

She seemed confused by what he was asking, as if she did not realize she had a gun in her hand, let alone that she was pointing it at him. She let her arm drop to her side a second later, but she did not release the gun from her grasp. In fact, the way her knuckles whitened around the grip Robert thought she was holding it even tighter than before.

"I can't believe it," Robert whispered looking around at the carnage.

Amber muttered something in response he could not quite understand.

"What?"

"Fools," she said louder. "Idiots and fools."

"Idiots?" Robert echoed. "These are police officers..."

"With what? A couple of decades of training under their belt?" Amber interrupted sounding disgusted. "Probably less? I've waged war for hundreds of years Robert. Real war, when there were no rules. During a time when there were no civil liberties. When there wasn't any concern or even consideration for preventing innocent casualties.

"They didn't even challenge me when I got out of the ambulance and walked right up to them. A few passing looks before turning back to whatever they were doing. A couple of questions and they handed me the person in charge. Then I just used the chaos to my advantage. See a medic running and you aim for whoever she's running away from, not realizing until it's too late that she was the threat all along. Even if someone looks like one of your own Robert, never trust them until you know for sure."

"Amber..."

"Please Robert, I'm tired," she said and as if to emphasize the point used her good hand, gun and all, to rub her temple. "I'm so tired. Go and find Jay and Walt. See if they're ok."

"Fine, but we aren't done talking about any of this," he answered.

Sprinting past the dead and seriously wounded Robert ran from patrol car to patrol car. He finally found the two men huddled on the floor in the back of one that was closest to the plane. Luckily for them it was one of the least damaged cars he had seen, but it still had not been enough protection for the female officer not moving on the ground behind it.

"We're glad to see you kid," Jay exclaimed when Robert opened the door and helped the two of them to freedom.

Jay was tall and wiry, but Walt was at least six inches taller and could have been a basketball player if he was not a solid wall of muscle that loomed over Robert when he emerged from the back of the car.

115

"You too," Robert told him with a genuine smile on his face. "I was worried I might find you amongst the bodies."

"As soon as the shooting started we hit the floor," Walt answered. His voice did not have the growl in it anymore, but it still sounded like the rumble of distant thunder.

Robert went to the back of the car and took a set of cuff keys from the dead female officer. Seeing the woman's lifeless eyes staring at nothing was going to haunt Robert for a long time, but he was thankful he did not see any signs of a wedding ring or where one might have been when she was off duty. He could not imagine, and did not want to think about, the constant fear loved ones had when their spouse or father or mother went into harm's way every day. Every time there was knock at the door or the phone rang, did they question if this was the call they had always dreaded? With hands noticeable shaking, he quickly unlocked Jay and Walt's cuffs before leading them back to where he had last seen Amber.

"You're a damn fool," Jay muttered walking up to her and looking her over with obvious concern.

"I couldn't leave you two behind," she whispered. "You know that."

"Yea I know, but you probably should have. We would have been alright."

"Next time," she told him with a crooked smile of teeth covered in blood. "Right now, I want you and Walt to get the plane ready. We need to hurry."

Not waiting to be told again Walt immediately started back towards the jet clearly eager to leave, but Jay lingered before Amber waved him off. Robert saw an unspoken conversation play out between the two of them, but he was not sure what any of it meant.

"Would you help me Robert?" she asked pointedly ignoring Jay's concerned backward glance.

Robert stepped in closer to her and she shifted her weight off the van to lean against him. He managed to get an arm around her waist which caused her to suck in her breath, but she did not complain. He figured any discomfort she felt with his arm around her paled in comparison to what the rest of her body must be feeling.

"I know why you came after me, but Jay was right about you being a fool for coming back here."

"I came back for them for the same reasons I came after you," her voice sounded even weaker now and softer as she spoke. She sighed a little as her body slid down slightly in his grasp. "I came back because they're my family. Because I love them and because they'd do the same for me."

"So, we're all family now?" Robert asked. In reality he was hoping she might say something that would help explain what had just happened, but he could tell she was getting weaker and he needed to give her something to focus on.

She laughed softly causing her body to convulse and cough up blood. Robert instinctively brought her closer to him trying to keep her upright as her legs began to give out. She managed to raise her head just enough to look him in the eyes. This enigma of a woman with her pale, intense blue eyes and scarred skin, who appeared to keep risking everything for him.

Is she really dying this time? he wondered. He had no idea what would happen if she did. The fact that she came

117

back to life once did not mean she could keep coming back, or did it? In his head, Robert kept trying to make sense of the massacre he saw and somehow justify what was going on around him.

Maybe she didn't really die when I shot her. Maybe the plane had landed in time for the medics to save her, he thought to himself. But trying to convince himself of that fact seemed just as unrealistic as her still walking now. *They did take her off the plane in a body bag. They don't take living people to the hospital in body bags.*

"I've watched you for a longtime Robert Kariot. Longer than you realize." As she spoke, blood began running from the corner of her mouth. Unable to hold her head up, she let out a sigh of resignation and lowered it to rest against his shoulder. She liked looking at his soft brown eyes. She always did.

It sounded like she sighed again, but Robert realized it was not a sigh at all. It was just her breathing turning shallow as it was slowly coming to a stop.

Every time she managed to fill her lungs she was struggling to buy herself a few more seconds. She wrapped her good arm around Robert's but her grip was weak and it took all her willpower to hold on to him. "No matter what happens Robert, I'll always come for you."

Then she was gone and the full weight of her dead body was falling toward the ground. Robert dropped with her and caught her in his arms. He brushed the hair out of face and lifted her gently so she was cradled in his arms. Jay met him at the plane's entrance with a look of anguish etched on his face as he stared down at her body.

"She'll be alright. It'll take a while for her to recover, but she'll get there."

"Jay...she's dead. These wounds..."

"She's going to wake up Robert," he said in a reassuringly fatherly way. "Don't ask me how because I don't know and I'm not sure I want to, but it's just like her not getting any older. She'll be alright. You'll see and then you'll be a believer in miracles too."

Robert looked at her still face. Her eyelids were partially closed and in a macabre sort of way she seemed to be watching him. He was not so sure if he believed Jay, but considering everything, he was not sure what he believed anymore. The only thing he was really sure of was that his enemies were not going to stop coming after him until he was dead.

"Does this thing have an auto pilot system?" Robert asked Jay as an idea started to form in his head.

"Sure. Why?"

"Can you program it to take off and fly a predetermined course?"

"Hey Walt," Jay hollered over his shoulder.

"What?" Walt replied from somewhere inside.

"Can you use the autopilot to take off and fly somewhere?"

"You could probably program the thing to dance if you wanted to. Why, you got a plan? Please tell me you got a plan."

"I've got an idea," Robert said as the engines announced their reawaking with a slow *whirring* call. "But I'm going to need both of you to help me get her out of here."

119

CHAPTER FOURTEEN

After receiving word that the ordeal was finally over Bishop Thomas, out of breath with excitement and forgetting the civility of his position, burst through the hall's doors to deliver the news to John David. "Your Grace!" he cried half running and half stumbling along the tile. "Your Grace!"

The Pope did his best to ignore Thomas's outburst from afar and continued to polish the tile floor, but that only seemed to make the situation worse.

"Your Grace! Your Grace! I have news!"

That does not trump common decency, John David thought and he intentionally nearly knocked his colleague over by moving to the next tile in the row. His irritation grew knowing the tile he left was not completely clean yet and made a mental note of which one it was so that he could return to it later.

Stumbling out of the way, and almost falling over himself in the process, the rambling Bishop fell silent at the sudden awareness of his behavior. Embarrassed, Thomas knelt next to John David, took a cleaning rag from nearby bucket, and began to polish the tiles in silence.

In his peripheral vision, John David could see Thomas repeatedly glancing in his direction with an obvious growing agitation and the man's labored breathing did nothing to help John David's tranquility. Thomas must have stopped and started his cleaning at least a half-dozen times in the span of a thirty seconds. He even started cleaning tiles that John David had already attended too.

"Oh, for Heaven's sake," John David glowered, breaking the silence. He looked at the floor with disgust. All his work had been ruined and he would have to start again. "Tell me what has brought you here in such an unorthodox manner."

"It's over your Holiness! It's finally over!" Thomas excitingly proclaimed clinching the rag before him. "Amber and Kariot are dead."

John David eyed his Bishop for a moment and then went back to cleaning the tile before him. "Perhaps, Brother Thomas, we should not rejoice too soon. It wasn't all that long ago that you and Sebastian had come to tell me this once before."

The simple rebuke was like a slap on Thomas's face.

"Tell me what you have learned," John David instructed as he placed a hand over Thomas's and gave his friend a reaffirming squeeze before his dignity suffered anymore. "And, if what you say is indeed true, then I will gladly join you in your bliss."

This simple kindness of John David taking his hand seemed to once more bring life to Thomas's good mood. The two men stood, leaving the rags and bucket where they were, and began to walk around the perimeter of the hall. It was a circuitous route that Thomas had become quite familiar with since John David came to power.

"Michael Dublin contacted us and said Sebastian had called and informed him Amber and Kariot had boarded a private jet and were heading for the east coast."

"Dublin. Our man in Homeland Security?" John David asked.

"Yes, Your Grace," Thomas confirmed with barely contained excitement. "The plane was intercepted and forced to land in Colorado. No one quite knows what happened after they landed. The initial report from Dublin was that Amber was already dead and that he had taken Kariot into custody.

"We're not sure what happened after that. We lost contact with Dublin and his partner Edward Burks. We do know an emergency call was made reporting of shots being fired and there were requests for backup and medical personnel. We think whoever was working with Amber was able to orchestrate an escape somehow and recover Kariot again. I believe Dublin and Burks were most likely killed."

"A steep price to pay," John David remarked but made no other attempt to interrupt. He told himself he would say a prayer for the two men later, but at the immediate moment he was more concerned with the outcome of Thomas's story.

"Yes, Your Holiness," Thomas agreed. "After it was discovered that the fugitives escaped, their plane was quickly intercepted, yet this time it was shot down. Which we believe took place over southern Nebraska or perhaps northern Kansas."

"Has the wreckage been searched? Have they identified the remains of anyone on board?"

"The authorities and the NTSB are on the scene now Your Holiness. The wreckage may be spread over a wide area and our supporters in the government have said it may take some time before they have more specific information to give. A day at least, perhaps more."

"And the press?"

"They're being told it was an accident for the time being, but I don't think it will be long before the plane and what happened at the airport are linked to one another." Thomas had expected a more positive response from the Pope, but he had only been rewarded with questions and silence. He grew more uneasy, and doubtful, with each circuit they made about the room.

"Where are Sebastian and the other Knights currently?" John David asked after contemplating the matter.

"I believe Sebastian has been joined by Sven Hurst. The others should not be far behind them. Would you like me to order them back to their original assignments your Holiness?"

"No!" John David snapped but said no more and they continued to walked on in silence.

Bishop Thomas was considered by many in the Vatican to be an excellent organizer, but to Thomas the ability was just second nature. He had always felt the need to exercise his mind and logistics just seemed to be a natural area that suited his desire. Early in John David's reign, during these long circular walks, Thomas realized that it took him two hundred twelve steps to navigate the hall's perimeter when he walked with the Pope. It was a constant, always the same, never more or less which he found amazing back then.

Most times he and the Pope would only traverse the course two or three times or, as Thomas calculated, at most six hundred thirty-six steps. When his current count reached one thousand sixty steps and his Holiness was still silent, Thomas began to grow concerned and stopped thinking of

123

the other items he still needed to see too after this meeting. When his count reached one thousand four hundred eighty-four steps, his concern had turned to worry. By the time the count was one thousand nine hundred eight steps his worry had turned to fear and it was not until he counted two thousand two hundred twenty-six steps, or ten and a half circuits around the room, that John David finally spoke and at that point Thomas was on the verge of panic.

"Why would they use the plane again?" John David puzzled aloud, almost to himself as if he had forgotten Thomas was with him.

"Um, I'm afraid I don't understand Your Holiness?" Thomas remarked, his voice shaking with nervousness.

"If they were discovered so quickly the first time and forced to land, why would they attempt to use the plane again?" John David asked again apparently oblivious of Thomas's discomfort.

"Perhaps they had no other option or speed was a necessity."

"Yes, perhaps, but I don't think so," John David replied and focused on that one question. "It's too convenient. Were any other planes missing from the airport or vehicles?"

"I don't know Your Grace," Thomas admitted. "I will have to make inquires."

"Perhaps the matter is finally settled Thomas. It may just be the paranoia of an old man, but I think it is more likely, or at the very least a possibility, that Amber and Kariot are elsewhere. So, until we know for certain that Robert Kariot died on that plane we must assume that he is still alive."

Thomas felt his early joy fracturing like a delicate egg being sacrificed to the fiery skillet. He dearly hoped the Pope was wrong and that the matter was finally ended, but what if it was not? What if Kariot was still on the loose? How were they going to find him again? Sebastian was no longer following them and any trail they had left behind was surely gone by now.

"I want you to contact Sebastian. I want to speak with him personally," John David instructed.

"Of course, Your Grace."

"Has Sebastian told you why he believes Kariot is heading for the east coast?"

"He believes she was taking him to a place called Harmony, Your Holiness."

"Harmony?"

"Yes, Your Grace."

"And what is Harmony?"

"I honestly don't know. It's not something that's been mentioned before as far as I can recall."

"Hmmm. Thank you, Thomas," John David said and led him to the door. He saw no point in asking Thomas anything further. If his friend had known anything else, he would have said so. "Inform me when Sebastian has called."

After Thomas left, John David continued to circle the room in quiet contemplation. *Harmony*, he pondered the possibilities of what that could mean, but finally pushed the thought aside out of frustration and retired to his own room. Whatever it was, if Mary had a hand in it, he was certain it could only mean trouble for the church. "*War*" she had told him on that night they met and he felt a chill run along his

125

arms at the thought. One usually did not find harmony until the war was over.

Almost an hour later John David was preparing a cup of Earl Grey tea in his private study. The smooth, bold flavor of the black tea combined with bergamot was comforting to him after a long day and, in his mind at least, it felt as if the days were getting longer and longer. Throughout the last several nights he had been visited by dark dreams. He often awoke in a sweat, yet he was never able to remember exactly what the dreams had been about, but he felt that God was talking to him. He knew he was being shown something important concerning the circumstances laid out before him and the terrifying outcome should he fail in the task God had given him. As he absently stirred a teaspoon of sugar into his cup his private phone rang.

"Yes," he said after picking the receiver up on the sixth ring.

"Sebastian is on the line Your Grace," Thomas informed him from the other end.

"Thank you, Thomas. Put him through."

"Yes, Your Grace. One moment." The line went quiet while Thomas switched the connection to a private encrypted line.

"Sebastian?" John David asked once the line came back on.

"Yes, Your Grace," Sebastian answered.

The man sounded calm to John David. He felt it was a good sign that Sebastian was not letting his emotions regarding the events that had transpired over the last few hours blind the Knight, like they had Thomas. "Is she still alive, Sebastian?"

126

"Is *who* still alive Your Grace?"

"I have no time for prattle Sebastian," John David reprimanded and slammed his spoon onto his desk. "You know her better than anyone. Do you think Mary and Kariot are still alive?"

"Yes, I do," Sebastian answered and then added, almost as if it were an afterthought "Your Grace."

"Why?" John David demanded and ignored the soft sigh that he heard coming through on the other end of the line.

"Amber isn't stupid Your Grace."

"Her name is *Mary*. And if I thought that was the case Sebastian we wouldn't be having this conversation."

"She no longer considers herself to be that person Your Grace and it would be equally dangerous for us to think of her that way as well," Sebastian explained before making a muffled comment to someone nearby. "What do your advisors think? Do they believe Amber is a fool? Is that the problem Your Grace?"

John David felt his anger rising at Sebastian's implied insult, but he forced aside the harsher admonishment he was going to issue, if only because of the simple fact that Sebastian was right. Believing Mary was dead was exactly what the bishops were doing. The order was happy, ecstatic, that the problem simply went away in a ball of fire even though they still did not know the outcome. The fools were already discussing plans for a future without the threat of *her* lingering in the shadows and threatening to pop out of nowhere.

"Your Grace?" Sebastian injected after John David did not respond.

127

"I asked you to explain your reasoning Sebastian."

"It's a simple matter of tactics Your Grace. Amber has an objective to achieve and her first attempt to reach it failed. She won't make that mistake again. Being in the field gives her the benefit of being fluid. She adapts to the situation as it changes," Sebastian explained and then added, "she doesn't have to wait for someone to tell her what to do."

"You sound like you admire the woman."

"No, Your Grace," Sebastian countered with a darkness that made John David realize he did not want to know how Sebastian really felt about her.

"If what you say is true, that she is still alive, then we've lost track of her. I need you to find her trail again."

"No, Your Grace."

"No?" John David stuttered before the anger that was simmering below the surface exploded. "No!" Who are *you* to tell *me* no? I want her found! You have no idea what is at stake!"

"I'm perfectly aware of what is at stake," Sebastian countered, but his voice remained quiet and hard. "I can't find her now because whatever incompetents that were sent to retrieve her from the plane failed. She should have been locked down on the runway and left for me to handle. As Your Grace said, no one knows her better than I do."

John David suppressed his next outburst. Instead he said nothing and let his heavy breathing tell Sebastian that he was still waiting to hear what he had to say.

"I know where she's going," Sebastian revealed after calming his own frustration. If he pushed the Pope too much he might be ordered back to the Vatican. He could not risk losing this opportunity to face Amber.

"Harmony," John David muttered.

"Yes, Your Grace."

"Where is it?"

"It's not a *where,* Your Grace," Sebastian answered. "It's a *what.*"

Six minutes after he hung the phone up, John David placed a call for Thomas to present himself. When he arrived, Thomas found John David at the window looking out over Vatican City.

"Thomas, please arrange a flight to the United States," John David instructed without turning to face his companion. "As soon as possible."

"Your Grace?" Thomas asked confused by the suddenness.

"Arrange for a trip to the United States. To New York," John David reiterated as he took up a position behind his desk. "And I don't want anyone not directly involved in this matter to know of it. Coordinate with Sebastian which airport he will meet us at."

"Traveling in secrecy..." Thomas began and then stopped himself leaving the difficulty of such a thing unspoken in the air between them.

John David slammed his fist on the desk causing Thomas to jump and take a half step backwards. "Isn't that what we're paying those bureaucrats in Washington for? To make sure our people can enter and leave the country unmolested? To keep prying eyes looking elsewhere and to deal with the ones who aren't?"

"Yes, Your Grace, but...but you're the Pope."

"That's correct," John David declared pulling himself fully upright. "I am the Pope, so make it happen. I don't care what it takes or who you have to entice."

"Yes, Your Grace," Thomas replied and resigned himself to the nearly impossible task he was given.

John David glanced in Thomas's direction when he did not leave. "Speak freely Brother. I think the time for formality has passed us at this point."

"Your Holiness," Thomas began, bowing as he did. He paused, not sure how to say or ask what was on his mind. "Are you and Sebastian of like minds then? Amber...I mean Mary and Kariot are alive?"

"Yes Brother. We are of a similar opinion in that."

"Then why must we leave for America? Won't Sebastian and the others be able to stop her?"

"I'm leaving because that is where I belong," John David answered and walked back to his window again. The wonderous view of the city beyond calling to him. He loved this place and would do anything to protect it. "I pray that our Knights will be able to once more smite those that try to oppose God's will Thomas, but for this, I'm afraid prayer won't be enough. We must leave and it must be soon."

CHAPTER FIFTEEN

Amber felt like she was being rolled gently back and forth when she started to wake up. From the muffled clacking sound and the way her body moved with the motion she knew she was on a train. She always enjoyed train rides, she even followed Robert on one a couple of years ago. What made it even better for her, was he was not going anywhere. He just wanted to get away and have a change of scenery. In Amber's opinion, it was perfect. Unfortunately, Kate had come along and she and Robert had another classic fight. Amber listened in behind a platform piling as Kate yelled at Robert at the first stop about how much she hated trains and him yelling back, demanding to know, why she had come. It ended with them leaving in a taxi. Amber hated Kate after that.

It was a peaceful feeling being on a train again and the sounds and the feel of it tried to tempt her to go back to sleep for a little while longer. It had been such a long time since she had felt any sort of peace in her life and she seriously considered letting herself drift off to sleep again, but she could not allow herself to. So, it was with a sense of loss that she slowly cracked opened her eyes just enough to take in her surroundings.

She was lying on a small, more hard than soft, padded bench seat, under Jay's navy-blue windbreaker he had on the plane. At least she thought it was his jacket from the faint aroma of his cologne that drifted across her nose. He never went anywhere without it, no matter how hot or cold it was, he would have it tucked away somewhere. She was in a compartment, about the size of a small walk in closet, and bathed in the dying sunlight of an approaching evening. A large window perched above her and a single, sliding door was closed at the other end of the bench. A narrow aisle barely wide enough for leg space spanned the distance between her and where Robert sat. Seeing him sitting across from her brought on a rush of unexpected excitement and swept away her lingering fatigue as her eyes flashed open.

He was sitting peacefully, or so it seemed, with a thick book in his lap. He had changed his clothes from the last time she had seen him. It also looked like he had shaved recently, no longer sporting the dark shadows of encroaching facial hair. She suppressed an urge to run her hand along his cheek to feel how soft his skin was.

"Where are we?" she asked as she stiffly pulled herself into a sitting position and let Jay's jacket fall to the seat beside her. Looking down at herself, she was shocked that her own clothes had been changed. The white, long sleeve shirt with an outline of a large pink heart on the front was not her style. Her hair fell over her shoulders as she looked down at herself and she ran her fingers through the dark, recently cleaned, strands.

"Somewhere in Illinois I think," Robert answered keeping his head tilted towards the book in his lap. When he finished what he was reading he looked up at her and smiled. "I'm glad you're up. We should be at the station in an hour or so."

"You changed my clothes?" she asked, her eyes locking onto his.

Her voice lacked the typical commanding tone, but Robert still felt compelled to answer. "Yea, well, didn't have much choice there. You were covered in blood and gunshot wounds so we thought it would better if it didn't look like we were pushing a dead body onto the train."

"We?"

"Jay and Walt are on board. They're in the next cabin over," Robert tilted his head toward the wall behind her.

"Great," she muttered. She took a deep breath and felt the bandages underneath her clothes tighten.

"If it's any consolation, it was just me doing the changing. Walt didn't seem too comfortable with it and Jay said he barely had enough coordination to get himself dressed, let alone someone else, but I have my doubts about that."

"And that makes it suddenly alright for *you* to do it?" she asked a little sharper then she intended. She did not know why she was so upset about it. Others had seen her in worse conditions, but for some reason those times were suddenly an entirely different matter altogether and did not involve Robert.

"Under the current circumstances, I'd say damn straight it does. It wasn't like we had a private suite and I had my way with you. It was in the back seat of a stolen car and I was trying my best to keep you from looking like some horrible surgery gone wrong."

"Guess you got a good look at the damage," Amber muttered turning to look out the window, her hair falling in such a way as to shield her face from him.

He did not know what she was, but *damaged* had not crossed his mind in the least after seeing what she was capable of doing. The bullet holes had closed over by the time they had gotten to the city. The shotgun wound needed more attention but was healing. He had to admit the scarring on her back looked worse comparatively. There were so many small scars they looked like one big scar with a few small spots of untouched skin that stood out of place.

"Actually, I thought you have surprisingly soft skin," he told her, truthfully. As surprised as he was about her back, he was equally surprised with the smoothness of her skin.

She turned her head just a little to peer at him and caught him quickly looking away and back towards the book in his lap. A hidden smile grew on her face as she sat quietly and watched him from the corner of her eye. She found herself wondering what his skin would feel like if she ran her hands over it, but quickly pushed the thought away. *What is wrong with me?* she thought and instead asked the first thing that popped in her head. "What are you reading?"

He closed the cover of the thick paperback and held it up to show her. In large, scripted capital letters the words *Holy Bible* were etched across the non-distinct cover in gold lettering. "Figured I should familiarize myself with what I'm dealing with. Know thy enemy sort of thing."

"You must be a fast reader."

Robert shrugged and tossed the book on the cushioned seat next to him where it landed with a noticeably heavy thump. "Not fast enough to get through this, but it helped pass the time while you were out."

"How long was that for?"

"A few hours. Which, considering how fast you recovered from getting killed earlier," he blew out a breath as he realized the insanity of that statement, "I thought you would have recovered sooner."

"I was barely able to move before having to face that tactical team. I don't heal instantly. All the damage adds up. It was mostly will power that was keeping me up."

Keeping his thoughts to himself Robert just gave a nodded reply but did not say anything further.

"What happened with the plane?" she asked.

"Decided we should take an alternate route. Turned out to be a good thing too since right now the NTSB is probably putting together what's left of it anyway."

She narrowed her eyes at him. "What does that mean?"

"I had Walt set the jet's autopilot to take off and fly for Canada. The train station had some TV's on when we were getting tickets and up popped breaking news about a plane crash in Nebraska, southwest of Mullen, wherever the hell that is. I figured if they found us once they could find us again, but this time they weren't taking any chances."

"What are you talking about, found us once? I woke up in a body bag, remember? And when I got out I saw you in the backseat of that car with Michael as you were pulling out of the airport."

"Agent Dublin?"

"Agent?"

"Yea, he said he worked for Homeland Security," Robert explained. "So I'm guessing you know he was knight?"

"Yea, I knew," Amber muttered. "I just didn't know he had bedded down with Homeland Security."

"Well, back on the plane Jay had come back to tell us a couple of fighters showed up. Which was just after you forced me to *shoot you*," Robert clarified, enunciating the last two words for affect. "Then he knocked me out."

"Jay knocked you out?" she interrupted, confused as to why Jay would knock him out.

"Yup. By the way, between you and him I'm starting to feel like a punching bag. Anyway, we were forced to land at that small airport back where you found us. You were...dead when that happened. When I came to, Jay and Walt were gone and they carried you off in a body bag. Guess you know how the rest turned out."

They sat in silence for a few minutes. Neither one looked at the other as the train continued rocking them gently back and forth. Amber was looking at the floor, lost in her own thoughts while Robert turned his attention towards the world beyond the window where the sun had set and night was rapidly closing in.

"Thanks, by the way," he said after a little while.

"What for?" Amber asked, roused from her thoughts.

"For saving me back there. Dublin flat out told me I was a dead man."

"Arrogant," Amber mumbled.

"Huh?"

"Knights are so arrogant," Amber spoke more clearly. "If they were smart they would have shot you first and then told you as you were dying why they did it. Saying anything beforehand only gave you time to think about how to get out of there."

"I'll take arrogant," Robert told her, clearly firm in his opinion on the subject. "I don't see how I would have made it out of there if you didn't come along."

"You would have figured something out."

"Maybe, maybe not. Guess as long as I'm still valuable to you I have a wild card on my side."

"What's that supposed to mean?" she demanded, her indignation clear.

"What?" Robert countered, his own defenses rising at her tone.

"You think just because I need your help I'd toss you aside once this is finished?"

"I'm not entirely sure. Would you? You've made it pretty clear on this little road trip of yours that what happens to other people really doesn't matter to you," Robert shot back refusing to back down.

"Where do you get off saying," she started to argue as a coldness touched her eyes that were now firmly locked on him, but he cut her off before she could say anything else.

"How about you threatening to kill the cop outside of my house if I didn't behave. Or that car you blew apart when the motorcycles were chasing us," Robert noted, flicking his fingers as he counted. "That guy behind the desk at the airport in Oregon, the *entire* tactical team and police force at that little airport outside Denver. Did you even think about who they left behind?"

"I told you, I'd do anything to keep you safe..."

"Until you're done with me," Robert shot in before she could say anything else.

Up to that point he had made it a point to look her in the eyes so he did not see her left hand come out of nowhere and smack him hard enough to make his head spin. One moment he had been staring at her and the next he was looking at his own reflection in the window staring wildly back at himself.

"Maybe we can't all be *perfect* like you are Robert," she scoffed as Robert turned to face her again.

He expected to see a lethal calm in her eyes, but she looked like she was going to cry. She shook her head, pushed herself to her feet and left the compartment without another word, slamming the door as she went.

Robert had no intention of going after her. Whenever he fought with Kate and went after her it only led to a bigger argument. Yet Kate never looked like she was going to cry when they fought. Which was why he found himself in the narrow corridor moments later instead of staying in the compartment and stewing in his own righteous anger. Amber was nowhere to be seen.

He flipped a coin in his head and went to the right, through a busy dining car and into the next passenger cabin before he decided he had chosen wrong and turned around. After going through several cars beyond their own he backtracked and climbed the stairs to the upper deck of the observation car, where he found her sitting alone at the far end. He walked past a young couple, too involved in each other to notice him, and approached her slowly. *It doesn't look like she wants to keep fighting*, he thought and considered his options. This was new relationship territory for him so he decided to not say anything and instead just sit down next to her. She said nothing to him and barely acknowledged his existence except for a quick glance at his approach.

The sun had fled beyond the horizon and now the reds and purples that pursued it were being transformed into shades of inky black. Night was descending quickly, casting its enveloping blanket over the train as it continued to rumble unerringly onward. The sky was mostly clear. A few patches of clouds, now dark shapeless forms floating against the sky, kept what lay behind them secret. Otherwise the curtains to the heavens were opening for the mere mortals on the world below to behold. Without the intrusion of street lamps and city lights the night sky became indefinable. A million, billion stars sparkled as the quarter moon started to make its appearance just above the eastern horizon in a futile attempt to catch the sun.

"It's beautiful," Robert whispered swinging his head to see the splendor of the universe laid out before him. "You never get to see this in the city you know. It's stuff like this that reminds a person just how alone we are in the universe."

"We're not alone," Amber whispered but said no more.

Robert lowered his head and sighed. Looking at his hands resting on his lap he rolled his fingers closed into fists and then stretched them out again.

"What are you Amber?" he finally asked when the silence felt like it was going to go on forever. "An angel? An alien? Some sort of government bio project gone rogue?"

"After everything you've seen me capable of doing, you think I might be an angel?"

"Why not?" he asked raising his head to look out at the night sky again. "Angels don't always do good deeds you know. And ruthlessness can be part of God's M.O. Look at Sodom and Gomorrah. The great flood. The Tower of Babel. The plagues of Egypt."

"I'm no angel Robert," she answered softly, keeping her gaze focused on anywhere but him.

"Then what are you? And how did I get involved in this... mess?"

She did not answer him.

The last few days had been rough on the two of them. Ever since she had seen that man, Sebastian, at the airport Robert knew something had changed in her. Yesterday she had been calm and in control. Almost carefree in her illicit behavior. Today Robert thought there was a subtle difference. The confidence was still there. The lethality was still lurking just under her calm demeanor, but the carefree attitude was gone. It had been replaced with an urgency that they were no longer just running towards something but fleeing something else as well and knowing there was something, or someone, out there that made her feel threatened gave Robert pause.

Am I ever going to have a normal life again, he wondered. The last time he felt like he knew what normal was, was a lifetime away now and he seriously doubted he would ever feel that kind of normalcy again. That was if he somehow managed to survive this suicidal adventure he was now on. A part of him said he should just stand up and get as far away as he could, but deep down he knew that was not going to happen. At least not yet. More than the fact that either the church or some psycho religious group was out to kill him he wanted to know the truth. All his life his parents had pushed him to look beyond what was right in front of him and find the truth behind the presentation. And here he was, on a train in Illinois, with the greatest enigma he had ever witnessed sitting right next to him.

While Robert warred with his inner turmoil, Amber watched his ghost like reflection in the train car's window. She saw his frustration clearer than what the blurred image in the glass showed. She knew that after everything she had done to him and put him through he deserved to know the truth. He was the key to it all and she needed him, but looking at his reflection she kept seeing her own failures and kept asking herself how she had fallen so far. Now she felt a fear she had not felt in a long time. She was going to have to open-up to him or she was going to lose him. Inside, she felt hurt and alone and she screamed at herself to do something, anything. All she had to do was reach out and touch him and she knew it would get better, but instead she just sat there doing nothing.

Amber's silence kept fueling Robert's seldom seen stubborn streak and he could feel it coming to the forefront of his personality again. It was a trait, according to his mother, that he had gotten from his father and by all accounts he did not see any reason not to believe her. Luckily though, his temperament was a toned-down version of his father's. He was not sure when he no longer became a hostage, or if he ever really was one to begin with, but somehow, he knew if he got up right now and walked away, she was not going to stop him. He still did not know what he was going to do when they reached Chicago, whether he stayed or left he figured he was screwed either way. The only thing he was certain of, was that this was his life and he was not going to sit idly by while events played out.

"I'm mostly human," she whispered out of desperation as he started to get up. She could not let it end like this. "At least I think I am."

Robert turned to stare at her, but she refused to look at him. He eased himself back down on the bench seat and waited.

"I don't have parents like you do, at least I don't think so, but I did have a brother."

"What happened to him?"

"He died a long time ago," she answered lowering her head and absently pulling a piece of fuzz off her jeans and casting it away.

"Died?" Robert asked wanting her to look at him, but she kept her focus in her lap. "He didn't heal like you?"

"No. But he could do other things that I couldn't. He had a gift for predictions," she told him sparing him a quick glance before turning to look out the window at the stars. She was not really seeing the heavenly bodies though, as her memory took her somewhere distant and out of Robert's reach.

"You're saying he was a psychic?"

"No, he wasn't a psychic, but you would have thought he was. He used mathematical probability to figure out what was going to happen. I didn't know that's what it was at the time, but I think that's how he saw the world. As one big equation, a mathematical formula, full of variables and outcomes that he could use to manipulate events to his advantage. Or just as importantly, he knew when the outcome of an event was not going to go his way, no matter how he stacked the deck."

"How'd he die?"

"Do you believe in God yet Robert?" she asked instead of answering him.

"Not really," he replied seeing that this was going to be a reoccurring theme in their relationship.

"I guess that means you don't believe in Heaven either."

"No, not Heaven," he admitted while collecting his thoughts.

"But something?"

"Something? *Something...*" he started but left the comment there.

"Tell me," she asked looking at him for the first time. "I'd like to know."

"It may sound a bit crazy."

"That's alright, I can handle crazy," she encouraged with a warm smile.

"Well, we're creatures made of matter and energy and they say matter can't be destroyed but can be transformed."

"I don't understand."

"It's a scientific law that matter can't be destroyed but can be changed. In order to change matter, you need to exert some sort of energy on it. Like when you heat water to make steam or freeze it to make ice. So, the way I see it anyway, people are born with the ability built inside themselves to transform into something else when they die. We're made of matter with all these electrical energy impulses shooting around so maybe we don't die. Maybe we just become something else."

"Like what?" she asked.

143

"I don't know. Maybe we just become a part of out there," he sighed waving his hand toward the night sky. "Maybe our energy merges with everyone else's that went before us and we help fuel the stars or something."

"Fuel the stars," Amber murmured sounding thoughtful.

"Or something," Robert responded with a small shrug of his shoulders. He had never told anyone that before. "Seems like a good way to let loved ones know we're okay and that we're waiting to greet them when their time comes. Especially out here, away from the city lights, the stars are limitless."

"I like that idea Robert. It's good," she said and turned her attention to the floor while he continued staring at the galaxy above them.

"And here I figured you as a pearly white gate kind of girl."

"Even if Heaven existed, I would be one of the last people to get in," she responded with a cryptic chuckle.

"You keep asking me if I believe and it sounds like you're the one who doesn't believe in Heaven?"

"Oh, I believe in Heaven Robert, just not what the Vatican's vision of Heaven is."

"You can be quite confusing you know," he told her even though he was sure she had heard that sentiment on more than one occasion.

"I know. Did you know that right now in the world there are scientists mixing different compounds together for the sole intention of creating life?" she asked, tossing her head to cast her long hair over her shoulder.

"That's not really my field, but I'm not surprised."

144

"When they succeed, not if, but when, how do you think those single celled organisms will look upon us?"

"I suppose you're taking the trek that we'd be gods to them," he said off-handedly.

"Yes."

"But what does that have to do with us Amber? You and me?"

"That's the whole point Robert. We're the single celled organism."

"Now, I really don't understand what you're talking about?" Robert was exasperated and his face contorted to reflect his frustration.

"I'm saying we're the single celled creature in the Petri dish. That God isn't what the church has capitalized on, but a higher being that succeeded in what the scientists here are trying to do."

"You think that you and I, and the rest of the planet, are just a bunch of single celled animals floating around in a Petri dish?"

"It's the best analogy I can give you."

"We live in an infinite universe..." Robert started but she quickly cut him off.

"No. We live in a universe that we haven't found the boundaries too yet, but it does end and it ends at a wall Robert," Amber said taking his hands in her own. "I need you to believe me."

"You want me to believe you?" he asked sounding incredulous. "I've heard some pretty far out stuff. Stuff even along the lines you're talking about, but I've never met someone fanatical enough to seriously believe it."

145

"I'm not a *fanatic*," she replied and let go of his hands.

"Yea, ok," Robert scoffed and stood up. "Look, Amber, I appreciate you looking out for me. I *absolutely* believe that a group of dangerous, powerful, people want me dead. And I can't even start to explain how it is that you can accomplish what you can in healing yourself, but I think I'm at my end with all this.

"A couple of days ago I walked into my house just wanting to take a shower and get a cup of coffee. Now here I am, almost to Chicago, and running for my life. I'm done." The pain he saw in her eyes as he spoke was crushing him and he did not understand why. He was supposed to hate her, wasn't he? "I'm getting off the train at the station and then I'm going to empty my bank accounts and find some quiet, isolated, part of the world until things blow over."

He could not look at her anymore without seeing his own failures so he took one last look outside at the stars instead. Billions of little sparkling lights reminding him of what was waiting for him one day. Robert was not sure how far away that day was, but considering his current situation did not help his outlook. "I'm sorry," was all he could say and began to walk away.

"Robert wait," Amber called, catching up to him before he had taken a half-dozen steps.

"Amber look..."

"Here," she interrupted holding up a tiny, very thin piece of metal. "Take this."

He clasped it lightly between his fingers and turned it around trying to figure out what it was.

"It's a handcuff shim," she explained. "I wish I could tell you that walking away will mean it's over, but it won't be. They'll never stop looking for you, but if you're lucky you'll get the chance to use this to try to escape."

"Amber..."

"Shut up," she rebuked, her voice cracking with emotion she was struggling to control. "Use the flat end and slide it in along the teeth of the cuff. If you do it right you'll hit the ratchet assembly and be able to open them."

"Thanks," he said and he meant it. "Hopefully I won't lose it."

"Slide it into the tip of your shoelace. Here," she said and took it back from him and knelt down to insert the small escape tool into one of his laces. "It's not something most people carry so nobody will probably even look for it."

When she stood back up again he leaned in and kissed her gently on the cheek. Robert was not sure why he did, it was mostly an impulse, and after giving her a tight smile he turned and walked away without saying another word. He was sure if he stayed any longer or said anything else he was going to lose his nerve and stay with her.

Amber watched him go, thankful he did not see the few tears she could not keep from escaping. Everything was coming to an end and she felt more alone than she had ever felt before.

CHAPTER SIXTEEN

Amber, Jay, and Walt silently stood near the exit door as the train pulled into the station. Amber was staring at the gray nondescript wall, lost in her own thoughts, while her companions individually wondered what their next steps were going to be. Somewhere on the far end of the same train car Robert was also waiting to disembark. Amber had seen him when she came down from the observation car just before they pulled into the station. Their eyes met, they held each other's gaze for a moment, and then she smiled at him. She thought she saw both relief and sadness on his face, but he managed a meager smile in return before they turned in opposite directions. Letting him go was the hardest thing she had ever done.

She thought she understood how he was feeling. Robert was not the first person who found what she had to say difficult or even impossible to believe. There was Sebastian after all, and even he was at the end of an already long list. She had not lied to Robert about him being important to her. He was probably more important to her in ways that she did not want to let herself think about. She understood she could have forced him to go along with them or forced the information that she needed out of him, but somewhere along the way she had let herself care too much for him.

But I've always cared about him, haven't I? she finally admitted to herself, which was why she was letting him go and why she was terrified about what might happen to him. Especially if Sebastian managed to find him before anyone else. Sebastian again. *Why did it always have to circle back to him?*

"Amber!" Walt's deep baritone voice broke into her thoughts as he prodded her shoulder.

Startled, she looked up at the two men across from her. "What?" she demanded.

"Don't get bitchy with me," Walt snapped back. "We've been talking to you for the last minute and you've been off in la-la land."

Her anger simmered down as the scary realization of just how inattentive she was washed over her. "Well, I'm listening now."

"Yea," Walt said in obvious disbelief. "What do you want us to do when we get off? Get tickets for Philly?"

"No," she told him instantly. "Being on a train restricts our movements too much. Get a car. We'll drive the rest of the way."

"What about Robert?" Jay asked. His head was tilted towards the train car's floor, but his eyes were turned up to stare at her.

"He's not coming," she told him turning to look out the door's window as the train slowed to a crawl.

"I thought we needed him?" Walt pushed.

"We'll find another way."

"That's not how you..." Jay started.

"Damn it, he's not coming. Okay?" she hissed making it clear she had no intention of continuing the conversation.

"Okay," Jay surrendered, turning his attention to his wristwatch.

149

"Suits me fine," Walt said to nobody in particular before looking over at Amber. "You've been acting strange ever since you brought him along anyway."

The train had slowed even more as the cold, gray, concrete platform crept into view. The universally standard yellow lines painted across the platform's surface warned passengers away from where the platform stopped and a quick fall to the tracks started. Posters and overhead signs decorated the concourse, but all that was only circumstantial and cosmetic. Amber saw the truth those things hid which was that the stone, like life, was hard, unforgiving, and merciless. If Amber was going to get them through what lay ahead she was going to have to be more like the concrete surrounding them.

"Well I guess you don't have to worry about that anymore," she muttered in reply and slid out the doors as soon as there was room enough to slip through. She did not bother checking to see if they were following her. She was more afraid of seeing Robert again then of Jay and Walt not following her.

She exited the South Concourse in short order and made her way toward Clinton Street and the car rental desk. If they took turns driving, and kept their stops to short breaks, they could be in the New York area by late morning. She had to assume that Sebastian was already ahead of them and she let the anger of his betrayal push her forward. She was almost at the Hertz rental counter when Jay grabbed her arm and jerked her to a sudden stop.

"What?" she hissed, happy and ashamed she finally had someone to vent her anger at.

"Get a hold of yourself for Christ's sake."

"Don't you dare use *his* name like that." she warned in a voice that had turned deadly and it was the eyes of a killer that focused on Jay.

He closed the already short distance between them to a few inches so that she could smell the coffee on his warm breath. He knew her too well and for too long to just back down from her anger. "Look at the tv behind the clerk."

Eyes narrowing, Amber gave him one last disdainful glare before glancing over her shoulder towards the car rental area. She scrutinized the entire scene. A young Asian woman, with hair even darker than her own, was positioned behind the counter unaware of the news unfolding behind her. For Amber what was on the tv was a nightmare scenario she could not turn away from.

A picture of Robert Kariot loomed in high definition. Amber knew the image well, it was from his university ID taken a few years ago. She had a copy of that photo in her files, it was a favorite of hers. The caption at the bottom of the broadcast read "WANTED FUGITIVE. IF SEEN, IMMEDIATELY CONTACT YOUR LOCAL AUTHORITES" in bold flashing letters.

"Get the car," Amber ordered and was moving before Jay had time to respond. Almost as an afterthought she called back over her shoulder, "Pick me up on Clinton Street."

She moved rapidly through the somewhat empty terminal hoping anyone who took notice of her would have the opinion that she was in a hurry, but not rushing. She kept her face emotionless as she continuously looked through the terminals stragglers and ignored the few comments that men who had too much to drink at happy hour referenced her way. She was beginning to worry that Robert had been able to leave the station when she finally spotted him nearing the Clinton Street exit. A wave of relief filled her, but it was short lived when she spotted two of Chicago's transit officers moving in that same direction.

She instantly knew the type of crooked cops the two men were. She had seen hundreds of similar types around the world and over the years, although lately these particular types of scumbags seemed to be multiplying. She saw the holy-than-thou attitude in their eyes and the way they swept through the station terminal, like they were untouchable kings overflowing with a false perception that they were better than everyone else.

A drug dealer who was generous with a few hundred-dollar bills could safely walk away from incarceration for another night. A prostitute willing to go down on her knees could keep waiting on her corner for a more profitable client. Yet anyone unlucky enough to be taken into custody by those two was guaranteed to arrive at the precinct in worse physical condition than they were before the handcuffs were put on. So, it was with a growing panic that Amber knew Robert might not arrive at the police station alive if they caught him.

She calculated that she was twenty-eight long strides from him and her feet were moving before she even realized it. At fifteen strides, she did not know if she was going to make it in time to keep them from seeing him. At sixteen steps, she realized she was not armed, but by step seventeen she did not care. At step twenty, if it came down to a fight, she had decided to use scumbag officer number one, on the right, as a shield between herself and scumbag officer

152

number two, on the left. As step twenty-three became twenty-four in her mind's plan she had already killed scumbag officer number one and was making the calculations to dispatch number two. At step twenty-five, as the transit cops narrowed the gap, she was not sure she had been fast enough to keep Robert from being noticed.

At step twenty-eight, only seconds ahead of the officers turning their attention toward her and Robert, she reached out, grabbed Robert's swinging arm, and yanked him to face her. She ignored his baffled expression, wove her hands around his head, and pulled him into a deep kiss. A moment before their lips touched, Amber swung just enough to give the officers a profiled look of her curved legs and jean enhanced buttocks which she was certain would keep their focus on her lower half and off Robert. Then her lips touched his and she forgot about the officers all together.

A feeling like electric fire raced down her spine and she instinctively pulled Robert tighter against her body. Some part of her mind protested that his kiss was not supposed to feel like this, that she was only trying to protect him, but she could not remember who she was trying to hide him from or why. Her tongue glanced across his semi open mouth and she was thrilled when he responded and pulled her against himself. Her eyes were closed against the ecstasy of his touch and the world disappeared in that blissfulness.

It was the need for a clear breath of air that finally broke their connection which left the two of them breathing hard and wordlessly staring at one another. Neither one of them knew how long they had been locked together, but just by looking at the other, they both knew they had experienced something similar. They saw the confusion, and hunger, in

153

the other's gaze and the danger if they lost themselves in that embrace again.

Clarity returned to Amber first. It was like a lightning bolt exploding in her delirium and panic caused her to whirl on the spot to locate the two transit officers. When she found them, they had already gone by and were at least thirty feet away now. A brief wave of relief rolled through her and she took that moment to grab Robert's hand and pull him with her towards the exit before he could protest.

"Amber, what are you doing?" he asked. He sounded a little confused, but he did not fight her as they hurried.

"You're on the news," she whispered drawing him closer and wound her arm possessively around his waist when she saw the doors that would take them onto Clinton Street. "I don't know if those cops were aware of who you are, but I couldn't take the chance. The church is moving faster than I'd imagined. It's turning into a nationwide manhunt so we're going to have to keep you out of sight as much as possible. Jay's getting a car. He'll meet us outside."

"So back there," Robert started but stopped when he noticed how oddly she was looking at him. "What..."

Before he could say anything else, Amber pulled him to her and kissed him again letting her warm breath and soft lips mingle with his. She barely had enough will power to break the connection, but the seriousness of the situation and the danger they were in helped her push him away. "Back there was wonderful," she answered truthfully, leaving her hands softly circled around his back. "Unexpected, but wonderful."

Before Robert could say anything else she pushed through the doors and pulled him into the recessed and sheltered entranceway that led onto the street. Holding his hand, she started walking ahead, but Robert pulled her back. She turned around to see what was wrong and the look in his eyes felt like a knife stabbing her in the chest. Her heartrate began accelerating and a desperate and unexplainable dread started taking hold. *Why am I feeling this way?* she demanded to know of herself, but no answer came.

"I meant what I said on the train Amber. I'm done." Robert stated.

"I know, but..."

"I'm not going."

"Robert, they're saying you're a terrorist," she exclaimed stepping closer to him. "They haven't been able to stop you so they're going to get the country to find you for them. They're going to kill you."

"Probably."

"Then let me help you."

"Why?"

"What!" she shouted as her own indignation flared at his stubbornness.

"Why should I let you help me? Why should I even *trust* you?" he calmly asked as he pulled himself free of her hold. "You won't even tell me the truth of what this is all about."

Completely dumbfounded, all she could do was stare at him. This, stubborn ass, standing before her infuriated her to no end, but at the same time there was a whisper in the back of her mind that he could drive away the loneliness she was always feeling. An emptiness that had

155

never left since Michael had died so many, many years ago. Gently, tentatively, she took his one hand in both of hers.

Her hands were soft, even after years of fighting and struggling, her body was constantly repairing itself. Robert's hands were rough from use, but not damaged from hard toil. His right middle finger, calloused on the side, told her he often held a pen or pencil in that hand and she wondered how many years she had written in the same way. The two of them were very different, but at the same time they were similar in so many ways.

"I've never lied to you Robert," she told him with a firm finality as she strengthened her grip on his hands and looked him in the eyes. "And I never will."

A maroon colored SUV pulled to a quick stop outside the short tunnel they were standing in and gave a quick beep of its horn.

"Please come with me Robert," she asked in soft gentle tones. "I'll tell you everything. You won't believe me, but I'll tell you."

"I think that's the first time you've said *please* to me," Robert declared.

She smiled at him and ignored the two more quick beeps from the SUV. "If you're lucky it won't be the last time either."

He shook his head slowly from side to side. "I really must be insane."

Her smile widened and chased away the apprehension and fear he had seen in her eyes moments before. He asked himself if he would ever get tired of looking in her eyes as she wound their arms together and he allowed her to pull him towards the street.

156

"Aren't we all a little bit crazy?" she asked him as they climbed into the back of the SUV, but he did not hear her as they fled into the Chicago night. He was still trying to overcome the revelation that he had started to enjoy looking in her eyes and making her smile.

A short time later they found themselves alone in the back of the car at a gas station near the entrance to Interstate Highway 90. Jay was outside, his back leaning against Amber's door, watching the digital readout on a gas pump spiral upward. Walt had disappeared into the gas station's convenience store to grab some drinks and food for the start of their long trip east. Amber had made a few quick calls to her supporters in the government who promised they would do what they could to counter what the Vatican's supporters were doing. For his part Robert remained relatively quiet not saying much of anything. He was still trying to figure out why he had gotten in the car with her.

"My mother used to tell me that the moon was full and there wasn't a cloud in the sky on the night when she and my father found my brother and me. She said it was a special night where a star had shown so brightly it was like a second moon had formed over the world and the night had transformed into day," Amber told Robert in a hushed tone after she hung up her burner cell. She rolled the window down just enough and tossed it outside and heard it being crushed under Jay's foot as she closed the window again.

"My childhood was pretty unremarkable, but it ended early by today's standards. I was sixteen when I was forced to marry a man almost twice times my age. Which is just the way things were back then and in some places, unfortunately, still are.

157

"Anyway, he wanted children, but for whatever the reason, I could never get pregnant. Even though I didn't love him, I tried to be a good wife and he was patient in the beginning, but saying my husband was disappointed with me for not being able to give him a son would be an understatement," she paused for a moment lost in some memory of that time. "It was when he started beating me every day that I finally left.

"So, with nowhere to go, I returned to my parent's home wearing just the clothes on my back. I was one of the lucky ones, they welcomed me with open arms, but it wasn't like that for most women. It still isn't really. Most got sent back to their husband. Some were killed for bringing that sort of dishonor back to the family's doorstep.

"I didn't stay at home for long. Perhaps because of the guilt and shame I was feeling, but mostly because my brother had already left, and something inside of me told me I needed to be with him. When I finally found him, I asked him why he left and had traveled so far from home. He told me that he felt compelled to leave. That it was as if there was a song playing that only he could hear and it was drawing him away.

"Even from an early age, perhaps even on an instinctual level, we both knew we had been born for a purpose. He always seemed to know what his was. He found fulfillment in educating people and trying to unite the world in brotherhood, but my purpose remained more elusive. I knew there was something I had to do, but what that was, was always just beyond my understanding. Somehow hidden behind a misty veil that I couldn't quite see through and it wasn't until my brother died that the veil finally vanished."

"How old were you when he died?" Robert asked when she paused.

"Thirty-three," she answered giving him a smile to say that she was okay. "A few days before it happened he took me aside to talk to me about the events that were about to happen. I was outraged that he had planned his own death. That he had manipulated and schemed the odds to make it happen. He stood there calmly telling me that at this pinnacle of events the outcome we had been working so hard for could still fail, but he was certain that his sacrifice could shift the odds in our favor. He told me I needed to be strong, that I would understand when he was gone. And, as always, he was right.

"The moment my brother breathed his last breath I understood what my purpose in life was. It was as if my mind was awakened from a foggy, hazed filled, dream by an explosion of clarity. God did have a plan for me and that plan was suddenly laid out before me in such detail that it was overwhelming at first. The magnitude of it, the sheer scope of what lay before me, I knew I was going to have to be patient if I was going to have any hope of success.

"My brother often told me I had to be more patient. I sometimes wondered if maybe he knew what God had intended for me all along and I often argued with him that he never gave me insight into what that plan was. It was only after he died that I finally understood I was wrong to feel that way. He may have known that God had a plan for me, but he never could have realized what that plan was."

Before she could say anything more Jay interrupted them with a quick series of raps on the window, receipt in hand. On the other side of the car, Walt closed in on them carrying full plastic bags in both hands. Amber gave a quick nod to Jay before turning her full attention back to Robert. "I'll tell you the rest later Robert. But needless to say, after that, it gets complicated."

CHAPTER SEVENTEEN

"How many are there Luc?" Mary demanded for the third time with growing irritation.

"Enough!" he shouted, causing the links on his chainmail armor to clank together. "More than enough."

"We'll have to disguise you."

She turned to glare at the other man with them who thought she needed his council. "You expect me to run Pierre?"

"Yes," he told her flatly. "I've brought you a servant's dress to change into and you should cut your hair as well. It is not much, but perhaps in the confusion you'll be able to escape."

"I have no intention..."

"Mary," Luc said in an eerily calm voice that made her break off what she was about to say. "The keep is lost. Pierre is right and deep inside you know he is."

She knew they were right, but that did not make it any easier for her to accept. She held up a hand to forestall them from saying more and turned to look out the archer slit again. Two stories below where she stood the clash of swords and pikes rang through the dark moonless night accompanied by the screams of the wounded and the dying. Michael was down there somewhere, whether he was dead or alive she could not know, but that is where she would find him if she were to go searching. *How did I not see this coming?* she asked herself again and slammed her first against the wall.

"She should change her name as well," Pierre whispered to Luc. "It may not mean much, but even the littlest thing can turn a defeat into a victory."

"We'll worry about that later," Luc muttered in reply.

Only half listening to them, Mary's hand went to the amber studded necklace around her neck that Michael had given to her only a few hours earlier. It had caught his eye in the markets and was just something that he thought she would enjoy. He had such a kind heart and even though she did not feel she deserved his love, she cherished it. If only he were with her now she would not have felt so alone.

Her eyes were drawn to a torch lit area in the courtyard where living shadows became substance. One of the Templar Knights, her knights, staggered backwards from a spearhead that had pierced his abdomen. Even mortally wounded he still fought the soldier holding the other end. It was not Michael, but that was all she could tell as the two men struggled back into the swirling mass of shadows once more.

"Amber," she whispered.

"What?" Luc asked.

Mary turned to face them. "You will call me Amber from now on."

Their eyes drifted to the necklace she was thoughtlessly caressing. They knew who had given it to her and where her thoughts were in that moment.

"Very well...Amber," Luc declared into the silence and grief that threatened to swallow all of them. "Now with that settled, we need to get moving. What little time we have available to us is growing short."

"We can take the servant corridor and leave through the kitchens," Pierre suggested and pointed further down the hallway to the left. "Then we can escape over the cliffside."

Amber nodded and took the lead before either of the two men could say anything further.

The keep had been built on a narrow, broken hilltop with the rear of it situated on a vertical drop that no catapult or trebuchet could reach. Even the sides of the keep were difficult to mount an attack on, given how rugged the terrain was to cross, and it made it impractical for siege equipment to be deployed. Not that those defenses had done any of them any good tonight. Only the day before, the soldiers that Amber's Templar's were now fighting had been allies. How quickly things had changed.

They ran like the devil was chasing them. Racing through the back corridors and down stairways once only used by servants and now by the desperate. The sounds and echoes of the fighting grew and fell in a chorus of chaos as they passed doorways and windows in their flight. Luc had taken over the lead early on leaving Pierre the position of rear guard behind Amber. The two men would be overwhelmed on the open field, but both were capable fighters and, if it came to it, could hold the narrow hall long enough if they needed to give Amber time to escape.

The stairwell Luc had chosen to take them to the ground floor spiraled below them and emptied out into the rear of the kitchen. At this late hour, the ovens were cool and the cook and his helpers had long since retired to the village not far away. Two more doorways exited from the room, one to the outside behind the keep and the other into a short hallway that lead to the Great Hall. They should have fled outside, but the three were stopped by the reality of the struggle they were trying to escape.

"Phillip!" Amber exclaimed and brushed past Luc to get to a wounded Templar who was using the cook's table in a struggle to remain standing. Two of the King's men lay motionless not far beyond him.

A slow but steady trickle of blood rolled down the left side of Phillip's face as he turned towards Amber. His tunic, once white, and the chainmail he was wearing under it were covered in so much blood that Amber could not tell where his wounds were. A painfully forced smile appeared on his face as she took his head in her hands.

"Phillip," she whispered ignoring the blood and dirt that clung to her fingers as she stroked his cheek.

"Ah, my angel comes to greet me," he managed to reply, each breath an endeavor, and the two of them slid to the floor as his strength finally failed him.

"Of course," she answered struggling to hold back the tears as she brushed his hair away from his face. "Be strong. We're going to take you out of here."

"Don't be foolish. Even I know I'm dying," he told her grasping one of her hands in his steel gauntlet. "I'm going to meet with your brother."

She smiled at him, but the happiness never entered her sorrow filled eyes. "Will you tell him hello for me?"

"Of course," he whispered as his life began to slip away. "It won't be long until they break through. You need to hurry."

"I will," she reassured him, she but did not move or let go of him until she saw his eyes lose their focus and his breathing stop. *You deserved so much more than this*, she thought. Phillip deserved to die as an old man peacefully in his bed instead of here, in this kitchen, and on this cold October night. She would have stayed there with him longer if Luc had not gently taken her by the arm and led her through the door and into the rear courtyard.

"No time for changing now," Pierre said, tossing the servant dress aside as they made their way towards the fortress's rear wall.

"I suppose not," Luc replied before turning his attention to a group of six handpicked knights waiting for them. "Has the way been checked Cariot?"

"It's clear," the young knight answered.

"I don't need to remind you of the importance of what you are about to undertake," Luc began.

"But you will anyway," Luc's son, Peter, murmured loud enough for everyone to hear from his place at the rear of the group.

"Not tonight," Amber whispered and the weight of even that hushed reprimand brought an end to anything else that may have been said.

Luc pointed out four knights, the young Cariot amongst them, and ordered them ahead. His son led the way and pressed on a nondescript stone in the fortress's outer wall while a second knight pushed on the adjacent section of wall. It swung outward revealing a short tunnel through the ten-foot thick wall and was just wide enough for a single person to traverse. Amber watched them disappear through the opening and came to the decision that she was going to have to separate herself from Cariot. After what happened tonight, she knew it was too dangerous to keep him near her.

"You go ahead as well Pierre," Amber instructed and waited until he disappeared before turning to face Luc. "You aren't coming, are you?"

"No, I'm not."

"You don't have to do this."

"Maybe not," he replied. "But I believe it is the right thing to do."

"What if I told you I needed you with me?"

Luc's soft laugh was nearly lost in the cold breeze. "There's only one person you need Mary and when the time comes he's going to need you just as much as you need him."

She threw her arms around him, pulling him close, and he returned the embrace until the sounds of approaching fighting signaled that her time to leave had come.

"If...If you find Michael. If you get the chance to tell him," she had to stop as her voice began to quiver and break.

"He already knows," Luc told her as he gently lifted her necklace in his hand. "But when I find him, I will remind him nonetheless."

"I will miss your stories," she told him with a forced smile.

"I'll share some more with you the next time we meet," he replied stepping away from her and pulled his sword free of its scabbard. "Now off with you."

She turned from him and, with head held high, strode away with the regal poise that had made kings bow to her. Luc would expect nothing less from her and she was not going to disappoint him in these final moments. As she pushed the secret doorway closed behind her, instead of feeling fear, her smoldering anger was beginning to alight. Perhaps her brother would have been able to handle the

166

players in this game better than she had, but he was long since dead and she was not her brother. If they thought this attack was going to break her then she was going to show them what they had unleashed.

The narrow passage was unlit, but she knew the short distance she had to cover was straight and the contrasting light at the exit acted as a guide. She emerged onto a narrow ledge overlooking a near vertical drop that plunged into the darkness. Three anchored ropes shook slightly as the knights ahead of her had already begun making their descent. Only Peter remained behind, waiting for her.

"Your father won't be joining us Peter," she informed him as he turned at the sound of her approach.

"I know," he accepted and removed a leather strap from under his tunic upon which a gold signet ring dangled.

"If you would rather stand by his side I would understand. I'll not have you holding it against me that you left him."

"I may not have my father's gift for storytelling, but you have my sword my lady."

"Then I accept your sword Peter and your companionship," she told him as she grasped one of the ropes and fearlessly spun herself out over the cliff face.

When she reached the bottom of the long descent her escort was already mounting their horses and making ready to depart. She could feel the somber mood as Pierre handed her the reigns to her own horse. She nodded her thanks and turned to watch Peter finish his descent, landing a moment later and tossing the rope aside.

"Where are we to go now?" he asked in both anger and disgust as he stared back up the cliff side.

"La Rochelle," she answered following his gaze. She could not see much beyond the faint glow a few braziers were giving off. "We need to reach the fleet."

"That's a quarter day journey on a good day," Peter pointed out. "They may have already struck there as well in attempts to cut off a means of escape."

"Perhaps," she replied cursing herself all over again. King Phillip had sent a man by the name of Antoine to lead the forces now attacking her keep. She had only met him briefly, but he did not seem the type to divide his troops, instead preferring to overwhelm each objective. "But I don't believe he has yet. We'll need to travel quickly though. Once Antoine has secured the keep I have little doubt he'll move quickly to secure the harbor."

"Especially since the treasury is empty," Pierre noted.

"Precisely," Amber replied swinging onto her saddle.

"Where will we sail to?" Peter asked as they began to pick their way through the dark. Fearing to reveal their position no one dared to light a torch.

"We'll stop in Portugal first and warn the order there. They can spread the word for us while we continue to Scotland."

"An odd destination," Pierre remarked.

"A stopping point Pierre," Amber acknowledged shifting her eyes to Cariot. "Nothing more."

"Where will we go from there?"

"West."

"To Ireland?"

"No, much further."

"What's west of Ireland?" Pierre pressed, but Amber ignored his question and the others knew that she was done discussing the matter.

CHAPTER EIGHTEEN

Pope Clement the Fifth felt his anger rising when he arrived outside his office chamber door and found that Julius was not at his post. He made a mental note that this lack of impropriety would have to be the first thing addressed upon the man's arrival. The present times were disturbing enough without his own men losing their sense of duty. He pulled the heavy oak door open and, frustrated, slammed it closed in his wake.

Clinching his jaw as he took a seat at his paper strewn pine desk he wrapped a heavy wool blanket around his shoulders to keep the chill autumn air at bay. The fire in the hearth appeared to have been stoked recently, proving Julius must have been here early, but today the heat from the fire did little to warm the drafty room. As he picked up the top most parchment and began reading its contents he had a feeling that the end to this year was going to be very cold.

It was November 13, 1307. A month to the day had passed since King Phillip had moved against the Templar order and the paper in his hand was yet another demand, in a line of never ending demands, that the Pope finally issue his proclamation for the damnation of the Templar prisoners that had been taken. Clement knew he would have to relent eventually. He saw little alternative to it now, but he could hold it off for at least a little while longer.

Suddenly a drop of blood fell onto the crisp parchment he was holding onto but no longer paying very much attention to. Instinctively he brought his hand to his nose, but found nothing wrong other than it was cold.

Another red drop fell. He moved his hand to his mouth, still nothing. A third drop raised his eyes to the ceiling above him just as a cloaked figure leapt from the ceiling beams and fell towards him.

With a cat's grace, the figure extended a booted foot that slammed into Clement's shoulder and sent the stout man tumbling, wide eyed, from his chair before he was able to scream.

"Please, spare me," he moaned, holding his injured shoulder while trying to curl into a protective ball.

"I have no intention of killing you...yet," a woman informed him.

Clement knew that voice, but hearing it brought him terror instead of comfort. An assassin would just kill him and be done with it, but *she* would deliver upon him a slow and very painful death. He slowly lifted his face from behind his arm to look at her. "Mary?"

A swift but glancing kick to the head sprawled the Pope on his back.

"Mary is gone Your Grace. You will no longer call me by that name. You nor anyone else who wears your blood-stained robes. Mary stood for what my brother believed, that humanity was worth salvation, yet that path is no longer viable. It is buried in my ruined fortress! From this day forward, you will call me Amber. You and all who take your place afterwards. Do you understand that?"

"Yes...of...of course...Amber," Clement stammered, nodding his head vigorously. His eyes darted towards the door. *Where are you Julius?*

171

"Go ahead and scream," she offered him with a twisted smile that chilled him to the bone. "No one will hear you."

"What have you done?" he whispered, but she only smiled more as if she savored the taste of his terror.

"First you fools allow Constantine to dictate what the word of God will be," she continued, pointedly ignoring his question.

"To help unify the people..."

"To help unify his empire," Amber scoffed. "How many teachings was he allowed to discard? How much of my brother's wisdom was lost? Only God's empire is eternal, Clement. The Roman Empire was already in decline. If that had been all, perhaps the future could have been salvaged, but then you traitors allow Gregory the Ninth to lead the church and release his inquisitors on France. How much blood did the church spill then? How many were sacrificed?"

"I had no part in that."

"No, *you* didn't. But you are the Pope now and you bend your knees to a king who sees gold instead of truth."

"Without a doubt Phillip is mad, but he is still king..."

"And a king is greater than God?" she hissed, putting her face only inches from his own so he could see the hatred in her eyes.

"No. No, of course not!" he cried, trying to shimmy away from her but the wall at his back left him little room to do so.

"And yet here the charges lay on your table!" she shouted and swiped her arm across his desk so the pages flew around him in a storm of parchments. "Heresy. Worship of a false idol. Denial of Christ! Accusations against those who you know understood and followed the way of the Lord because they followed me!"

"Phillip's charges..." he croaked.

"Charges that you will ultimately sign. Isn't that right? Isn't that what a sniveling coward like you does?"

"No, I won't. I won't sign," Clement whined. *Where are you Julius?* he was sure someone must have heard the commotion. "I swear...I swear I'll..."

"Silence!" Amber bellowed and Clement obediently fell silent. "You're weak and unworthy to stand in the light, priest. The final ties that have held your order and mine together are no more. Instead let there be war between us from now and until judgment day."

"Am..Amber, please. You don't know what you are saying."

She stood looking down upon him with nothing but disdain in her ice blue eyes. As she spun away from him, her cloak opened for an instant revealing a belt of bloodied knives strapped around her waist. She strode toward the door and placed her hand on the weathered iron handle. "War, Your Grace," she pronounced and fearlessly flung open the door before vanishing into the hall beyond.

CHAPTER NINETEEN

High Inquisitor Fernando Magill emerged into the stifling heat of summer after having spent the last several hours shivering in the cold of the catacombs deep beneath the remote village's small Spanish church. He believed that the residents of this humble town would describe it as a *grand* church, but Fernando had seen the glory and magnificence of ones much greater. These country churches, chapels really, no longer captivated him as they once had when he was a child. He did however appreciate the privacy that the catacombs of this particular cliffside church provided. It made his mission so much easier if those under questioning could be isolated which was not always an easy feat in the country villages and towns.

Of course, having the accused tucked away from loved ones offered other benefits that Fernando could partake in. Like the physical offerings a local woman would provide to free her father, or brother, and even a husband. As far as Fernando was concerned, such promiscuity only solidified the guilt of the individual such a woman was trying to help. An immoral woman was but a reflection of an immoral household in Fernando's mind. Sill, such trivial things did not prevent him from enjoying such spoils when they were offered and it pained him little to have the offending woman arrested when he was through with her.

The fact that Fernando was nearing the point of putting Father Pedro to the questioners himself was exactly why he had decided to withdraw himself from the stale, damp tunnels so early and he hoped he would be able to find a suitable companion for his bed so he could relieve his frustrations. Father Pedro had been infuriatingly impatient since Fernando's arrival earlier in the day, practically whisking the inquisitor into the church before his carriage had come to a stop. The fool's eagerness was subdued quickly enough when he discovered his error in summoning Fernando to begin with.

"To think the idiot thought that whelp of a girl was the one I was after," Fernando muttered to himself as he entered the church proper and looked around.

Unfortunately, the church appeared empty of attendants this afternoon. Most of the residents were probably working on their farms he thought or, more likely, had closed themselves away now that the inquisitors had arrived. Not that hiding would do any heretic in this village much good. Fernando was certain the inquisition would find them in the end. It was only a matter of time really. Even if that girl Pedro had uncovered was not this Amber woman he had been ordered to hunt down, she had still confessed to several other crimes and immoralities. Fernando was sure there would be a few more sinners to unearth here, he just had to turn over the right rocks to find them.

Annoyed at the lack of immediate prospects, he had almost given up on the chance of finding a suitable woman for his bed, when he noticed a young lady kneeling and lighting candles in a secluded alcove near the church's entrance. Her long, dark black hair fell around her downcast shoulders and hid much of her face, but her stance depicted a certain sadness or sense of loss. Fernando felt an instant arousal and began circumventing his way through the battered wooden pews to her. He noted her green dress was

175

simple but was certainly made specifically for her by a seamstress. A local noble's daughter perhaps? If that was the case Fernando may have to have her father brought in for questioning in order to get her to respond favorably.

"Who do you pray for child?" he asked with the best display of concern he could muster as he approached.

"Loved ones who have gone before me, Inquisitor."

Fernando nodded in feign sympathy, keeping his face neutral, but he bristled at her defiance. *Who is she to call me Inquisitor?* Oh yes, he was going to have her begging to please him before he tossed her into a very dark cell and forgot about her.

"So many candles." he continued when he noticed the five candles flickering in front of her. "You are too young to have suffered so. Who were they child?"

"This one is for all those who fell defending my keep from usurpers who came on a moonless night," she explained pointing to the first of the candles and then moved along the row. "This one is for Pierre who gave his life to defend me two years later. I lit this for Luc who was like a brother to me and whose stories I dearly miss and this one next to it is for his son Peter, who became just as good a story teller as his father and, thankfully, died an old man surrounded by loved ones."

"And the last?" Fernando queried. Even her voice was alluring and he was beginning to think that his trip to this village was not in vain after all. A few nights, and perhaps days, with this woman waiting for him in his bed chambers certainly held the potential of making up for the inconveniences he had suffered so far.

"This one," she began but paused. "This candle is for Michael, who gave his life so I could escape when my keep was lost. Michael, even though he knew who I was, loved me, Mary, just because he wanted to."

"I'm truly sorry for your losses," Fernando whispered in a low, and hopefully, sympathetic voice. "Your name is Mary then?"

"Not any longer Inquisitor Fernando," she corrected turning hard pale blue eyes towards him. "My name is Amber and I understand you've been looking for me."

Before Fernando could react, there was a flash in his eyes from the sunlight glinting off the steel of her knife. He gasped and clutched at his belly where she had cut him. Warm blood, his blood, gushed from the wound and he crumpled to his knees trying to keep his insides from spilling out. He struggled to say something but whatever it was died on his lips as he fell backwards. His open eyes no longer saw Amber as she rose and stepped over him on her way towards the catacombs.

* * *

Father Pedro found himself cowering in a corner and praying feverishly for his own salvation a short time later. Even with his eyes clasped shut he could still see Inquisitor Santiago's entrails spilling to the floor when the man had tried to apprehend the woman who had disturbed them. If only that horrible child had not warned her about Inquisitor DeLeon's presence. Unfortunately, the girl's warning was heard and it caused DeLeon's dagger to only find its mark in the woman's shoulder instead of the back of her chest. The man paid with his life just as quickly as his comrade had moments before.

Terrified, Father Pedro bolted for the stairs, but one look into the woman's pale blue eyes as she turned to stare at him chilled his blood and sent him scurrying to the corner furthest away from her. He was sure, beyond any doubt, that this was the woman the High Inquisitor was looking for. Pedro had never seen her before, he was certain of that. So, what had brought her here? The girl? He found it hard to believe that the little scrap of a girl had any value to this woman.

Ignoring her shoulder wound Amber retrieved a large key off a small warped oak table that held vials of ink, quills, blank parchment, and the little girl's confession. She held the document up and scanned over the contents before lighting it on fire in the table's candle and let it drop from her hand. She casually walked to where the girl was secured to the wall and gently began to unlock the shackles that held her hanging an arm's length off the ground.

Amber's eyes softened at seeing the harm done to the frail wisp of a child. Her forearms were cut from where she dangled from the shackles. Fresh blood mixed with old where the Inquisitor's whip had fallen. Blackened skin, blistered and bubbled, from where hot iron rods had been placed. Amber's rage at the sight threatened to boil over, but the girl cowering before her had seen enough hate and cruelty to last her lifetime and Amber was not going to add to that burden any more than she had to.

"Thank you for warning me," she whispered as the girl practically fell into her arms. "It was very brave of you to do that."

The girl only nodded as she buried her head against Amber and began crying hysterically.

Amber gently encircled her arms around the child. A moment of kindness for the girl now, a display showing her that the world still held some good in it, could make all the difference when the nightmares and sleepless nights ahead of her came. It was a brief moment of comfort. One that she wished could have lasted longer, but it could not. Someone was going to find the Inquisitor's body upstairs and she meant to be well on her way before the town guard could be organized. Even small hamlets like this had some sort of guard, probably only a volunteer force led by the elders, but she wanted to avoid any further confrontations if she could.

Only hearing the muffled crying of the girl Father Pedro cracked his eyes open to witness Amber's show of affection. He watched her softly caress the girl's hair and hold her close to herself. It was a motherly act. *Is she the girl's mother?* he wondered, but that was impossible. The couple, who had fought so hard to keep them from taking the girl, professed to be her parents and Pedro had little doubt that they were telling the truth. But perhaps he was witnessing a relationship here nonetheless and it was a source of information that he could somehow use to his benefit. The stairs were nearby. Perhaps this tender moment the woman and the girl were sharing would provide him the brief time he needed to escape. *Fernando must still be close by*, he thought. All he had to do was find him. He would know how to deal with this demon.

He slowly began to uncurl himself so he could flee. His first thoughts still focused on finding Fernando, but one look at the bodies of the two other inquisitors gave birth to a fear that Fernando could very well be dead himself. Pedro focused on the steps. *Of course, Fernando was still alive,* he told himself. *This woman couldn't have killed him.* He brought his feet underneath him, making ready to flee, but a shadow cast over him as the woman broke free of her embrace with the girl and turned her unholy eyes upon him, froze him in his place. She stepped towards him, a knife suddenly appearing in her hand and he felt his bladder give way. *Why have you abandoned me Lord? Am I not destined for things greater than this? Am I to die in these dank tombs?*

"Do you know who I am?" she taunted leaning over to place the tip of the blade under the fat man's nose and hoisted him to his feet.

Pedro tried to nod his head that he knew her, but when he did she pushed the knife point even higher forcing his head back even further. "You're the devil's mistress," he managed to stammer.

She tossed her head back and broke out into a laughter that reverberated along the stone walls. The echoes built upon each other until it sounded to Pedro that he was surrounded by a hundred of her, all of them mocking him. The blade she held to his face barely moved as she laughed. If anything, she forced him to tilt his head a little farther back until the only way he could see her was to look down his own face.

"Tell me something Father," she smiled sinisterly. "Do you want to live?"

"Yes," he answered his voice cracking as he grasped at the hope for life she offered. *Please dear God, please let me live. Stay her hand almighty Father. Let me live. Let me live.*

"You're going to be my herald," she told him and took a step closer until he could feel her hot breath upon his face and clearly see the hatred buried in her eyes. "You will deliver a message for me. And if you fail to do so I will hunt you to the ends of the earth and you will wish for death every moment that I allow you to live after I have found you."

"I'll do as you ask," Pedro promised as tears began to roll down his chubby cheeks. "I swear."

"You will seek out Tomas de Torquemada," she instructed.

"The Grand Inquisitor?" Pedro interrupted displaying even more horror on his face than he had already.

"Yes," Amber whispered with a knowing smile. "You will tell him that Amber sent you with a message for him and then you will read Psalm thirty-five, verses four through nine to him. Do you understand?"

Pedro tried to nod, but the way she held the knife kept him from doing so. "I understand. Psalm thirty-five, verses four through nine."

"Very good," Amber praised, but there was no kindness in her voice. "Remember that, Psalm thirty-five, verses four through nine."

Let them be confounded and put to shame that seek after my soul: let them be turned back and brought to confusion that devise my hurt. Let them be chaff in the wind: and let the angel of the Lord chase them. Let their way be dark and slippery: and let the angel of the Lord persecute them. For without cause have they hid for me their net in a pit, which without cause they have digged for my soul. Let destruction come upon him at unawares; and let

181

his net that he hath hid catch himself: into the very
destruction let him fall. And my soul shall be joyful
in the Lord: it shall rejoice in his salvation.

"Now go." Amber commanded and lowered her knife. "Go and do not stop herald until you give Tomas de Torquemada my message. Tell him no matter what he calls his hunt for me, no matter how many people he burns, he will fail."

Father Pedro needed no other urging and practically fell over himself trying to get up the stone stairs. More than once he found himself using his hands and feet to catapult himself forward unaware of the how the rough stone cut and scraped his skin. Amber watched him until he disappeared from her sight and the noise of his stumbling subsided before she sheathed her dagger. When she turned around see found the little girl had retreated into a corner and curled into the smallest ball she could.

"Are you ready to go home little one?"

Through tears the girl looked at her with both hope and fear. "The priest said you belong to the devil."

"That is what he said," Amber said kneeling down several steps away so not to frighten her. "And I will not lie to you. I have indeed sinned and there is no place for me in Heaven, but they say I belong to the devil only because they can't have me."

"I want to go home," was all the girl could muster.

"Then let's get you home. I'm sure your mother and father are sick with worry."

The girl allowed Amber to pull her to her shaking feet and support her as they made their way up the spiraling stairwell. Once they entered the church, the girl looked around with renewed fear expecting a trap was waiting for them and as they neared the exit she clung even tighter to Amber's dress. Amber gently stroked the girl's hair and did her best to shield her from seeing Fernando's body as they approached the two ancient timber doors that Father Pedro had thrown open in his haste to escape.

Outside, the sky was clear blue and cloudless which provided no relief from the pounding heat of the sun and the still air offered little in the way of reprieve. The initial shock of sunlight forced both women to shield their eyes, more so for the girl who had spent the last week or more in the poorly lit catacombs. Amber pulled her into the folds of her dress and slowly guided her toward the cobblestone street at the bottom of the wide granite steps.

"So, this is little Amber," a lanky man with dark skin and thick mustache stated matter-of-factly as Amber and the girl approached. He was holding two brown, sleek mares loosely by the reins.

"Her name is Francesca, Julian," Amber curtly replied even though her attention was focused on the surrounding empty street. There were people out in the hamlet, but they were staying clear of the church and giving Amber's group suspicious glances from afar as they made their way about their business. No one stared openly, it was too dangerous to draw that sort of attention to oneself in these dark times, yet they knew something out of the ordinary was happening. Amber would have liked to believe she could have found sympathy amongst these people for the girl she kept next to her, but she knew that was not going to happen.

"You can call me Julian too," He told Francesca with a quick, easy smile before handing the reigns of the slightly shorter mare to Amber. "The priest came out of the church at a near run just before you. He practically accosted the Inquisitor's coachman and the two were racing out of town like the devil was chasing them."

"Good," Amber replied taking her horse's reigns from him. Kneeling so she could be face to face with the little girl, she turned Francesca's attention to her. "We're going to ride from here ok?"

Francesca nodded, her eyes growing wide.

"Have you ever ridden a horse?"

She quickly shook her head no.

"Alright, you're going to ride in front of me."

Amber waited until Francesca gave her a small nod that she understood before she gingerly lifted the girl onto the saddle. The mare was well trained and remained firmly rooted where she stood while Amber mounted behind Francesca. Amber took her time making sure the girl was comfortable, whispering short instructions as she placed the girl's legs and arms so they would be out the way. When Amber nodded to Julian he mounted his own horse and the little group turned away from the false sanctuary of the church.

Julian did not bother to hide his eagerness to be away, but Amber was purposely taking her time. In part for Francesca's sake, due to her wounds, but more so to show the people of the village she was not afraid. If they were going to think that she was a witch she was going to make them see she was the strongest and most feared of them all. She returned the look of anyone she saw watching her, silently daring them to interfere with her, but every gaze she met quickly looked away and the person found a reason to get off the street.

"How do you like riding?" she asked Francesca after handing her a bright red apple from her saddle bag.

"It's a little scary," the girl replied enthusiastically sinking her teeth into the juicy fruit.

"Scary? Really? Why is that?"

"I'm so high off the ground," she mumbled through a mouth full of apple.

"Mmmm. I remember the first time I got on a horse. I fell right off the other side and landed in a mud puddle," Amber told her. Which was the truth even if it was a lifetime ago, but the old tale was received with a giggle and Amber smiled. Not because of the memory of that first horse riding lesson, but because if Francesca could still laugh then there was real hope that she was going to be alright in time.

When Francesca finished her apple, Amber handed her another and then offered her water skin to wash the meager meal down. Occasionally Francesca would point in the direction they were supposed to go to get to her home and Amber, who already knew the way but kept that to herself, pulled the reigns as the girl guided them. The entire journey from church to the farm only took four fingers of sunlight atop the meandering horses and it ended with the girl sliding from the saddle and falling into her parent's outstretched arms.

"It won't be safe for them to remain here any longer," Amber told Julian when he brought his horse abreast of her own. "The girl looks too much like me."

"She's just a child."

"With dark hair, olive skin, and blue eyes. That's all the inquisitors care about Julian."

"We're going to take them with us then?"

"I want you to take them. I can handle the other matter myself."

Julian gave a snort to tell her what he thought of that, but whatever else he was thinking he wisely kept to himself. "When should we expect to see you again?"

"Before winter," she answered and turned her horse back in the direction they had come from. "I think dark times lay ahead for Spain so travel as quickly as you can. May the light guide you my friend."

She spared another glance towards Francesca who was crying and clinging to her mother's dress while her father knelt next to her, stroked her hair, and spoke softly to her. At least this time Amber was sure Francesca's tears were from the happiness of reuniting with her family again. *I wonder what sort of woman you'll become,* she pondered as she rode away.

CHAPTER TWENTY

Amber woke with a start as the ship plummeted over another enormous wave. The storm driving those dangerous walls of water had raged for almost two days and had threatened to sink the twin mast vessel on more than one occasion. At least the heaviest of the rain had finally subsided, yet the winds still howled and the waves rose and fell with little remorse for those who cowered inside the belly of the ship. The captain had told her in no uncertain terms that it was not a hurricane, but a fierce storm that had occasion to strike at the east coast of America and all they could do was to ride it out and pray. Amber was unable to recall the last time she had prayed, but she did not tell the captain that since, like praying, it would only have been a waste of her time. Francesca would have laughed at her if Amber had told her that.

How Amber missed Francesca's laugh. She had been afraid Francesca's time with the inquisitors was going to ultimately lead her to live a lonely life in seclusion, but quite the opposite had occurred. There were times, in the woman's younger years, when her spirit could rival Amber's own so it was no wonder they had become such good friends. *No,* Amber corrected herself. *We were more than friends. Sisters.* Sisters was a much more appropriate description of what their relationship had been.

She had done her best to look after Francesca's family after her death, but as the decades had passed it had become an impossible task. Especially when she considered all the children, grandchildren, and great-grandchildren that Francesca had. Still, Amber did what she could to make fortune shine upon them and the legacy they had built in those years was one that she believed Francesca would have been proud of. By sheer coincidence, some of Francesca's descendants were on the same ship as Amber was now. Maybe that was why she had been dreaming of her.

This was not Amber's first long sea voyage to the vast new continent they were calling America. She had seen its shores long before Christopher Columbus discovered the tropical islands far to the south or Amerigo Vespucci landed in Brazil. Her first expedition was after the Knights Templar had fallen and she had enlisted the help of the Vikings to aid in her escape with the Templar treasure. That had also been a harrowing experience, but before she could think more on that journey a loud pounding on her cabin door brought her attention back to the present.

"Come," she called, lowering her hand to a dagger she had secreted away inside the sleeve of her dress as the door opened and a scruffy faced sailor poked his head inside.

"Pardon the intrusion me lady, but the captain said I should inform you that land is in view."

"Thank you, Mister...?"

"Oliver, me lady."

"Thank you, Mister Oliver. If you would be so kind as to inform the captain I will join him presently, I would be most grateful."

"As you say," Oliver replied, disappearing back into the hall and softly closing the door with a surprising nimbleness on the rolling ship.

Amber took her time preparing herself before she exited her cabin. In part because she was not used to the sea being so turbulent or the dramatic rolling of the ship that accompanied it, but she also had to keep up the appearance of being a *proper* lady. It seemed that a commoner, man or woman, could be hard as nails, but a lady was believed to be more delicate. It was a preposterous notion in Amber's opinion, but one that she could not discount in public. After donning the proper rain attire, she half walked and half stumbled her way onto the deck.

Oliver was waiting for her as she exited, his wide stance allowing him to roll with the rocking vessel. Ahead the clouds remained gray and unfriendly, but here and there a break allowed the sun to cast a ray of light upon the world. The shoreline she had been longing to see was still only a thin streak of darkness on the horizon that appeared and disappeared in the rolling waves and offered little for her eyes to gaze upon. Yet those fleeting glimpses were enough to calm the nervousness she had locked up inside.

"Having second thoughts about coming above deck?" a stern and gruff voice called down from atop the quarterdeck. Holding her oiled leather bonnet with one hand Amber arched her neck to see the man speaking to her.

Captain Victor Brice stood almost directly overhead, both hands holding the weather worn railing, gazing down at her with his dark eyes as the salt water spray dripped off his weather proof coat and hat. He was perhaps the tallest man on the ship and the skinniest too, but he left no doubt in anyone's mind that he was in charge. For those only making a single crossing Victor Brice had the reputation of being a hard and unyielding devil of a man. Looking at those wild eyes, Amber could easily see how he had gained such a reputation, but she also saw the capabilities beneath that demeanor and she had little doubt the reason they had successfully weathered the storm lay with the skills of Captain Victor Brice.

"Not at all Captain," she yelled back over the thunderous crash of another wave against the bow. "May I join you?"

"From what Mister Oliver told me, I was under the impression I did not have the option of saying otherwise."

"I meant no offense Captain. The ship is yours and by right you may order me below once more."

Brice's eyes narrowed as he considered her for a moment before replying. "Very well Miss, you may join me. Oliver get back to your post."

With barely a pause Oliver sprang across the deck towards the mast leaving Amber to make her way alone to the stairs built along the side of the ship that led up to the quarterdeck. *So, you wish to test me Captain Brice,* she thought as she slowly moved towards the stairs. Her first steps were unsteady from the mix of wind, slick decking, and rolling waves all working together to make it a treacherous place to be, but by the time she reached the railing she displayed little discomfort. She understood it was a dance, much like a fight, where moves were met with countermoves and opportunities taken until a winner was decided. One hand on the rail, one still holding her bonnet in place, she climbed the steps with the air of a woman attending a ball. From the half smile Captain Brice had allowed to slip through his cold exterior she believed that she may have finally earned a degree of respect from the man.

"Welcome Lady Magdelene," He said, reclaiming his air of authority as he extended a hand towards her.

"Thank you, Captain," she responded taking his hand. Her grasp was firm, but not clinging letting him know that his gesture was welcoming, but not needed. "Please, call me Amber though."

"If it pleases you Lady Amber."

"It does."

"Very well then," Brice said with a nod of his head. "But in that case, I must insist you call me Victor."

Amber nodded her acceptance to the conditions of their arrangement and then turned her attention towards the bow of the vessel and the shore line in the distance. "How far are we from shore Mister Victor? Two Leagues?"

"Closer to three. If we were crossing land I would be inclined to agree with you, but distance is always farther on the sea. A ship must sail over and down many valleys before reaching her destination."

"Will we be able to make port today?"

"I believe we will make the evening tide into Boston. Now that the worst of the storm has passed we'll use what's left of its winds to gain on some of the time we've lost thus far."

"Excellent. Then you'll be able to join me for dinner then."

It was the first time on the voyage that Amber had seen Captain Brice startled, even if he recovered from the surprise quickly. It told her that he had little dealings with a bold woman like herself.

191

"I'm afraid I must decline Lady Amber. The first few hours in port are often the busiest and I would be unable to leave the ship."

"Tomorrow then," Amber instructed and when it appeared Brice was about to refuse once more she quickly cut him off. "Captain Brice I assure you my intentions are honorable. This new land is vast with opportunities for those who can take advantage of them and men such as you will be the key to that success."

Brice looked at her as if really seeing her for the first time. It was only a glimpse, but Amber had seen that look before. He knew she was a woman of importance and wealth and, in an instant, hundreds of thoughts flashed through his mind of new possibilities previously closed to him.

"The day after tomorrow. I will be otherwise engaged until then," Brice countered.

"Magnificent," Amber smiled and then looked across the bow with a sigh. "With your permission Captain, I'll leave you to see us safely to port. I'm afraid the view from three leagues leaves something to be desired, but it still is a comfort to behold."

"I'll send word when Boston is in sight."

"Thank you," Amber replied with a small incline of her head. Walking steadily towards the stairs she paused before taking the first step down and turned back to him. "The day after tomorrow Mister Victor. It would be a shame if I found out you had left port and I had to send privateers to bring you back." She almost laughed at the stunned look on his face, but she only showed him a crooked smile before she twirled and descended back below deck.

True to his word, as she knew he would be, Victor had the ship anchored in Boston harbor well before sunset. Before disembarking, Amber finalized her dinner arrangements with the good captain for two nights from then at her manor house. She then found herself in a longboat with a dozen other people racing towards shore under the powerful strokes of the men manning the oars.

Boston had grown since she had left in the fall, and now, with her midsummer return, she took a moment to trace the changes. The shadowed outline of new buildings scattered amongst the old. The vast number of masts that dotted the harbor and the new docks that welcomed them. To some the continued expansion from Europe would be a concern, but to Amber she knew she had made the right decision to move her operations to America because of the untapped potential this new world offered.

Unsurprisingly, she found her manor steward, David Thatcher, waiting for her with not one but two coaches. Sometimes she swore that man could tell you what the weather would be the week from next if asked. Dressed in a simple brown cotton overcoat with matching hat he seemed to have grown a good deal older over the winter. His tall, lanky frame was slightly more stooped and his hair seemed a little grayer than the deep brown she last remembered.

"Mister Thatcher," Amber hailed as she accepted his hand off the longboat. "I hope you have been well in my absence. I see you have not lost your uncanny ability to know when a second coach would be required."

"I fair better than a great many these days Miss," he stated flatly and seeing her gaze darken quickly added, "As to the latter, tis little more than an old man's intuition."

Letting matters be for the moment Amber turned to gather the family she had traveled with. "May I introduce you to my steward, Mister David Thatcher," Amber announced once she had gathered them around her. "And Mister Thatcher, may I introduce you to John Kariot, his wife Claire, and their daughter Judith. And this is John's brother, Richard Kariot, his son Peter and daughter Elizabeth."

Not fairing as well as Amber had, the small group still appeared seasick and pale from the rolling waves and the storm filled final days of their voyage. They were clearly relieved at finally being on land once more, but it was Claire, who was only weeks away from delivering her second child, who looked more relieved than the rest.

"A pleasure," Mister Thatcher acknowledged giving a tip of his hat. "If you'll follow me, I'll show you to your carriages."

"Carriages?" Claire whispered eyeing the two simple black coaches nearby. Each was a closed cabin and were drawn by two deep brown and well cared for horses. Looking at the smartly dressed attendants manning each she took hold of her husband's arm and drew him down to her level. "We cannot accept her Ladyship's carriages Richard. Not after all she's done for us."

"I insist," Amber interrupted. "My estate is a half day's walk from here and even at this time of year it would be after dark by the time you arrived."

"If you insist," Richard hesitantly replied. "But at least allow John and I to ride on the back so your Ladyship will have a coach to herself. Claire and the children can take the other."

"I prefer to ride on horseback," Amber replied. "And I have other matters to attend to here in Boston with Mister Thatcher before I follow along. I'll see you in the morning for breakfast where we'll further discuss your new life here."

"Now that the matter is settled, come along," Mister Thatcher insisted after recognizing Amber's dismissal.

While Mister Thatcher led the small group away Amber turned her interests to the second longboat tying up and the people disembarking onto the docks. They were a varied group between very young and very old. The state of their well-kept clothes and the few articles of jewelry the women wore marked them as neither poor nor rich, but somewhere in between. The little attention they paid to the motion of the boat and the sureness of their steps when they transitioned from the water to land marked them as members of the sea merchant's guild.

"Mister Grace?" Amber inquired approaching the oldest of the men she had seen. Although age and lineage had covered the ancestry she was sure she could see a little of Francesca in his face.

"Yes Miss," he answered removing his hat. His voice was raspy from years of barking orders, but it still contained a good deal of strength for his age. "Do I know you Miss?"

"I do not believe so sir, not personally in any case. I am Lady Magdalene and I have had dealings with the Grace shipping company in England for many years now."

"Pardon me Grandfather," one of the middle age men declared stepping alongside his elder, but his attention was directed towards Amber. "The voyage has been long Lady Magdalene. Perhaps this discussion could take place tomorrow or the day after."

A glimmer of uncertainty flickered across the old man's face, but it was gone just as quickly. "I will decide when and with whom I speak with Jacob," the old man decreed with an edge to his voice that left little room for dispute. "Take the rest of the family on and I will join you shortly."

"Grandfather..."

"Now!" the older Grace growled and stamped the foot of his cane on the dock for added measure.

"Yes Grandfather," Jacob responded, but threw an icy glance at Amber as he left to join the others in his party.

Amber's eyes followed him as he went. *I'll have to keep an eye on that one.*

"Please forgive my grandson Lady Magdalene," the old man requested drawing her further along the dock and away from the others. "He does not mean to offend. His concern for my health gets the better of his manners at times."

"It tells how much he cares for you."

"Bah, I'm old. Not something he need concern himself with."

Amber laughed, it was something that Francesca would have said. She encircled the older man's offered arm and they began to walk.

"I recall," he began after they had walked for a time in silence. "When I was very young, spending time with my grandmother at a harbor not unlike this one. I was named after her you realize and she was very near to my heart. I still cherish those memories of visiting her often as a boy during the winter months when the harbor was not as busy and my duties fewer. At times, I would spend weeks in her company."

196

"Your grandmother must have been a special woman to impart such warm memories."

"She was Lady Magdalene. She most certainly was," he answered stopping to look over the busy harbor. "Sometimes her dearest friend would be there as well. A beautiful woman with olive skin and eyes the color of the palest blue. Ah the stories the two of them would tell me on those cold nights as we warmed ourselves by the fire." He tipped his aged face towards her. "Now shall we continue with this charade of being strangers *Aunt* Amber or shall we get down to business?"

Stunned by the old man's revelations, Amber let go of his arm and stepped away from him. "How is it possible that you remember me at all Cisco? You were so young when last we saw one another."

"I was young when *you* last saw me, but I've caught glimpses of you through the years."

"How did you know it was me and not another?"

"It's your eyes. Not so easily forgotten to an impressionable young boy who thought you were the most beautiful thing he had ever seen. Nor were the stories of your agelessness that grandmother told me when you were gone."

"And you never spoke a word of it? Were you not afraid?"

"Afraid?" the old man laughed but it quickly turned into a hacking cough and Amber moved in close to offer her support, but he waved her off. "You're as bad as my grandson," he mumbled as the fit subsided which earned a smile from her. "I have faced death countless times upon the oceans. I've seen things I cannot explain or begin to understand how they exist so far from shore. Therefore, after seeing how my grandmother's eyes sparkled when she spoke of you, knowing the bond you shared, why would I have any reason to fear you?"

"Your grandmother was a dear friend to me. The sister I never had."

"And you to her," Francisco countered. "These are strange times we find ourselves in, aren't they? New lands. New opportunities."

"New probabilities," Amber whispered as her eyes fell on Captain Brice's vessel at anchor.

"Probabilities?"

"If you were a man to wager, what odds would you give that there was a reason you and I were to meet like this after all these years?"

"I'd be a wealthy man if I had bet a shilling on those sorts of odds." Francisco answered with an equal mix of disbelief and sarcasm.

"Exactly. What brought you and your family here Cisco?"

"Opportunity. My nephew William controls the shipping company in England now. With what America appears to offer, a contact point on this side of the ocean only made sense."

"Do you have merchants and ships under contract?"

"No merchants as of yet. Or ship's captains for that matter. We had three vessels nearly built when we left. Once the company can get them captained and fitted they'll join us here. By October perhaps. Do you have something in mind?"

"The future is about resources Cisco. This continent has more to offer than most realize."

"Perhaps, but it will take time for us to establish ourselves here. It will be months before we could be of service to you. That is if you have plans on continuing to work with my family."

"It may not take as long as you think my dear nephew," Amber smiled and glanced once more towards where Brice's ship was anchored in the harbor. "Would you care to join me for dinner the night after tomorrow?"

"Of course, it would be my honor."

"Excellent!" Amber replied with a bright smile.

On the short walk back to where Francisco's grandson waited alone, their discussion turned quickly from business to family. Although expected, to hear the names of the deceased saddened Amber, but to hear how Francesca's family had grown brought a genuine warmth to her heart. She realized she had the unique perspective to see the impact one person could make upon the world and she counted herself lucky to have known Francesca.

"Until the day after tomorrow," Francisco reaffirmed with a bow to Amber when they neared his grandson.

"I'll send my coaches for you and your family," Amber told him and gave him a gentle embrace and kiss on the cheek.

He waved his grandson over. "Jacob, we'll be dinning with Miss Magdalene the night after tomorrow, would you provide her our address so she may send her coachman."

"Unnecessary," Amber interrupted.

Francisco opened his mouth to question her but fell silent and smiled as she arched her eyebrow at him. "I suppose it is," he chuckled taking his grandson's arm and tipped his hat to her. Amber watched him as he disappeared into the dwindling evening crowd before turning to locate where Mister Thatcher had positioned himself so she could find out what he had to tell her.

"Very well Mister Thatcher, out with it," she ordered double checking that they were far enough away from any ears that could hear them.

"There are trials going on out by way of Salem. Witchcraft trials," Mister Thatcher informed her in a hushed tone even though they were alone. "I believe..." he began again, but she quickly brushed whatever comment he was going to make aside with a wave of her arm.

"How many dead?" she demanded in muted anger that hid the growing rage within.

"My lady..."

"How many have gone to the gallows Mister Thatcher?" she demanded. "Or have they reverted to burning people at the stake?"

"Six, Miss. One in June and five in July. There may have been more since, there have certainly been enough arrested for it, but I have not heard word of late. Master Saltonstall's in town presently and I let it be known that you may want to speak with him on the matter upon your arrival."

"Nathaniel Saltonstall?"

"The same Miss. He was a member of the special court Governor Phips had set up to hear the cases, but he removed himself in June."

"Governor Phips," Amber muttered with obvious dislike. "Where is Master Saltonstall?"

"At Master Collin's residence."

Amber's snort told Mister Thatcher what she thought of that arrangement.

"Very well Mister Thatcher, let us pay Nathaniel and his host a visit."

"As you say, Miss."

A quarter of an hour later Amber was striding past the granite lions guarding Henry Collin's wrought iron gate while Mister Thatcher waited along the street with their horses. The well-tended yard, stained glass windows, and brick constructed home spoke of the wealth that lay within. It was meant to impress and intimidate visitors, but it did neither with Amber as she took hold of the polished brass knocker and drummed upon the door.

Before the door was even halfway open Amber brushed the white haired male servant aside and entered the grand foyer where a crystal chandelier cast candle light in twinkling rainbow hues. A majestic stairwell, lined with portraits of the family's patriarchs, spiraled upward to a second-floor landing where the head of the household could greet his visitors from on high. Ignoring the silver candle holders that perched on the walls and nearby mahogany table Amber turned to the flustered servant that had answered the door and deftly swung her cloak from her shoulders and handed it to the man.

"Inform Master Saltonstall that Miss Magdalene has come to call upon him," she commanded before the man could protest her rudeness and stared into his shocked face daring him to challenge her. Clearly frustrated, he quickly folded her cloak over his arm and strode into one of the adjoining rooms.

201

"Yes, I heard her quite clearly Anthony," a man announced from within before Anthony could take two steps over the threshold. "Please show her in."

"Thank you, Master Anthony," Amber acknowledged as she floated past and entered the house's formal living room where two men waited for her.

To Amber the formal living room, like the foyer, was another extension of Collin's proclamation of wealth. Three stuffed purple velvet chairs and a long purple couch were arranged to form a close conversation area near the center of the room. A grand piano sat quietly unattended in the far corner, polished to a shine. Two large arched windows, flanked by ten-foot high cherry wood bookcases, looked out onto the front gardens and the stone wall that partially blocked her view of the street. White silk curtains waiting to be drawn left the ornately stained glass in the window's arches clearly on display for both those within and those passing by outside. The remaining wall space was covered with even more paintings of the Collin's family, both the living and the dead.

The younger of the two men, a man in his mid-thirties, stood next to the piano and idly twirled a half full glass of deep red wine. The other, an older gentleman with a decade's experience on his young counterpart, sat upon one of the purple chairs with a thick book opened halfway and carefully balanced across his knees. In Amber's opinion, the young Collin's displayed a certain cocky amusement on his face and lived with the false perception that his money offered him an untouchable sanctuary. Nathaniel though eyed Amber with a cautious, calculating gaze, attempting to gauge whom the lioness had come to feed on.

"Thank you for such a prompt welcome Henry," Amber announced to the younger man with a slight incline of her head.

"Certainly," the young man responded raising his wine glass a few inches in reply. "Perhaps one of these nights you will call upon me, instead of one of my guests."

"Perhaps," Amber told him, but they both knew no such event would occur.

"I already spoke with your Mister Thatcher on the matter Amber," Nathaniel began, holding up a hand to forestall what she was going to say when she turned to face him.

"I'm aware of that Nathaniel. He told me your version of events on the way here."

"Then you know everything I do."

"The question I have is not what you have already explained, but where you think the course of these events will travel?"

"Why trouble yourself over Salem of all places?" Henry interjected. "Witchcraft. Blah. They are not even Catholic. What does it matter what the heathens do to one another?"

"For one who has not witnessed these matters first hand I would not be so quick to brush the hand of the Quirinal Palace aside Master Collins," Amber retorted. "Catholic or not."

"This will pass Amber," Nathaniel interrupted before Henry could antagonize her further. "This is the new world and far from the inquisitions of Europe. Reason will win out in the end. Even now there are people openly questioning the proceedings and that number will only continue to increase."

"You see Amber," interjected Henry after upending his glass of wine, "a little patience is all that is needed. Even the Puritans aren't beyond redemption. So, you have no need to fear for your vast holdings."

"Patience, Master Collin? My *patience* for these witch hunts ran out long ago," Amber retorted before turning her attention back to Nathaniel once again. "No matter what you call it Nathaniel, an inquisition is an inquisition."

"Amber...," Nathaniel began to protest, but this time Amber raised a hand to forestall him.

"I will take you at your word on this matter Nathaniel and I will attempt to be more patient, for now."

Nathaniel nodded his understanding, a look of relief crossing his face.

"Well, now that that little matter is settled," Henry announced, "shall we adjourn to the dining room? We're having fresh pheasant this evening Miss Magdalene, would you care to join us?"

"Thank you for such a generous offer Master Collin," Amber announced turning to face her host with a feign smile. She and Collin both knew that neither of them wished to spend any longer in the other's company than necessary, but there were formalities that needed to be observed. "And for allowing my late intrusion, but I must decline your offer and return to my *vast holdings* as you put it. Perhaps another night."

"Oh, very well. We'll make arrangements in the future," he replied with just enough sincerity so as not to be insulting.

Amber gave Nathaniel a nod and exited into the foyer to retrieve her cloak from Anthony who stood near the front door waiting. Amber allowed him to place the heavy wool garment upon her shoulders and she slid a number of gold coins into his coat pocket with a whispered word of thanks. The act of generosity would no doubt confuse Anthony, but to Amber each coin that was placed in a pocket only grew her spider web larger.

"A strange bird that one," Henry remarked watching her walk down the path from the living room window. "I suppose when one is as wealthy as she is one can afford to be strange. Still, whenever anything occurs with a hint of the church's hand in it she's ready to go to war."

"You should truly tread more carefully with her Henry," Nathaniel replied after emptying his own full glass of wine in a single long swallow.

"You cannot be serious Nathaniel," Henry scoffed turning away from the window. "I'll grant you that she has money and perhaps influence, but she's still only a woman after all."

"With reasons as good as anyone for feeling the way she does and the influence to make things happen."

"If I did not know you better Nathaniel I would believe you feared her."

"Feared?" Nathaniel asked aloud as if hearing the word for the first time and trying to understand its meaning. "No Henry. Not fear, but something far greater."

Henry stared at the back of Nathaniel's head for a long moment. To say he was baffled by the whole episode would make the matter sound trivial. He could understand Amber's oddities, but he could not understand what had gotten into Nathaniel. Shaking his head, a sly grin formed on his face, as he made his way back to the decanter and the lovely red wine it held. *Perhaps I am the only sane one here tonight,* he laughed to himself.

Outside Amber found Mister Thatcher, exactly where she had left him, casually stroking the horse's manes. Even in the gloom she was sure he was looking at her sideways, waiting to hear, or not hear, what came from the meeting. She knew when she had caught him as a child trying to steal her coin purse that he was going to be useful and Mister Thatcher had not disappointed her over the decades.

"As always, you are well informed Mister Thatcher," she commended.

"Thank you, Miss," he replied with a tip of his hat. "Will we be making plans for a trip then?"

"No."

"You are not concerned over the matters in Salem?"

"Troubled would perhaps be a better description," she answered as she took hold of the reigns he offered her. "I have become little more than folklore to any but the Pope and his inner circle. Too much time has passed, too many generations, since I was a constant thorn in their side that they've lost track of me. When I appear from shadow and deliver reminders that our war is not over, all the Pope can do now is throw a wide net and hope to catch something."

"A person could use such obscurity to one's advantage, Miss."

"Oh, I do intend to do just that Mister Thatcher. Perhaps not in the way you are considering, but it is an advantage I have no intention of squandering while it is in my possession."

CHAPTER TWENTY-ONE

"Who, exactly, was your brother?" Robert asked. They had pulled off the highway a short while ago to refuel. It was the middle of the night, but even as they closed in on the east coast they still could not escape the heat of the summer. Amber had Walt and Jay drop her and Robert off at an empty park to avoid any unwanted attention. The never-ending highway and stress was wearing on them all so a break was certainly in order. "You've mentioned him a few times now and he seems to have a bigger part in all this than you've wanted to say."

"You've heard of him Robert."

"Oh really? How about a clue?"

"Jesus Christ."

"Look, I'm just trying to wrap my head around this. You don't need to get an attitude because I asked you something personal."

"I'm not getting an *attitude*," she scoffed. "Jesus Christ is my brother."

Robert stared at her not knowing how he was supposed to respond to that. It was absolute madness, but she had said it with a finality that left no room for argument. When she turned to look at him a moment later it was a given that she expected him to think she was crazy. He could see it written all over her face. She was waiting for the confrontation, expecting it.

"I told you I was old Robert," she said when he did not say anything. "My brother and I were babies when Mary and Joseph found us on their way to Bethlehem. There were no angels whispering of things to come. No wise men bearing gifts. Just two loving people who saw a sign from God and found us. The guiding star spoken of in the scriptures was just a remnant of God introducing us into the equation."

In a million different ways Robert wished she had never started telling him any of this. The more he knew, the more it felt like the black hole beneath his feet kept getting wider and wider. Now the question was, when was he going to fall through it?

"Just as scientists here are working to create life on Earth, God is out there doing the same thing with the universe. He isn't some all-knowing and all powerful being Robert and he isn't what is depicted in today's bible. My brother and I never believed that, but the church isn't based on what we believed anymore.

"All, well most, of the scriptures that mattered were lost after the Council of Nicaea. Not that it matters, but I should have known then that this war was inevitable. Anyway, that's history," she said shaking herself free of old memories. "What matters now is that you understand that Earth is a speck of dust in the Milky Way Galaxy and while the Milky Way is a speck of dust in the vastness of the universe, our universe is a speck of dust in something larger."

"A person is a person, no matter how small," Robert whispered under his breath.

"What?"

"Nothing. Just a line from a Doctor Seuss story."

"My brother, Jesus, was the Alpha. Two thousand years ago was his time in the proverbial spotlight. He was trying to unite the world together and if he had succeeded think what could have happened. Think of what a unified humanity might have accomplished in two thousand years. All the good that could have come about if there was no war. All of the diseases that could have been cured with the money that the world's governments have spent on their militaries."

"Let's, for a moment, say you're not crazy," Robert began and saw a momentary smile play across her lips before it disappeared almost as quickly. "What about the other two thirds of the world's population? The ones that aren't Christian. What about their religious beliefs?"

"Christianity and Muslim beliefs both began with my brother. Not that it matters really. What does any belief, Christian or otherwise, have to do with the truth? It doesn't matter what title you give God, Robert. He isn't the poster child for humanity's spiritual personifications. I told you he's more like a scientist. He's the creator of all things, plain and simple."

"Alright fine," Robert conceded. "He's the creator of all things blah, blah, blah. Why are you so desperate we try to talk to him?"

"Have you ever carried out an experiment that didn't work?"

"Yea," he replied like it should have been obvious. He gave up counting his mistakes before he even graduated college.

"What did you do when it happened?"

"Analyzed the results I did get."

"And then what?"

"I suppose I rethought the problem and tried again using what I had learned."

"So, what do you think will happen to this world, this universe, if God doesn't hear us? He's out there right now working to create life here in our universe Robert, but he doesn't know he's succeeded. I don't know how I know that, I just do."

Robert did not answer her as he considered the implications.

"It will be the end of time Robert. Judgment Day, when God wipes out this universe and starts anew. If my brother had been able to bring the world together we might not be in this situation, but it was mankind that couldn't come to terms with what he was offering. Think about the Ten Commandments. Don't worship another god. Don't build idols. Don't curse. Remember the Sabbath. Don't kill. Don't cheat. Don't steal. Don't lie. Don't covet your neighbor's goods. If the world just followed even *half* of those beliefs or even showed common courtesy and decency to one another, regardless of religion, the world would be a much better place."

"Hold on," Robert interrupted. "You're saying Jesus was some sort of a catalyst?"

"What do you mean?"

"You're saying that God is some bio-engineer mixing things together to create life and he added your brother as a catalyst to start a bio-chemical reaction that would achieve the result he wanted."

"That's putting it rather oddly but I suppose so, in a way," she thought about it before continuing. "It's why he and I were put here. He was the alpha plan. I'm the omega."

"It's been two thousand years Amber..."

"Two thousand years for us Robert. I have no idea how long God has been looking for us. It may only be minutes to him."

211

"Well how are you supposed to unite the human race?"

"I'm not."

"What do you mean you're not?" Robert stopped himself short as his thoughts took a different, dawning, direction. "You told me the church was after me because *I* was going to destroy the world."

She nodded.

"But how does that fit into what you're supposed to do?"

"I'm the Omega," she told him as if that explained it all.

"But what does being the Omega mean?"

"Once you destroy civilization, I will conquer what remains and finally unify humanity," she told him as if the plan should have been obvious.

"Whoa, let's stop right there," Robert objected placing a hand on her shoulder to emphasize the point. "Let's assume that I believe you and we're on the top of some dandelion in a bigger world. I don't have any intention of destroying the world."

"This isn't about intentions or mystical beliefs Robert," she told him coolly. "It's about mathematical truths."

"Mathematical truths?"

"Nothing in this world is true until it can be proven mathematically."

"Yea, well the *mathematical* odds of me destroying the world calculates out to zero."

"No, they calculate out to you," She countered. "Revelations Chapter 13, verse 18."

212

Here is wisdom. Let him that hath understanding
count the number of the beast: for it is the number
of a man: and his number is Six hundred
threescore and six.

"You think I'm the Anti-Christ!" Robert shouted a fraction of a second before she finished.

Before he could keep shouting anything else and bring any more unwanted attention to them Amber kissed him. It had the desired effect of shutting him up and it was something she knew they were both enjoying when Robert pulled her closer to him.

"The Vatican thinks you're the Anti-Christ Robert," Amber replied after pushing him away from her before things went any farther. "That's why they'll do everything they can to stop you, but that's not what that verse really means."

"I think it's pretty clear," Robert snapped, clearly still annoyed, but at least he was not yelling.

"Will you just shut up and listen to me," she cautioned, finally becoming exasperated with him. "You are *not* the Anti-Christ. If anything, you're the complete opposite of him. That verse was a clue my brother left me, in the form of a mathematical equation."

"A mathematical equation for what?"

"Most people think it's a fancy way of saying six hundred sixty-six, but that isn't how the verse was supposed to be interpreted. The *number of a man*. It's an equation and a riddle all at once."

Robert looked blankly at her.

"I won't bore you with the math, but it ultimately refers to the six hundred sixty sixth child in a specific lineage line. Which really doesn't mean much, unless you know where the line starts."

"And you know where it starts?" Robert challenged.

"Of course, I know. I was there, remember?" Amber said moving closer to him. "The key to it, what the church failed to realize, was that it all began with his daughter and not his sons."

"Whose daughter? And what does that have to do with me?"

"I can trace your family's lineage back to her and the time of the Disciples. That's where all this starts. That's why you are so important."

"The Disciples?"

"*Kariot* is based from the last name *Iscariot*."

"Okay."

But it was clear to Amber that he had no idea what she was talking about. "Iscariot was the last name of one of the disciples Robert," she paused and bit her lower lip before going on. "You're the six hundredth sixty sixth descendant of Judas Iscariot, the disciple who betrayed my brother."

CHAPTER TWENTY-TWO

Unable to find the words for what he was thinking Robert could only stare at her. His expression was unreadable. Looking in her eyes he wanted to find some sign that she was kidding or playing some sort of twisted practical joke on him. There was none of that in her face. Her eyes, her expression, the way she stood there, everything about her said she was serious and at the same time worried.

His eyes flared with unsaid anger and he stomped back towards the street entrance. He did not see any houses nearby where he could use a phone and the dimly shining park lights, spaced farther apart then they should have been, did not show him a way out of this mess. As he stood beside the gravel path trying to take deep, steadying breaths, he gazed across the shadowy grass fields and felt like his life should be somewhere out there, beyond a clear path or a guiding light. That was where he belonged now. Mixed in the shadows of a never-ending nightmare. *If I hadn't gone for that run, would things have turned out differently? Would I still be here now?* He doubted much would have changed. It was like being in a Chinese finger trap where the more you struggled against the coils the tighter they got.

Mathematical truths, Amber would have called it. The events that brought him to this moment may have changed a little, but this was where he was going to wind up. Perhaps Justin would still be alive. Maybe all the cops at the airport too, but ultimately, he would still be standing here in the middle of the night, looking out across a landscape, and wondering how his life had gotten so screwed up. All he ever wanted was a quiet life. A life where his bills were paid and there was a little left over to enjoy the countless simple pleasures that waited. It seemed like such a foreign idea to him now.

"I'm sorry," he heard Amber softly tell him.

He glanced over his shoulder at her. "For what?" he demanded. The anger had cooled, but his tone still did not fit in with the quiet of the park.

"Everything," she answered and sighed.

He looked away from her again and released his own long breath, one that he did not realize he had been holding in. His shoulders sagged as his head fell to his chest. He stayed that way, his eyes shut, before finally lifting his head backwards to look at the night sky. The universe lay open, a silent witness to his dilemma. A billion stars, whose vastness was incomprehensible to most people, silently waited for his decision. *How can one truly envision infinity?* Robert wondered.

"You told me what I wanted to know. Nothing to be sorry for," he said to her as the last of the anger left him and a cold emptiness filled into the void that its leaving left behind. In a way, he welcomed the lack of feeling. Being dead on the inside helped to make things a little more bearable at the very least, or so he thought, but he was not really sure of that either.

"I wasn't sure you would believe me," she told him as she came to stand next to him and took hold of his hand.

"You said you'd never lie to me."

"I meant it too."

"They're not going to stop? Even if I walked away right now they'd still come after me, wouldn't they?"

"They would have come after you eventually just because you're an Iscariot. It was only a matter of time really. When the Vatican realized they couldn't stop me they started systematically killing the entire Iscariot line. It was the only clue they had to go on."

"What about the rest of my family?" the dawning fear of what might have already happened to them staggered him. "My parents, my brother and sisters? They could already be dead."

"No! No, they're ok," She reassured him gently taking hold of his cheek and turning his face towards her. "The Pope knows you're with me by now so they're probably being watched to see if you show up or make contact, but otherwise they're fine."

"How do you know?"

"I told you I've been watching you and your family for a long time Robert. I know how important your family is to you so they're important to me." She squeezed his hand reassuringly. "My people are keeping an eye on them and are ready to intervene if need be. I promise you, they're alright."

"The Pope," Robert muttered trying to see if he could picture what he looked like. It was a fuzzy memory. He never paid much attention to the man. "You're certain the church is still going to try to kill me? There's no other option?"

"You and I are two of the church's greatest threats and now that we're together they'll be putting all their resources into finding us so they can finally end this, but I'm not going to let that happen," she said with a cold determination in her voice.

He raised their entwined hands to his lips and kissed the back of her hand. Her skin was soft and warm and he wondered if the rest of her felt that way. "We all have to die sometime."

A few hours later, with still no sign of the endless highway coming to an end ahead of them, Robert sat awake and staring out at the dark Pennsylvania countryside that lay hiding beyond the dull yellow drone of another rest stop's flood lights. Walt and Jay had vanished inside leaving the wanted fugitive and his once captor alone in their rented escape vehicle. Robert pondered about the humor in that for a while. He had never seen a blockbuster movie where the characters stopped to get a car rental before fleeing across the country.

Amber had her head resting on his right shoulder and both of her arms entwined around his arm. She had been that way for some time now, but Robert could tell she was still avoiding sleep like he was. Her body was too alert, her breathing too controlled, and the grip on his arm, though soft and comforting, was too tight for someone who was asleep.

"Can I ask you something?" Robert asked her without turning his head away from the window scene.

"Mmm-hmm," she hummed back.

"The scars you have on your back," he started to ask but stopped after he felt her arms tense for just a fraction of a second. "Never mind. I guess it doesn't really matter anyway."

"No, it's ok," she told him shifting her head a little.

"Was it Sebastian?"

"No," she answered with a huff. "Did I tell you that he was actually on our side once? Or so I thought, but that

218

was a long time ago. You can't see the scars he left. The ones on my back I got when I was younger."

"Care to elaborate?"

"Not right now."

"But why didn't they heal?"

"Until Jesus died I could get hurt like anyone else. It was only after he died that my body was suddenly able to heal itself."

Knowing not to push the subject he directed his next question back to an intriguing remark she mentioned. "Sebastian was really on your side once? What happened?"

"He turned on me when I wasn't expecting it. Not that I was expecting it at all really."

"It's kind of hard to imagine anyone getting the jump on you."

"We were lovers," she clarified with the casual tone one would use to discuss laundry.

"Oh," was the only thing Robert could think to say.

Amber lifted her head from Robert's shoulder and slumped down in her own seat. She pressed her knees into the seatback, crossed her arms just below her chest, leaned her head back against the seat, and stared up at the ceiling.

"You don't have to say anything else. I was just wondering," he told her as he scanned the parking lot again for the umpteenth time.

"It's ok Robert. I know everything about you after all." she briefly smiled in reply, but the smile faded quickly. "I was lonely Robert, so I indulged in something selfish. I know, hard to believe, right? I'd spent centuries with the Templar Knights, more than anyone else in my life. I watched them being born and growing old. I saw them die.

They were family to me and then suddenly, in one night, they were taken away. You can't imagine that sort of loss or losing something so integral to who you are. It has its own sense of kindred irony I suppose. Anyway, I've had a few meaningful relationships since then, but I've always kept my distance with most people."

"Close but not too close," Robert summed up.

"Yea, something like that," she answered. "Honestly I think I'd go crazy if I lost that much again. Jay was the first one to get really close in a very long time and it's been wonderful having that sort of companionship again, even if it's a little fatherly sometimes. Walt came later, he's pretty quiet, but he has a way of growing on you. Then there was Sebastian, third's the charm, right?"

She did not say anything after that and Robert did not press her. It would come out in her own way and at her own pace. Instead he continued to look out across the parking lot where his attention kept being drawn to the dark areas just outside the glow of the parking lot's flood lights. The shadows seemed to shift every so often and he wondered if it was real or just a trick of the mind. Then there was the occasional car that would pass by their parking space, coming from one way or going another, its lights breaking up the car's dark interior for a few seconds, and Robert would find himself eyeing each one with suspicion thinking that it might be carrying a knight on the hunt for him.

"We met in France," Amber started explaining suddenly, catching Robert by surprise. "There was a group of knights on the way to kill a distant cousin of yours and I was trying to get there before them. It wasn't the first time they had tried to kill him and I had already moved him a couple of times. But this time... this time I was too late. Or maybe not late enough. I stumbled onto the group on the little side street where he lived as they were leaving. It was more like an alley really.

"Five knights to one of me, close quarters, practically surrounded, with little to no cover. Not really good odds for me, but then Sebastian came. All I saw was some guy in a uniform lay into the two knights that had gotten behind me. He was fast, they didn't know what hit them. The other three didn't stand a chance. Even though we had never met he and I made a natural team. Anyone watching would thought they were watching a choreographed fight scene from a movie.

"We had dinner that night within sight of the Eiffel Tower. I know, crazy, right?" Amber remarked at seeing Robert's *your crazy* face. She wondered if he had always been that easy to read. She did not remember being able to tell his mood with a glance before. "There we were having a dinner without a care in the world in a city probably crawling with knights at that point. After so many years laying low and coordinating everything behind the scenes it was amazing being out there in the open, acting like we ran the place.

"So anyway, we sat there, sipping wine long after the restaurant had closed. Turns out Sebastian had just gotten out of the Foreign Legion. He didn't have any family, nowhere to really go. Figured he'd wind up in some merc army sooner or later so I made him an offer to come along with me and he took me up on it."

"Is that how they found me?" Robert asked.

"No," Amber answered and tapped the side of her head with her finger. "This is the only place that information has ever been and I haven't shared that with anyone."

"Not even Jay?"

She smiled at him. "Not even Jay."

"When did it turn ugly?"

"A few months later. Jay never liked him from the start which should have been a tip off. Ruthlessly efficient he had once said to describe Sebastian. With an emphasis on ruthless, but it had been a long time since I had been with someone like Sebastian. A really long time.

"I was getting ready for bed. We had been intimate for a while, we shared the same bed, but early in the evening we got into a big fight. He'd seen me take some pretty big hits and within hours it was like nothing had happened to me. He wanted to know why and kept pressing. He just wouldn't let up about it. I finally had enough of it so I picked up a steak knife, cut my hand, and held it up for him to see the wound close.

"Sebastian doesn't really show his emotions, but when he saw my cut heal he couldn't hide the look on his face. I didn't know if it was shock, or fear, or revulsion, or what. I'd never seen it before and I didn't like it so I told him to sleep on the couch and then went to our room.

"He came in about ten minutes later. I was just pulling the covers down but didn't bother to look at him, I was still pissed. He handed me a shot of vodka and put his arms around me. Part of me wanted to throw the drink in his face and throw him out. The other just wanted to curl up with him in bed. I should have thrown him out," she paused for a second then more vehemently declared, "No, I should have gutted the bastard right there."

She shifted closer to Robert and took his hand in hers. She entwined their fingers together and thought about the roughness of his palms. He did not look like the type of guy to work with his hands, but she liked the fact that he did.

"I'm so sorry Robert," she whispered.

"For what?"

"My entire life has been spent preparing for you and...because I was..."

"What?"

"I almost destroyed everything Robert. Sebastian was a Vatican Knight and I didn't know it. How could I not have known? The vodka was spiked. He probably thought if he killed me it would all be over. He didn't know back then just how hard that is to do, but if he did, then I wouldn't have survived and when they came for you, you would be dead. All because I was stupid and lonely," She turned into him, kissed his cheek, and whispered, "Please don't hate me. You don't realize what it's like finding people you care for and love, and all the time knowing they're going to die while you keep living. That there's nothing you can do to stop it. Centuries worth of people, Robert, and the list of names keeps getting longer and longer. And I remember them all. I can see their faces. I can hear their voices and their laughter, and sometimes their crying.

"I try to be strong Robert. I try *so* hard, but sometimes I can't be. Sometimes I need someone to hold me and I hate myself for being that way, but I can't help it. I'm sorry. I'm so so sorry. Just don't hate me, okay? I can accept anything else, just...*please* don't hate me."

Robert lifted her chin with his free hand so he could see her face. He saw the fear in her eyes and the tears freely falling over her cheeks. He thought he should hate her. He had every right to after everything he had been put through, but he did not. Instead he leaned down and gently kissed her lips. When they parted, she wrapped her arms around him and buried her face in his shoulder and he ran his hand through her hair and whispered reassuringly that everything was alright.

It did not take long before her breathing evened out and she curled up against him before completely falling asleep. He gently eased her down until her head was laying in his lap and he wiped her cheeks dry. *This is madness*, he thought. *Complete and total madness*. If he really was smart he never would have gotten into the car back at the train station, but for some reason he was glad he did. Robert had never felt someone need him, or love him, or believe in him as much as Amber did. Not even Kate.

CHAPTER TWENTY-THREE

Walt and Jay returned soon after. Jay looked alert with a cup of steaming coffee in one hand and a couple bags of rest stop fast food in the other. The old man glanced toward the backseat and gave Walt a quick flick of his head in Robert and Amber's direction.

"Looks like she's got the right idea," Walt whispered to Robert. "Can I put my head in your lap too?"

"Shut up and go to sleep," Jay admonished as he keyed the engine to life.

Robert was starting to think he understood why Amber felt how she did about the two of them. They made a natural team.

Jay quickly left the parking lot behind, hastening them once again through night, and Robert drifted off to sleep thinking about the cruel Sebastian. His nightmares shocked himself awake as the eastern horizon was beginning to lighten with the approach of dawn. He looked around, attempting to orient himself to the real world, when he noticed Jay staring at him in the rearview.

"Nightmares?" he asked Robert, keeping his voice low.

"Yea."

"Is she still asleep?"

Robert glanced down to look at Amber and brushed aside a stray strand of hair that had fallen across her eyes. "Looks like it."

"Guess that means you're part of the club now. Congratulations."

225

"Huh?"

"In case you haven't noticed, Amber doesn't trust many people. If she fell asleep on you like that then it means she must trust you," Jay answered while he checked the sideview mirrors.

"You're the one that found her, weren't you?" Robert asked not being any more specific.

"One of the worst days of my life," Jay acknowledged keeping his eyes on the road ahead but he spared Robert a quick glance letting him know he understood exactly what he was talking about. "How'd you figure that one out so quick?"

"Just a feeling. She said Sebastian tried to poisoned her."

"As always, it seems she left out the details."

"Like what?"

"You sure you want to know kid?" Jay asked considering him in the mirror. "It wasn't pretty."

"I'm in this up to my neck already Jay."

"Alright. Just remember you asked. He didn't poison her, he drugged her so she couldn't put up a fight. I came by the house the next morning and as soon as I went in I knew something was wrong. That ever happen to you? You go into some place and it just doesn't feel right. Well that's what it felt like, it was too quiet inside, and when she didn't answer me I knew it was going to be bad. I just didn't know how bad.

"I found her in the bedroom. The sick fuck had cut her open from her belly up to her throat. What kind of sick psychopath does something like that? Her insides were hanging out of her, and the smell, I'll never forget it. Death has a smell kid and its god awful. I've been in war, I've seen death. I've seen bodies. But this was totally different. It was more...ritualistic the way he left her there.

"I thought she was dead. Her eyes were staring out at nothing for the longest time, but then she blinked. It scared the crap out of me when she moved her eyes to look right at me and when I saw her breathing I nearly lost it.

"Then the screams came. I've never heard anything like it and I think that's when I *really* did panic. I don't know how I was able to keep it together. I called in some favors. And Walt and me did what we could to patch her up, which wasn't much. We kept her drugged and tied her to the bed just to keep her from thrashing around and reinjuring herself."

"Why didn't you take her to a hospital for god's sake?"

"You've seen what she can do Robert. Do you think a hospital is the right sort of place to take her?" Anger was underlying Jay's soft-spoken words as he talked, but Robert knew it was not being directed towards him. "Besides doing that would have been like calling up the Pope and saying here we are at St. Joseph's Hospital send your goons to finish the job your lap dog couldn't."

Robert thought on it for a moment and decided Jay was right. "How long did it take her to heal?"

"You don't really heal from that sort of thing, but she walked out of her room the next afternoon if that tells you anything."

"Yea," Robert said more to himself than to Jay. "How long ago did all this happen?"

"It's been awhile. Several years."

227

"That's crazy."

"We're all crazy kid," Jay answered matter-of-factly catching Robert's eye in the rearview mirror. "It's the insane ones that you have to watch out for. They're the ones that really know what the hell is going on."

It was late morning when they pulled off the Pennsylvania interstate and fifteen minutes later into the parking lot of MJ's Diner. The faded awnings extending over the faded red paint of the building told a story of a place that had seen plenty of years. It was a warm sunny day, not overly hot and oppressive like it had been. It was the type of day people looked forward to being outside on and when Robert saw how full the parking lot was he knew he was not the only one to feel that way.

"We good?" Walt asked turning to look at Amber.

"All clear," she replied and Walt slapped his hands and quickly rubbed them together.

"Wonder what the special is today?" Jay pondered.

"Who cares," Walt rumbled opening his door. "Whatever it is will be better than that fast food crap we've been eating."

"Can't argue with that," Jay echoed as he climbed out.

"Come on Robert," Amber said smiling and opened her door.

"It's safe?"

"Safe enough," she told him as she exited. She raised her hands over her head and arched her back in a long stretch and caught Robert watching how her body curved with each twist and bend. "Ready?"

"As I'll ever be," he answered.

"Amber Lynn!" hollered an African American woman with salt and pepper hair as they came through the door. She was setting down plates filled with sandwiches and fries at a table in the middle of the room and left the customers to figure out whose dish belonged to whom so she could come over and greet the newest arrivals.

It was a packed house. From the old to the very young, with seating few and far between. The mid volume chatter that had greeted them when they first entered dropped to a noticeable hum as heads turned to look at the newcomers. Robert's anxiety level shot up when the door they had just come through made a noticeable bang and dozens of strange eyes looked them over. Yet just as quickly heads turned back to their meals or their companions and the noise levels crescendo back to a dull ruckus.

The approaching woman threw the white and green striped dish towel she was carrying the hot plates on over her shoulder and opened her arms wide. "Come here you," she ordered Amber.

For trying to remain unnoticed, they were not being very subtle and Robert was equally surprised when Amber opened her own arms in greeting.

"Mary Jane!" Amber yelled back just as the two met and embraced.

"Let me look at you girl," Mary Jane instructed, holding Amber by the shoulders as she looked her up and down. "You lose weight? You did, didn't you?"

"No..."

"Tyrone, put on the special. The cat done dragged in a scraggly bunch," Mary Jane yelled over her shoulder.

229

"Honestly girl. How do you expect to get yourself a man looking like a breeze could snap you in two? Then again," Mary Jane murmured as her eyes fell on Robert. "Maybe your man likes you just the way you are. Hmm?"

"Shut up MJ," Amber teased and headed towards the service counter before Robert could see her face flush.

"And who do we have here?" Mary Jane smiled, extending her hand towards Robert.

"Robert," he replied taking her hand. She had a strong grip and calloused palms from years of hard work.

"Hey Jay. How you doing you old codger?" Mary Jane asked as Jay slapped Robert on the shoulder and kept walking by.

"Same as always," he answered without stopping.

"Hi Momma," Walt said and gave the woman a warm kiss on the cheek in passing.

"Hi sweetheart," Mary Jane responded returning the kiss without taking her eyes off Robert.

Even with a room full of people Robert felt oddly alone standing there facing her. They had stopped going through the motions of shaking hands, but Mary Jane tightened her grip when he tried to let go. She was a strong woman.

"So, Walt is your son?" Robert asked just to break up the silence.

"Mm-hmm," Mary Jane hummed with a slow nod of her head.

"Um, what are we doing?" Robert asked feeling awkward.

"Waiting," she replied.

"Waiting for what?" he asked looking around the room.

"To see if she's put a claim on you yet?"

"Nobody's got a claim on me."

"You go right on believing that sugar. Don't make it true though," Mary Jane told him and pulled him closer to her. "Now a man can talk to another man all he likes. But when a woman has another woman's man all to herself, it don't matter the color of her skin, how old she is, or how important her status. A woman has to make the boundaries clear."

Robert was about to protest when he spotted Amber making her way back towards them over MJ's shoulder.

"See sugar," Mary Jane whispered with a sly smile. "It's written all over your face. I don't even need to look to know she's on her way."

Mary Jane laughed loudly at the mixture of embarrassment and annoyance that showed on Robert's face.

"So, does he pass the Mary Jane test?" Amber interrupted. Seeing Robert's expression and reddening face her eyes narrowed suspiciously. "What are you two up to?"

"Nothing sugar. Nothing at all. Now let's get you two set up with some of Tyrone's cooking." Mary Jane said and led them back through the crowded tables to where Jay and Walt were sitting at the long service counter. "From the way the phone's been ringing I don't imagine you'll be staying long."

"Who's been calling?" Amber knew immediately whatever was going on was not going to be good.

"Said his name was Christopher," Mary Jane answered. "Called a couple of times in the last hour. Once to

231

see if you were here. Then again to leave you a message. Wouldn't say what it was about, just said if you pass through you need to call him, ASAP."

"Who's Christopher?" Robert wanted to know, but a glance from Amber told him now was not the time to talk about it.

"Why don't you get something to eat Robert?" Amber suggested and kept walking towards the kitchen. "I'll be back in a minute."

Robert made to follow her, but Mary Jane stepped in the way and unceremoniously got him to sit down on an isolated red vinyl stool so no one could interrupt them. "Always wanting to be by your woman's side," she purred. "I knew I liked you from the moment I saw you Robert."

"She's not my woman."

"And don't you forget that. No *woman* belongs to no *man*. I don't know where you fool men ever got that idea in the first place," Mary Jane proclaimed as she walked behind the counter. "Now what can I get you to drink?"

"Water will be fine," he answered but his eyes strayed to the door swinging shut behind Amber.

"You can call her Amber or even the angel Gabrielle himself, it don't make no difference. She's one of God's lieutenants mark my words," Mary Jane proclaimed as she filled Robert's water glass and watched him look to where Amber had gone.

"His right hand ...woman huh?"

"You see this place?" she asked him and circled her arm in the air to indicate the diner. "I always wanted a place like this. A place for Walt, Tyrone, and me. A way to get out of the city. Away from the crime and the drugs. A place where

232

Walt could be a kid and not running around in some gang. All of this is because of her you understand."

"How did that happen?"

"Long story short, because of Walt," she said tossing a warm glance towards her son seated further down the counter. "There's not much hope of getting out of the inner-city. You either live as a prisoner in your own home or become what the street says you're supposed to be. It was the street for Walt. No matter how hard I tried I couldn't be there looking over his shoulder all day and night. Not if we wanted to keep a roof over our heads and food on the table.

"I don't know what Amber was doing there, but she crossed paths with the boys Walt was with and they were looking for trouble. Well they found it for sure," she laughed, but it was a sad sort of laugh. "I don't suppose they ever came across trouble like Amber Lynn. So here I am coming home after work, it's late you understand, and I find the two of them waiting outside the front door for me. Right off I know its trouble and as soon as Walt saw me he knew he was in for it. It was an amazing thing seeing him launch into excuses and going dead still when she looked at him. Whatever happened that night put the fear of God in him alright."

She fell silent for a few minutes absently wiping the counter as Robert sipped at his water and he thought about what Amber had told him earlier about watching loved ones die through the centuries. *So, she had met Walt when he was a kid*, he thought. He had grown up in her life and was a young man now. Jay had been a young man when they met and now he was old. She had invested so much time, decades, just in those two relationships and it made Robert wondered how many funerals she had gone to. How long was the list of names she told him about? It was hard for him to wrap his head around the sheer number of people she must have known, and mourned, in her life.

"There we all were sitting in our tiny apartment telling her about ourselves and our dreams. A complete stranger. Isn't that the damnedest thing?" Mary Jane asked once she broke free of whatever memory had captured her attention.

"It makes you wonder, that's for sure."

"Yes, it does," she agreed. "And do you know what happened after that?"

"I'm guessing this?" Robert answered with a wave of his hand indicating the diner.

"Exactly Sugar, this." She said looking around with pride. "A fresh start. Especially for Walt being a teenager in such a quiet town and all, but whenever he started to stray one call to Amber always put him back on the path. Oh, it was hard starting out, don't get me wrong, but it was worth every drop of sweat and tears."

"Was she through here a lot?"

"Mmm, a fair bit," Mary Jane said as the cook rang the ready bell. She whisked the food off the kitchen window and slid it in front of Robert. He had no idea whose food this was, he had not asked for anything, but Mary Jane did not seem to care. "We see her every few months I suppose. Stops in for a meal on her way to wherever she's going."

"Does Walt ever talk about what they're up to?"

"Not much. I hear a piece here and there," she told him turning more serious. "But I don't need to hear anything. I know danger when I see it."

CHAPTER TWENTY-FOUR

After Amber was out of sight behind the swinging door that led into the kitchen she quickened her pace to Mary Jane's office in the back corner of the building. Tyron, still as tall and as lean as she remembered, acknowledged her with a bob of his head but otherwise kept up his hurried pace at the stove. The two sous chefs he had with him were too busy to do even that as she hurried by. The office was not large, about the size of a small bathroom, but it had a door for privacy that Amber pushed closed and locked once she was inside.

She took a hanging picture of Jesus off the wall. Amber thought it was a horrible rendition of him accepted by today's mainstream, but it served its purpose to conceal a steel gray safe hidden behind it. Where a keypad should have been, a recessed finger print scanner was embedded. Amber placed her thumb on the scanner and watched a pale red light come to life indicating it was comparing her print to the ones locked in its memory. She moved her hand when the light turned green then quickly opened the door when the locks released.

A pistol, already loaded with a bullet in the chamber, was set inside ready to be quickly drawn in an emergency. If things got really bad, another three, hollow point loaded, 9mm clips were attached to the inner door just in case. Amber was not interested in either the gun or the clips and ignored them. Her only thoughts were on the remaining item inside, a small polished silver smart phone sitting in a charging cradle.

She grabbed the phone off its base, depressed the power button bringing it out of sleep mode, and watched the screen. It flashed twice the code letting her know the link had been secured and automatically opened the dial pad. She ignored the keypad and hit the send button, it could only dial one number and any attempt to call elsewhere would cause the phone to explode. Hopefully taking care of the security breach when it did.

"Control," A monotone artificial intelligence program announced before the phone rang even once.

"Phoenix one-one-two-seven-five," Amber said.

"Confirmed," the faux voice acknowledged.

"Herald nine-ten."

"Standby."

Almost immediately the phone on the other end of the call began to ring. Once. Twice. As the third ring reached its end the call connected. Amber remained silent. It would take the phones a few seconds to establish a secure link and it was not until the person on the other end of the line said anything that she would know if it had worked.

"Herald nine-ten," a winded sounding man began.

"It's Phoenix one-one-two-seven-five."

"Finally," the man on the other end proclaimed with noticeable relief.

"What's wrong?"

"They took the sparrow."

"Fuck!" Amber snarled. "Who took her?"

"Like I went up to them and asked for an autograph," came the sarcastic reply. "This assignment was supposed to be a no brainer."

"It should have been. There was always a chance something might happen, but I figured it would be slim at best."

"Yea, well..."

"Chris! When did they take her?" Amber demanded before he could complain about anything else.

"A few hours ago. Two guys. A quick snatch and grab."

"Did you recognize them? What did they look like?"

"No, I don't know who they were. The first guy was a pale Caucasian. Tall, easily over six feet with blond hair, pretty well built, looked European. The second guy was shorter. Definitely not as pale. Wide shoulders, bodybuilder type, and bald."

Sebastian, Amber thought when she heard the description of the second man. There were a few candidates for the first man. "Alright alright. Any idea where they took her?" she asked running a hand through her hair.

"Atlantic City."

"Atlantic City?"

"That's what I said. I followed them to the airport and bribed the shit out the place. These guys are definitely funded. Private hanger. Private jet. There was already a flight plan filed for the trip. Atlantic City International. It's in South Jersey."

"I know where it is," Amber snapped. It was also the one airport in the region that she did not have any of her people at and Sebastian knew it. It should have been one of the first things she changed when he fled, but she did not, and now that decision was coming back to punch her in the gut.

"Fine. What do you want me to do now?" Chris asked breaking into her moment of self-loathing.

"Evac."

"To where?"

"I'm lighting the furnace."

"Are you shitting me?" she heard him exclaim before she cut the connection. That should be a good enough answer for him she thought staring at the phone as the screen faded to black. She placed it back in its cradle, pushed the safe door closed, and put the picture back into place. *Why did you have to leave this to me?* she asked the picture of Jesus and the memory of the real man it represented.

She started to leave the office, but stopped with her hand on the door handle. She rested her head against the door, closed her eyes, and slowly banged her head against the reinforced metal frame. She did not want to tell Robert what had happened. She knew she would have to, but she did not have to like it. They were finally moving ahead together and this could throw all that out the window.

She wished her brother was with her now. He would have said something to comfort her. Pointed out some statistical chance of success to reassure her. She took a deep breath, pulled the door open, and trudged her way back to the dining room, stopping at the service door to look out the dirty window at Robert. She had been watching him from a distance since he was born, but in the last few days that past, obscure, life had become alien to her. He had always been a means to an end, but now he was so much more. She had beaten the crap out of him only a few days ago, held a gun to his head, and thinking about that now horrified her.

Sitting at the counter, Robert continued to listen patiently to Mary Jane regale him with stories of Walt growing up. She definitely had a flare for it and Robert figured out pretty quickly, considering how quiet Walt was in comparison, that he probably took after his father. Maybe if things were different, and he was not being pursued across the country, he could have enjoyed this moment of normalcy more.

"Come with me," Amber whispered walking behind and startling him with her sudden appearance.

Mary Jane grew quiet and followed Amber with her eyes. "It's ok if a woman makes you wait, but you should never make her wait for you, especially Amber, or you'll be left behind."

Robert took a long drink of his water before getting up. "That's the one thing I'm pretty sure I *don't* have to worry about," he told her before snaking his way between the tables to catch up.

Outside Amber closed her eyes and turned her face to the sun. Even though the day was hot already, with the barometer easily pushing itself into the nineties, the extra heat and the lower humidity felt good on her skin. She wondered what the next few minutes were going to do to her and Robert's fragile relationship. The diner door opened and swung closed with a dull bang and Robert stood next to her a moment later.

"There's no easy way to put this Robert," Amber said with a heavy sigh. "Sebastian is doing his best to stack the deck against us. He kidnapped Kate."

"What?" Robert shouted. "Why would he go after Kate? That doesn't make any sense."

239

"It makes perfect sense."

"No, it doesn't. They're after me."

"Look what just knowing is doing to you. Look at the guilt starting to eat you up. This is how Sebastian is going to get to you," Amber tried to explain. "Sebastian is the perfect hunter Robert. He's fast. He's strong. And even more importantly he's smart, really smart. He knows people. He can figure out what they're thinking, how they're feeling, and uses it to his advantage. Trust me I know. I'm sure he's read a psychological profile on you by now."

"How the hell did he get a psychological profile on me?"

"You think the Vatican only conducts Masses? They're one of the wealthiest institutions on the planet, they can afford the research."

"But why Kate?"

"Sebastian knows the type of person you are. He knows what it takes to pull your strings and he's doing just that. Plus, I don't care about her."

"What do your feelings have to do with it?"

"This," Amber barked, waving her hands back and forth between them. "It creates tension between us. It weakens us. Look I know. I understand how you feel."

"You understand? *You* understand? I find that pretty fucking hard to believe," he sneered, batting aside her hand as she reached for him.

"Well maybe I don't!" she challenged as her own temper started to rise. "And it would be so much easier if I just let it go but…"

"I'm sure it would. You wouldn't lose any sleep over it," he interrupted.

She stepped in close to him and grabbed his shirt when he tried to step away. "You're right. I *wouldn't* lose a minute of sleep over it, but you would so it affects me too," she shoved him away and faced him with her hands on her hips. "So now it's something I have to deal with."

"I'm responsible for how this crap affects the people in my life Amber. I can't just cut my feelings off and walk away like you."

Amber managed to keep her face neutral but it felt like he had just slapped her.

"Do you love her?" she managed to squeeze out. Not that it really mattered. It was not going to change what she was going to do, but she wanted to know. She needed to know and she dreaded the answer.

"I did, yea."

"Do you *love* her?" she demanded.

"No. Not anymore. I don't love her anymore," he answered and the fight seemed to leave him just as quickly as it had come. Admitting it out loud to someone was painful in its own right. It meant that he was no longer the man he was, he had changed somehow, lost a part of who he used to be. He did not want to think he was different. He did not want to admit that the chaos that had been their relationship and the fiery end of it had altered him so much, but it had. "But you can't expect me to just stop caring for someone who was in my life for as long as she was."

"I don't expect you to," she replied and moved closer to him again hoping it would reassure him that he was not alone. That she was with him. That they were in this together. "I just needed to know."

"What difference does it make?"

241

"You have no idea how much I was hoping it wasn't going to affect you like this."

"For god's sake Amber…"

"I know Robert," she cut him off and turned away to think.

"We have to do something. We have to try to rescue her or something."

"There are some favors I can call in," she said to him while she mulled over her options. "If we leave now and only stop for gas we *might* beat them to the airport."

"You know where they're going?"

"Atlantic City."

"Isn't that kind of like Vegas?"

"That's kind of like comparing a tree in your backyard to a forest, but yea. The airport isn't actually in Atlantic City. It's nearby, but it's a small hub which will work for and against us."

"How?" Robert questioned.

"It will be easy to find Sebastian but it'll be easy for him to see us coming too."

"What makes you think he's going to be looking?"

"He knows where we're going," she admitted. "I don't know how he figured it out, but he knows. What he doesn't know is where we are now. That trick with the plane you guys did back in Colorado wouldn't have thrown him off. He's smart, a true hunter, and now having Kate he knows he'll have some leverage. Either by keeping you from getting to Harmony or stopping you once we're there."

"Well if he knew where we were going all this time why isn't he sitting there waiting for us? Why didn't he just start there?"

"That is a very good question," she contemplated. *Why didn't Sebastian just come after me? Or better yet, why didn't the Vatican?* she thought before answering her own question aloud. "They don't know."

"Who doesn't know what?"

"The Vatican."

"The Vatican doesn't know what?"

"The Vatican doesn't know about Harmony," she answered even though it was more for herself than him. "If they did the place would have been a war zone. Sebastian didn't tell them."

"Like that makes any sense."

"For Sebastian it does. He hates to fail. I mean he hates it with a passion. They sent him to assassinate me and he failed. I survived, I got away. It's become a personal vendetta for him."

"Why do I feel even more worried now?"

"Because you're smart too," She told him with a smile. "He didn't come after me because he couldn't. The odds were stacked too much against him."

"And how does taking Kate change that?"

"It doesn't exactly, at least not with me, but it does give him an edge over you. And if he can get to you then he knows he can get to me too."

"Why didn't he just go after someone in my family? My parents? My brothers or sisters?"

"They're too well protected. He would know I'd have your family pretty well guarded so he went after a softer target."

"I thought you were only watching my family."

"I am," she shrugged ignoring the underlying question.

"So, what are we going to do?" Robert asked changing the subject back to Kate. He was sure he did not want to know what Amber's idea of *watching* his family really meant, but right now he was thankful for whatever it was.

"We're going after him," she said with a wicked smirk and gave him a quick kiss on the lips before going back inside to get Jay and Walt.

CHAPTER TWENTY-FIVE

Five hours and two speeding tickets later Robert found himself staring blankly at an aisle full of Lego's. From the bottom shelf to the top, in boxes and bright plastic bags the world of plastic imagination cried out to be noticed. The simple Lego's, the ones from his youth that consisted of plain old building blocks appeared to be in short supply and easy to miss unless a person was actively looking for them. Some of the themes on display Robert knew, like Star Wars, but others were less familiar and he found himself wondering when it was he had stopped being a kid.

"Would you look at this," Jay exclaimed from farther down the aisle. "They have Lego's that are motorized now."

Robert responded by aiming a blank stare toward his chaperone.

"Don't give me that look Robert," Jay defended. "When I was a kid Lincoln Logs were a big thing. Kids today don't know how good they got it."

"I think the Lincoln Logs are in the next aisle," Robert remarked and turned his halfhearted attention back to the tiny plastic figures before him.

Jay walked up beside him, but continued to glance around in an almost childlike wonder. It was at that moment, seeing Jay's expression, that Robert realized he did not know much about the man. Sure, it had only been a few days since they had met under less than ideal circumstances, but Robert did not even know the guy's last name, or if he was married, or if he had children. It was obvious to Robert that Jay had not been in a toy store in quite a long time, but what did that mean nowadays. Robert could not remember the last time he had been in a toy store and he found that fact somewhat depressing.

Kids had such an innocent outlook on the world around them. They were filled with wonder and a desire to explore and interact with the world. The world really was a giant playground to them and Robert truly missed feeling like that.

"What's your last name Jay?"

"O'Tool," he answered as he picked up a box depicting the Star War's legendary Hoth battle.

"Jay O'Tool, huh."

"Phillip actually," he corrected as he put the box neatly back on the self.

"Your first name is Phillip?"

"Yup."

"Where did Jay come from?"

"That was Amber's idea. She said I looked more like a Jason than a Phillip so she's been calling me Jay ever since. Guess it kind of stuck. Why do you ask?"

"No reason really. I was just wondering," Robert answered losing himself in thought for a moment. "What time is it?"

"Six and half minutes from the last time you asked," Jay offhandedly replied. Then in a more serious, yet fatherly sort of way, he continued. "It's almost four Robert. I know the waiting is tough. Hell, it's the hardest part sometimes, but in a situation like this *not* hearing anything is a good thing."

"That's what you said six and half minutes ago."

"And it was just as true then as it is now."

"Why is it we have to wait in a toy store of all places? Why couldn't we just go along?"

"First off Robert, Amber's not going to put you in any greater risk than absolutely necessary and going head to head against Sebastian is pretty damn risky," Jay explained as he picked up another Star Wars set of the First Order's AT-ST. "Secondly, if you were looking for you, would you think to look in a toy store?"

"I suppose not."

"Which is exactly why we're here."

Here, as Jay had eloquently stated, turned out to be a toy store in some town located in southern New Jersey. As Robert understood it, they were not far from the airport where Sebastian was supposed to land, but he still did not know where it was. There was a moderate sized two-story shopping mall across the street from where the two of them were held up and several shopping centers and plazas all around them. There was supposed to be a college nearby too which probably added to the overall craziness of the area. In Arizona things could get hectic too, but this was a whole new level from what Robert was used to. The lifestyle of the people here turned out to be a benefit for them though because no one seemed to notice or take a particular interest in either one of them.

Robert was going to point out the obvious fact that he was in fact not looking for himself. That the reality of the situation was that a pack of over enthusiastic zealots were the ones that they needed to be concerned with and where they would be looking that he and Jay needed to be worried about, but he never got to voice the thought. When Amber

247

whipped across the end of the isle a second later and came to a skidding halt, the thought was a forgotten memory.

"Let's go," she ordered in a hushed tone and began heading towards the exit without turning to see if they were following.

"What happened?" Robert asked after he rounded the corner and caught up to her. She did not look hurt to him, but he could tell from the way she was trying to get out of the store as quickly as possible without drawing too much attention that things were far from over.

"She's outside," Was the only response Robert got, but he took that as a good sign that Kate was alive. If she had been killed in the rescue attempt he was certain Amber would have left her behind. He did not press her for any more information and instead chose to silently follow along. Subtlety was not one of Amber's strong points and he could tell she was in no mood for answering any more of his questions. That time would come once they were on the move again.

When Robert did not see their car outside he felt a twinge of panic in his chest. Amber on the other hand made a straight line for a nondescript grey SUV at the far end of the parking lot that he had never seen before. It was parked a few spaces away from anything else in the lot as if the driver was trying to protect it from accidental damage. Its rear windows were tinted so he could not see who or what occupied the inside and his apprehension only grew as he got closer. When Amber opened the rear door Robert's relief turned to fear at seeing Kate lying in a motionless heap on the bench seat. She was on her left side, her bruised right arm dangled towards the floor, and her swollen right eye only gave a faint twitch when Robert reached out and gently stroked her dark brown hair. He felt like his chest was tightening and his throat was closing over. This was his fault.

"How bad is...," he began to ask.

"She's alive," Amber answered before he could even finish asking. "Now get in the car Robert, we have to get going."

"Where's Walt?" Jay interrupted.

"Buying us time," Amber whispered not looking at him as she opened the driver's door and hopped into the seat.

Gently lifting Kate's body Robert carefully climbed onto the seat behind Amber. Once he was in he carefully laid her head across his lap. He whispered softly to her and told her she was going to be alright, that it was over and no one was going to hurt her anymore. Deep down he hoped he was telling her the truth. He looked up as the they swung out of the parking lot and caught sight of Amber quickly shifting her eyes away from watching him in the rearview mirror.

"How bad?" Jay asked as they entered the main highway and headed east.

"Bad," Amber replied. "We met up with Frank and his gang and he got us onto the field without any problems. We were set when the plane landed, but then a half-dozen cars started pulling up."

"Knights?" Jay interjected.

"Yea, I recognized most of them. Looked like everyone who's in North America was there. We got as far as seeing Sven get off the plane with Kate before people starting shouting and guns were getting pulled. Frank and his guys took the center while Walt and I flanked Sven."

"Where was Sebastian?"

"I didn't see him and trust me I was looking."

"Okay, so then what?"

"Sven didn't see us coming and once we had Kate we headed for the closest way out and by then the other knights were on us. Walt covered me so I could get away."

"You just left?" Robert asked. "You killed how many cops in Denver while being half dead and you just took off and left Walt behind."

"It was that or risk getting your girlfriend killed," Amber snidely remarked.

"The Vatican's boys are bad enough Robert," Jay interrupted before Robert could say anything else. "But you have to remember too that they're not the only ones they had to worry about. Even if the fight only lasted a minute or two, that amount of time can mean a lot when it comes to who arrives in the meantime. The TSA is there and you've got local law enforcement too. That was why Walt told her to go. The longer he could keep everyone else's attention focused on the airport the better the chance we have of getting you and Kate out of here. You can't just sit around and discuss this stuff when the bullets start flying. You commit yourself to an action and pray you don't wind up dead."

Robert wanted to argue Jay's point but figured it was pointless. What Jay said made sense and Robert did not know enough to argue with him. Still, he did not feel good about leaving Walt behind. He considered that whatever happened to Walt was on his shoulders now too and the weight of his guilt was growing.

"I wonder if Sebastian was even on the plane," Jay considered aloud.

"Same thought crossed my mind," Amber said as they got on the north bound lanes of the NJ Garden State Parkway.

"You know what that many knights in one place means."

"Yea."

"And you're still going through with this?"

"We don't have a choice Jay. I'm pretty sure Sebastian already knows about the plant anyway." Amber flatly told him.

"And we're still going?" Jay asked in obvious angered amazement.

"It's got to be now. It's the only shot we'll get."

"But they could be there already. Waiting for us."

"They're not. I talked to Sara and she said it's business as usual."

"This is insane," Robert muttered from the backseat.

"Whatever you may think Robert, even I don't have the resources to stand up to the Vatican in a direct confrontation. They have more resources and political pull than you realize. It would be suicide."

"Not for you, you're immortal," Robert scoffed.

Amber slammed on the breaks and jerked the car onto the grass shoulder of the highway. Jay braced himself against the dashboard, but Robert had a hard time keeping himself in place while he struggled to keep Kate from sliding off him. Amber rammed the car into park and threw open her door before jumping down and yanking Robert's open.

"Get out!" she growled.

251

"Amber..." But before he could say anything else she grabbed him by the shoulder and unceremoniously started pulling him from the car. He had just enough time to make sure Kate did not fall to the floor before Amber was hauling him behind the tailgate.

"I didn't make myself this way!" she seethed. "Don't you understand that?"

"I know," Robert admitted breaking free of her grip. "I know, but they know where we're going and you're still taking us there. It's a death sentence!"

"This is the only chance I'll get. I've bet everything on this, on you."

"I know..."

"You don't know!" she declared cutting her arms through the air between them. "It's been over two thousand years Robert. Two *thousand*. And, finally, everything I've set out to accomplish is right here in front of me. I wish it was different. I wish we could find somewhere quiet and just be in love with each other, but that can't happen yet. Or maybe ever."

"You love me?"

At a loss for words, Amber stared at him. She did not realize what she had said until just then and it left her wide open before him.

"Damnit!" she shouted. She grabbed her head and forced her herself to take deep breaths. "Alright, yes. Yes, I care about you. I'm not going to lose you Robert. Do you hear me? I'm not losing you! I'm not losing you to Sebastian! I'm not losing you to the Pope! And I'm not losing you to *her*!" she finished with a defiant jab towards the car. "I know I'm not the easiest person to be around. And maybe I am a little broken, but when we get through this, I...I'd like to start things over with us and see where it takes us. So now that you know, maybe you need to think about how you feel about me."

She gave Robert a second to challenge her, but the stunned and surprised look on his face must have been satisfying enough because she whirled towards the car and got in without another glance at him.

Back in the car, Robert settled into a combined state of frustration and confusion. He leaned his head against the window and watched the outside world race by. With all the woods surrounding them he could see why they called New Jersey the Garden State. It was not what he was really expecting. He always had a picture in his head of crowded towns and cities. It was all he ever saw on the news, when the news was major enough to make a rebroadcast out west. After a while Jay turned the radio onto a light rock station, but kept the volume low, and Amber made a few brief phone calls as she drove.

Robert did not know who she was talking to, but it sounded like she was having the same conversation more than once. He wondered how big her plans really were and how many people were involved because, whatever those plans were, he felt they were coming to a head and it was like being on an out of control freight train.

He was not sure when Kate woke up, but suddenly Robert found her staring up at him. He gently brushed her hair away from her swollen eye and allowed the back of his hand to caress her cheek which elicited a smile from her.

"Hey," he said and smiled back.

"Hey," she replied, her voice soft and groggy sounding.

"I'm so sorry you got mixed up in all this."

"So am I," she declared. She started to pull herself up and had to grit her teeth against the pain. She slapped Robert's hand aside when he tried to stop her and used his body to push herself into the other seat. Almost immediately she saw Amber and her face contorted into hatred. "You!" she hissed and balled her hands into fists.

"Yea. Sooo... for what it's worth, I'm sorry," Amber told her in an empty emotionless voice making it clear she was not all that sorry about anything.

"You're sorry? Sorry! Do the words *drop dead* mean anything to you?"

"Well, you're feeling better." Robert observed remembering Kate's temper.

"Shut up Rob," Kate ordered.

Robert hated being called Rob and Kate knew it. He could not help but feel slighted at the remark. After all they had done to free her, even if Kate did not realize the totality of it yet, he had expected a more gracious reunion.

"What happened?" Jay prodded Amber from the front.

"She didn't give me much of a choice."

"I didn't give you much of a choice! Really?" Kate challenged her voice rising with each word.

"Kate?" Robert broke in, clearly frustrated with how quickly the situation was dissolving around him.

"She's the one who gave me this!" Kate spat while pointing to her bruised eye.

"I said I was sorry," Amber snapped with a touch of her own venom making it more of an insinuation that Kate should just accept her apology and drop the matter. "If you hadn't turned your head it wouldn't have been so bad."

"You little, fucking..." Kate yelled, rising from the seat, but Robert quickly interceded to bring the argument to a close.

"Enough! That's enough from both of you!" he barked so sharply that the two women fell silent, but from the poisonous looks Amber and Kate gave each other it was clearly far from over for them. "Kate, what happened?"

"You tell me Robert. I was in my bedroom getting ready for work when there was this huge crash in the living room. I ran down the hall to see what fell over and the next thing I know I'm on my butt and there's two guys standing over me aiming pistols at my head. The tall blonde guy Tasered me and I woke up on a plane. Blondie thought he could persuade me to give them some answers about you, but the other one kept him in line. Most of the time at least."

"Did they talk to anyone else?" Amber broke in, but Kate just glared back at her reflection in the rearview mirror.

"Kate," Robert intervened again. "Did they talk to anyone else? It's important."

"What's going on Robert?"

"Kate please."

"No alright! No," she shot back. "No, they didn't talk to anyone else. At least not near me. There was one time when I caught the end of a conversation with some guy named Thomas, but I don't know what they were talking about."

Robert looked towards Amber's reflection to see if the name meant anything to her.

"The Pope's personal assistant," she answered.

"Did anything else happen? Did they do anything to you?" Robert probed. "Hurt you or anything?"

"They didn't rape me if that's what you mean," she derided back, but the look on her face clearly meant that it was a question Robert was supposed to answer.

"Yea, that's what I meant," he replied lowering his eyes.

"Now, you better fucking tell me what's going on."

"In a nutshell," he started taking Kate's hand like he always did when he really needed her to pay attention to what he was saying. "The Vatican thinks I'm the Anti-Christ and they want to kill me before I bring about the apocalypse."

She started to respond then she stopped and just stared at him. "Maybe you should give me the long version."

The long version was not any easier for Robert to explain. More than once he found himself backtracking to clarify a point he had forgotten to mention or stumbling through something he did not really want to explain in the first place. Some parts he skipped altogether. He said as little as he could about Amber and Phoenix Industries, and especially about how close they had become, but from the way Kate kept glancing at her it was clear she knew there was more of a connection there than what he was telling her.

When he was finished, no one said anything. Kate turned away to look outside. Robert could tell from her reflection in the window that she was thinking. She always got a certain look on her face when a dilemma arose. She had a temper, but Kate was a strategist at heart.

"So, what do we do now?" she asked him when she turned back around.

"What do you mean *we*?" he countered.

"Exactly what I said," she challenged. "What do *we* do now?"

"*We* don't do anything. You think I want to be here? Hell no. So, there's no way you're getting involved."

"In case you haven't noticed Rob, I already am."

Robert ignored her. It was already escalating into another argument that was just going to go around and around and ultimately lead to nowhere. Even with the threat of death looming it appeared some things would never change between them. Instead of carrying on in what was going to become an ugly fight he turned his desperation to Amber who had been staying silent through their exchange. "Amber?"

"If you think I'm going to listen to what the bitch has to say, you're dead wrong," Kate bristled.

"That's exactly what's going to happen to him if you stay Kate. He's going to die," Amber told her nonchalantly.

"How would you know?"

"Because I've watched your relationship self-destruct over and over again. I've seen what it's done to Robert. If you get involved, he's going to try to do something stupidly heroic and get himself killed."

"Hey!" Robert protested, but Amber ignored him.

"Tell me I'm wrong Kate and I'll let you stay. I was able to keep him away from the airport and you saw what happened there, but where we're going now Robert's life is going to depend on your answer."

Kate looked away without responding. Occasionally she'd glance at Robert or threw a glare at Amber, but mostly she looked at the floor. Turning what Amber said over and over in her mind she thought about her past life with Robert and all the good and bad times they had gone through. She thought about when they fought because Robert put his nose into something she never wanted him to and she wondered if he would ever realize that sometimes she wanted to fight her own battles.

"Fine," she huffed refusing to look at either of them. "I'll leave."

"Kate," Robert protested but stopped himself when she turned to face him with a challenging glare. *Typical us,* he thought. The constant contradictions could define their relationship and why it exploded. Her leaving was the best outcome possible he reminded himself. He had never wanted her involved in the first place.

"It's alright Robert," Kate assured him. Her face softened and she took his hand and gently squeezed it. "It's the right thing to do."

"I know," he answered and left it at that.

"So, what now?" Kate asked Amber, the gentle tone she used with Robert now gone.

"North Star?" Jay offered.

"That could work," Amber hesitantly agreed, although she did not seem happy about it.

"What's North Star?" Robert asked.

"My yacht," Amber answered. "It's off the coast."

"Sounds cozy," Kate muttered with a touch of scorn.

"State of the art," Jay told her turning around in his seat to look at them and contemplate Kate's black eye. "Great doctor who can look at that eye of yours too."

"Doctor?" Robert wondered aloud. "How big of a yacht is it?"

"It's... cozy," Amber echoed with a small, lopsided smile that tugged at the corners of her mouth.

CHAPTER TWENTY-SIX

Their little group arrived at a massive power plant an hour later and they were greeted like dignitaries in their stolen car. As Robert sat in the backseat and waited for the formalities of passing through the security gate to get over with, he read the sign attached below the security station's window with mixed emotion; "Welcome to Phoenix Industries" which was followed below in smaller letters with "The Future Starts Here". Knowing what sort of storm was coming Robert was not convinced which was more accurate, that the future was going to start here or end here.

There had been a few introductions after they parked and went inside. Robert forgot most of the names and faces almost immediately. A helicopter was already waiting to take Kate to Amber's yacht and their goodbyes to one another in a way echoed their breakup with unspoken truths being passed in looks instead of words. He was a little surprised at his lack of sadness at seeing her go, but Kate was going to be safe which was what mattered in the end.

He thought she would probably hate him for a time. A long time maybe when she discovered what was really going on, but then she might get over her anger and only harbor some form of resentment and blame somewhere deep inside. He could not hold that against her. He had known for a long time that the two of them were not right for each other. Fire and ice. He should have put an end to the rollercoaster relationship they had lived through sooner, but what he should have done was beyond him now. At this point, he was tired of thinking about it any longer.

"You better take care of him," Kate yelled at Amber over the sound of the whirling helicopter blades. "If you don't you're going to have to deal with me."

"You won't have to worry about dealing with me if I don't Kate because I'll already be dead," Amber shouted back.

It seemed to be the one thing they both agreed on.

"She won't hate you forever Robert," Amber commented as if reading his thoughts while they watched the helicopter turn east and drift away.

"How would you know?"

"She's stubborn and temperamental, but I imagine she has a softer side too. A private one, meant for only someone special to see."

"Yea. When times were really good at least," Robert agreed, but, if he was being honest, those times did not happen very often.

"That's how I know she won't hate you forever. Only special people get to see the softer side and special people always hold a special place in a person's heart."

"That's probably the wisest thing I've heard you say."

"Well I've been around long enough to make some mistakes and learn a few things," she remarked with a smile before turning serious again. "Now let's get going."

"Lead on," Robert replied sparing one last look at the helicopter growing smaller and smaller in the distance.

Neither said too much as they got back in the car and drove off. She drove him though the streets of the complex's massive primary station, two square miles of storage tanks, support buildings, and miles upon miles of

261

pipes all within view of the Manhattan skyline. When she finally stopped at a smaller substation, Robert knew he was about to came face to face with his creation: Harmony. There were a few more introductions as they entered. A few more names and faces for Robert to forget. Always in the back of his mind was the question if the people he just met really understood what was going on. If they really knew what Amber was planning?

It was a surreal feeling being surrounded by the manifestation of his idea. Up to this point, he had believed only a few prototypes of his drill heads had been created for testing which was so far off from the truth. As he approached Harmony's control room, he thought it resembled a giant spider from a distance. Massive steal support beams arched away from the suspended globe shaped control room like an arachnid's legs. The pipe work running beneath it scattered in all different directions, crisscrossing the plant's floor like a web. It was like some new age artist's steam punk vision brought to life.

"This entire extension was built to support the control room," Amber told him as they walked down one of the many narrow alleyways that crisscrossed the massive room. "It's been in operation for about six months now."

From the way everything seemed to gleam, Robert would have said it had only been turned on a few days ago.

"We told the inspectors that it was part of an expansion to the plant's new geothermal system," Amber continued. "And that the control room was a monitoring room for it. In reality most of what you see deals with Harmony itself. I fast tracked this project as much as possible, but I'll admit I don't have as many drills online as I'd like."

Robert knew the stakes she was playing for and that she was going to leave as little to chance as possible. There was only so much that could be done in the time she had so she was stacking the deck in her favor anyway she could.

He had designed Harmony to be a supplementary system to contemporary drilling methods. It worked on the premise that sound was a force that could be directed in such ways that the resulting sound waves would literally shake and pulverize their way through the Earth's crust ahead of the drill making it easier and faster to reach target depths. The real breakthrough though came when he discovered a variable harmonic system for liquid amplification which allowed for frequencies to build on one another and increase their overall effectiveness and strength. In layman's terms, if modern day drilling was the equivalent of using a pickaxe, he had invented the jackhammer.

"Pretty impressive huh?" Amber asked as they walked up a set of metal stairs to a bridge that led to Harmony's control room.

"Bigger than I had envisioned."

"Your original set up was fine for a few drill heads, but we needed to make some modifications for all the drills we're using here."

"What sort of modifications?" Robert asked turning to look at her. "And how many drills?"

"Thousands," she admitted with a sense of accomplishment and stopped just inside the control room. "My rigs are maxed out with them and every one that can be put in the ground has been. I made a deal with the Chinese to get access to their quantum satellites, but that meant we needed to upgrade the system's communications and processors. Phoenix's shares dropped fifteen percent for that particular market quarter announcement. But now, we have instantaneous communication with a large number of the drills and near the speed of light for the rest of the system."

Robert had to admit that was impressive. Keeping communications uninterrupted and as fast as possible was critical. It was so important he made of point of highlighting the fact in the reports he sent in and it appeared Amber was doing her best to make sure all the issues he raised were addressed before she executed her plan.

"I won't bother asking how you're dealing with any of this," she remarked in a gentle tone.

He half laughed. Seeing his designs in the metaphorical flesh, and being used, drove the final nail in the coffin. She really did expect him to destroy the world.

"But there's still one element missing, Robert."

"A harmonic equation that would encompass the planet's surface."

"Your research papers were pretty well detailed for handling particular layers of rock and the harmonic computer can handle drilling a few simultaneous shafts pretty decently, but planets are on a whole different magnitude."

"And what makes you think I know it. It's not exactly simple mathematics we're talking about."

"I said I'd never lie to you Robert. It would be nice if you showed me the same consideration from time to time."

"I didn't say I didn't know it," Robert shot back. "It's entirely theoretical, it won't do you any good anyway, the planet's crust is way more complicated than trying to drill through some layers of rock. One station wouldn't be able to handle it. Even with the number of harmonic drills you're using here it's *mathematically* impossible."

She smiled at him. "Let me show you something," she told him and held out her hand for him to take.

He did not bother taking her hand. Instead he just waved her off and followed her to the front of the control center. Within the suspended globe the control room itself was a small, circular room ringed in thick glass that overlooked the plant floor. A half-dozen computer operators manned stations that lined the front half of the room, each person was monitoring a multitude of computer monitors displaying multiple windows of information. In the back of the room humming softly in the air conditioning stood the master computer host linked to the harmonic computers.

Amber tapped a young thirty something woman with long brown hair on the shoulder. She swiveled in her seat at the interruption and looked at them with sad brown eyes. "Sara, bring up the station status board please."

With only a quick nod of her head and a couple clicks of her mouse the thick glass wall beyond her terminals gave life to a multicolor translucent overlay.

"It works on HUD technology, Heads-Up-Display," Amber informed Robert as he looked over the information. "What you see on modern day fighter jets, only bigger and a little more refined."

The main image he was looking at was ghostly pale blue and depicted four rows marked Stations Alpha, Bravo, Charlie, and Delta. Each of those stations had a growing percentage bar next to it. Alpha and Bravo had already reached one hundred percent which was emphasized with a flashing *System Online* at the end of the bar. Station Charlie was not too far behind the first two with an estimated completion rate of eighty percent. Station Delta appeared to be lagging well behind the rest.

"Conquest and War are online with no reported problems," Sara announced as she scanned through secondary information displayed on her own terminals. She sounded tired as she read off the information. "Famine will be online in one hour thirty minutes plus or minus a few. They're going through final harmonic alignments. We're still two hours, thirteen minutes from being fully operational. All drill heads are finalizing individual alignments and complete system harmonic alignments will begin in approximately thirty-eight minutes."

"Four stations Robert," Amber whispered in a sort of reverence. "Conquest, War, Famine, and Death as foretold in book of Revelations, chapter six."

"The four horsemen of the Apocalypse."

"I thought it would be fitting. We're at Station Delta on the border between New Jersey and New York. The other three stations are in Southern Europe, Indonesia, and Mexico and each of those is in control of several sub-stations. The configuration isn't ideal, but it's within any margin of error and the field tests so far have been positive."

"Field tests? What kind of field tests?"

"The exact kind of tests that you're thinking of," she told him with a cold hard edge returning to her voice. "As you know, modern drills can dig in any direction we want so we've tried different configurations, various depths, overlays, that sort of stuff. Some of the earthquakes and tsunamis

266

you've heard reported on in the news recently have been caused by these stations. We haven't been responsible for all of them over the last year, but enough of them. The environmental groups have been pushing hard for disclosure, but my allies in Congress have been able to keep any serious inquiries at bay."

"But how?" Robert found himself asking without even realizing it. The enormity of it all loomed over him and threatened to come crashing down. *How many people have already died because of me?* he wondered as a sick feeling grew in his stomach.

"How else? Money. Billions of dollars. But you have to admit a person with my particular traits has an advantage is some things," she said almost causally before turning serious again. "I've spent my entire life preparing for this."

Robert felt numb. He did not care how she had accomplished it, all he wanted to know was how she could kill millions so indiscriminately. The last few days had been unbelievably dreamlike, but now he had entered some sort of indescribable, nightmarish, twisted reality where nothing made sense any longer. He kept staring at the translucent display counting down and the people working so nonchalantly at their stations. "What about them? Do they know what you're attempting to do?"

"Yes, they know," Amber answered as if that should have been obvious. "Everyone working directly with this part of the facility does."

"Why?"

"Why? Why what?"

"Why...why..." but Robert could not think of anything else to say. He found himself sliding down into an unoccupied chair and his face fell into his hands. The air had grown thin and tasted stale making it difficult for him to breathe. His invention was supposed to help fix the world's energy problems it was never meant to deliver apocalyptic devastation.

"Guys, give us a few minutes please?" Amber called to everyone in the control room. "Thanks."

Robert could hear the footfalls of everyone exiting and feel their stares, but he did not look up. He was unsure what he would see on their faces, pity or scorn, but he was not interested in what their opinion of him was. The door slid silently closed and Amber knelt in front of him. Her hand stroked the back of his head in a vain attempt to comfort him.

"Why would they help? Is that what you want to know Robert?" she asked sympathetically and sighed. "They all have their own reasons. Sara was gang raped in front of her husband before they killed him and left her for dead. Mike, the man that was next to her, has a lifetime of sins he's seeking to find redemption for. Some of them are just straight up anarchists, but they're all looking for something Robert. Some meaning or answer to it all, to life. I don't even really know myself what's in their hearts, but this is something real and tangible to them."

"I still don't understand such blind loyalty to this kind of cause."

"Faith, Robert, not blind loyalty," she corrected.

"Call it whatever you want Amber. I still can't believe they're throwing everything away for a story about a god looking at us through a microscope."

"They don't know that part. That was for your ears only. The rewards they're getting in return are more mundane."

"Yea? So, what's in it for them?"

"They get a VIP entry pass into the new world order."

Robert laughed. "They're sacrificing everything for that. They're going to let anything that's ever mattered to them, their families, their friends, fall off the face of the planet just so they can pretend to be kings."

"Do you really think I'd let things happen that way?" Amber asked sounding disappointed. "This year is Phoenix Industries' sixtieth anniversary and, right now, there are a few chartered cruise ships floating around the middle of the world's oceans to celebrate. Onboard each one of those ships is anyone who mattered to the people at these stations. I even made sure that the employees that don't know what's going on, who are just peripherals to this cause, and their loved ones are on them as well.

"We've been running the shore-based plants with skeleton crews for the last two weeks. Production and delivery is at an all-time low. Maybe you haven't seen Phoenix Industries' stock price lately, but it's nose diving because I've been spending money like its water to make this day happen. The Department of Energy is breathing down my neck threatening investigations, not like it matters now."

"But you're still going to kill a few billion people."

"Yes I am."

"What if they knew the truth?" Robert pressed raising his head to watch her reaction. "What if they knew about all the God stuff?"

"It wouldn't matter," Amber replied returning his stare with one of her own. "Their parts are done. The drills are installed and all the stations are coming online together so the only two people with the power to do anything about it are in this room right now."

The coldness of her words struck him like a punch in the face. He was angry. Angry at everyone. Angry at Amber for dragging him into this. Angry at the church for making it impossible for him to escape. Angry at himself for not looking at the fact that someone might try to weaponize his research.

Deep down he knew someone or some organization might try to twist the science he had developed. There was always a mad dictator who wanted to destroy another government. What better way then to be able to blame a seemingly random act of nature. Yet whenever Robert let himself think about that consequence, he kept telling himself it would not turn out that way. That the level of technological difficulty was insurmountable. That such an endeavor would be financial suicide. That his research would only be used for what it was intended for. It was a judgement clouded by the money that was offered to him.

It was just too good, too real, to pass up. He should have known better right then. If it looks too good then it probably is and there was always a catch. Why did he ignore that feeling so deep in his gut? Because now he could finally admit to himself that he had become a victim of one of the deadly sins, Greed. He still remembered that day, when the man in the tailor-made suit came to the college. The check was in his hand and with it was a secure future for Robert. The people at Phoenix Industries had read his research papers and were interested in securing exclusive rights to his designs for their deep-sea drilling and geothermal operations. He signed the contract with the college lawyers a week later.

"What about what I want Amber? Doesn't that mean anything?"

"Of course it does Robert. More than you could possibly realize, but this is more important than what either of us wants. It's God's decree."

"I won't give you what you want. I can't be responsible for the death of billions of people."

She stared quietly at him. Robert could tell she was weighing her choices in her mind. He did not know when he started picking up on the subtle differences in her, but he was certain she was thinking about just how hard to push him. It did not take long before she smiled her crooked smile at him and shook her head slowly. "The question you should be considering is how many more billions are going to die with me at the controls instead of you? The system's coming online in about an hour and I'm turning it on. I never wanted you to operate it Robert, but what I want is irrelevant. You're the only one who knows enough about it to contain the damage and make sure there's something left when it's all over."

She stood up and headed toward the door. Robert watched her walking away but did not follow her. She stopped with her hand on the door frame and turned back to him before leaving him alone. "It's the second coming Robert, only God sent Jesus's sister in his place."

CHAPTER TWENTY-SEVEN

Only a few miles away at what could be considered a quiet section of Newark Liberty International Airport, or as quiet as it could be in the heart of the industrial northeast, an Italian airliner made its final turn off the taxiway. The orange glow from the airport terminal's floodlights bathed the surroundings in a toxic haze which even the brilliant radiance of nearby New York City failed to penetrate. Watching the nonscheduled private jet rolling towards him, Sebastian waited in a massive repair hangar located well away from the commuter terminals. He eyes constantly scanned the surrounding area and shadows nearby, looking for anything or anyone that should not be there. One could never be sure who was watching, even from the secrecy behind the Vatican walls leaks had occurred from time to time, and they were well inside Amber's domain now.

The whine of the quad engines drowned out all the other airport noises as the plane came to a stop in the middle of the bay and the large hangar doors began to rumble closed behind it. Sebastian's eyes lingered on the temporarily borrowed and well-paid ground crew springing into action. He analyzed their threat potential and quickly disregarded each of them in turn. To them it was just another secret flight, at the end of a long list of secret flights. It was a meager crowd compared to those that would be typically awaiting the arrival of the Pope. He would be more accustomed to huge crowds, thousands of the faithful, waiting to cheer, throw flowers, and profess their love in his presence. After which, with a quick wave to the gathered devoted, he would promptly enter his security vehicle and be whisked away to more stately matters. Tonight held none of that pomp and circumstance.

Only Sebastian and five other Vatican Knights were here to greet John David. There should have been more, but three had been killed, including Sven, when Amber sprung her little rescue plot for Robert's ex. Two more had been wounded and were taken to the nearby hospital, both were expected to recover. At least five of Amber's faithful had been put to rest and the others had either been taken into custody or rushed to the hospital, including his former comrade Walt, so his own losses were not a total waste in Sebastian's opinion.

The door of the jet swung open as the engines wound down and the first of the Pope's twelve personal body guards exited. Each one of them had been handpicked from within the ranks of knights from across the globe for being the most skilled and loyal follower. Each one wore an identical custom handmade Italian suit whose dark cloth mirrored the hardness in their eyes. Amongst the rest of the Vatican security forces these twelve were secretly called The Disciples.

Sebastian stepped up to the bottom of the mobile staircase and greeted each of the Disciples with a slight nod of his head as they passed. In return, each one pointedly ignored Sebastian's existence. He had been the first, and only knight, to ever decline an offer to join their ranks and the insult was never going to be forgotten. Sebastian had kept his reasons for declining to himself at the time, but he compared the Disciple's loyalty to fanatics. He could respect an individual who possessed drive and determination, but he

273

had little tolerance for the blind faithful and wanted no part of it.

John David was not wearing his typical white robes when he emerged a few minutes later. He had chosen simple black pants and a light gray, long sleeved, shirt to wear along with the golden Pectoral Cross hanging around his neck. Normally a site to behold, the hellish haze from the hangar's lights gave the symbolic jewelry a tarnished look. From the jet's doorway John David locked onto Sebastian's eyes and began to slowly make his way down the steps as he proclaimed;

> *And he saith unto him. Verily, verily, I say unto*
> *you. Hereafter ye shall see heaven open and the*
> *angels of God ascending and descending upon the*
> *son of man.*

"John, chapter one, verse fifty-one," Sebastian answered as the Pope took hold of his outstretched arm.

"Very good my son," John David acknowledged trying not to appear too out of sorts. The secretive flight, the long hours spent incased in a metal tube at thirty-five thousand feet, and even the abnormally quiet arrival left him feeling strange and unclean in some way. "I've heard of what transpired in Atlantic City, Sebastian. It's already breaking news. By tomorrow, if not before, the church is going to be linked to it and then it will be *world* news. This is not the service I've come to expect from you."

"My apologies Your Grace. It was an unfortunate turn of events which I did not foresee. I take full responsibility of course. By tomorrow though this war will be ended and the sacrifices justified."

"You have found Robert Kariot then?"

274

"Yes, Your Grace. They're both at Harmony."

"Harmony," John David said aloud to no one as his thoughts drifted to the conversation he had had earlier with Sebastian. "Are you certain Sebastian?"

"I have no doubt Your Grace. The surveillance team saw them enter."

"So, this is truly the end then," John David murmured coming to a stop and releasing Sebastian's arm. "Thomas," he called turning to the priest shadowing them.

"Yes, Your Grace?" Thomas asked, clearly uncomfortable in the situation he had found himself in.

"Thomas, once the last of the munitions are offloaded have the rest of the men join Sebastian at the rendezvous point outside Harmony," John David instructed. "And Thomas..."

Noticing the pause Thomas broke the growing silence. "You're going with them to Harmony, aren't you?"

"Yes. Yes, I am, but you are not, my friend. I have a more important task for you to accomplish yet I promise we will see one another again either here or in the kingdom of heaven once this is finished."

"Certainly, we will, Your Grace."

John David could not help but smile at his companion and friend of so many years. Even though Thomas's fear was clearly evident, he was not going to try to stop him. Thomas would understand better than anyone else why he needed to do this.

"Here," John David began sliding the ring from his finger. "I want you to protect my ring."

"St. Peter's ring! Your Grace, I couldn't," Thomas protested.

275

"The ring of the fisherman is a symbol Thomas, just as I am. What we are about to face will not fear a symbol. Should something happen to me I couldn't bear the chance that it may be left behind."

"Nothing will happen to you," Thomas whispered as he closed his hands around the small treasure.

"Then I will collect the ring from you on my return," John David said and warmly smiled as he took Thomas's closed hands in his own. "God bless you my friend. You have indeed been a beloved companion for all these years."

With a final shake, John David released Thomas's hand and turned to Sebastian, taking the younger man's arm in his own. "It seems that, in one way or another, the end is upon us Sebastian."

"Yes, Your Grace," Sebastian acknowledged. "But if I may remind Your Holiness of Revelations Chapter 2, verses 26 through 28."

*And he that overcometh, and keepeth my works
unto the end, to him will I give power over the
nations. And he shall rule them with a rod of iron:
as the vessels of a potter shall they be broken to
shivers, even as I receive my Father.*

"*And I will give him the morning star,*" John David finished and laughed softly. He lightly patted Sebastian's forearm in understanding, but the two said no more. They exited the hanger where Sebastian helped John David into one of the waiting vehicles before climbing in himself. Moments later, from a small window in the door, Thomas watched the motorcade vanish into the shadows of twilight with a dire sense of dread growing within his heart.

It was a short, twenty minute ride and John David found himself standing on the edge of a nondescript void of land and looking at a maze of industrial pipework on the outskirts of Phoenix Industries. His mind and emotions were adrift and restless. A part of him wanted to be back at the Vatican polishing the floors, but for the moment that simple joy was out of his reach. *Perhaps soon though*, he told himself. *Perhaps I will be able to return to that life.*

She's somewhere inside there with Robert. And Harmony, he reminded himself. Had it really been only a few short days ago that Kariot had been exposed. It was hard to believe. He was certain the tension within the Vatican had been building for longer, but his sense of time no longer seemed as reliable as it once was. Perhaps it had been hidden away somehow in the daily stresses of Vatican life and responsibility. Or perhaps the tension had always been there, but he had not noticed it until recently. Whichever the case, it had grown thick and heavy these last few days and he felt its weight pulling at him now.

Sebastian silently appeared, a shadow walking in the darkness. He had changed from his crisp Italian suit into a black tactical outfit. Even with the additional bulky composite body armor, with its steel plates woven into the fabric, Sebastian's hands were comfortably clasped behind his back as he came to stop a respectful distance from John David and waited for the Pope to address him first. There was a time when John David would have questioned the enormous expense the Vatican paid in preparing for war, but now he was thankful for it.

"One often forgets," John David announced. "That some missions are meant for the young."

277

"If I may offer my opinion Your Grace, you are too unforgiving of yourself," Sebastian countered. "This trial has been hard and you have stood firm where others would have fallen."

"Moses faced Pharaoh when he was eighty years old. It is the Lord who will give me the strength to stand and it is the Lord who will see me through this to the end."

"Yes, Your Grace."

"Is Robert still inside?" John David asked steering the conversation back to the matter at hand.

"We have been unable to get a positive sighting of him since he entered the complex, but I'm certain they're still inside," Sebastian answered.

John David looked over the massive energy plant before whispering to himself. "How did you keep this a secret Mary?"

"Your Grace?"

"Never mind. When will you be ready?"

"We already are. We're just waiting for your blessing to proceed."

"Then you will have it."

John David presided over a short prayer in the dirt and gravel strewn field, surrounded by junk and the smell given off from all the industrial buildings running twenty-four hours a day. He took the time to bless each individual knight and delivered the Eucharist. It was a quiet ceremony with none of the pomp and circumstance one would find in a cathedral. Although the undertaking that lay ahead of them was more vital than any Sunday mass, it was just that level of importance that made a simple and solemn ceremony carry so much more weight. God had gathered them together in this field and although John David spoke the words to them he was certain it was God who was really carrying out the blessing.

"I'll inform your Grace once we have secured the site," Sebastian told him as his men climbed into the vehicles.

"You're very much mistaken Sebastian if you think I'll be staying behind."

"Your Grace," Sebastian protested. "It's far too dangerous."

"This is all of mankind's judgment day Sebastian, not just yours," John David rebuked. "The fate of all humanity rests in our hands and I'm not going to cower before the darkness."

"I only meant that we won't be able to guarantee your safety. I did not mean to imply that Your Grace was a coward."

"Sebastian, God is my protector, not you."

"Yes, Your Grace," Sebastian relented and, knowing he had been dismissed, bowed slightly before moving off to adjust the plan for the Pope's accompaniment.

CHAPTER TWENTY-EIGHT

Robert was leaning on the bridge handrail just outside Harmony's control room when the countdown timer inside closed to within thirty minutes of the system being fully ready. He had kept to himself for the most part since his brief discussion with Amber. He could see her out of the corner of his eye, on the ground below, standing next to the steps leading to the bridge he was on. She was talking to Jay and Sara about things he was sure he did not want to know about. She was still moving ahead with her plan even though he had not agreed to help. The third station had been brought online just before he left the room and he knew without a doubt when the fourth station was ready Amber was going to throw the proverbial switch whether Robert helped or not. He was still trying to figure out how to stop her when the first explosion went off.

Robert whipped his head in the direction of the noise, but everything in this section of the plant looked normal to him. Whatever had happened, it was outside somewhere, but considering how loud it was in here whatever it was had been big. When he looked back towards where Amber had been he found that she was already running up the stairs towards him taking the steps three at a time. He knew explosions and power plants were never a good thing when put together, but seeing the look on her face he knew that whatever was going on was much worse.

"What is it?" he yelled at her. "What's going on?"

She did not stop when she reached him like he thought she would, but instead grabbed him as she passed and pulled him into the control room. Emergency warning lights sprang to life all over the plant bathing the area in glaring yellow beams of light that twirled in a never-ending circle. Amber grabbed the nearest phone and punched in triple nine before putting the receiver up to her ear.

"Security," said the voice on the other end.

"It's Amber, what's going on?"

"LNG tank 24 blew," The security guard informed her. "Fire teams are in route. What the...front gate was just compromised. Multiple vehicles are in the perimeter."

"Get all security personnel to H-Block."

Another explosion, closer this time, reverberated through the room. "They just hit cooling tower three," the security officer told her clearly becoming more frazzled.

"Did you hear me?" Amber practically screamed into the phone. "Get all security personnel to H-Block!"

"All security to H-Block, yes ma'am," the man acknowledged and Amber hung up the phone.

"Let's go Robert," she ordered and stormed out of the control room.

"What the hell is going on?"

"It's Sebastian," she called back over her shoulder before leaning over the rail looking for Jay. "Jay!"

"We're leaving?" Robert asked, shocked.

"You're leaving," she corrected and grabbed hold of his arm and pulled him across the bridge after her.

"You can't stay here either," he protested pulling free of her grasp but continued to keep pace with her.

She did not bother to answer him. As long as he was still following her, she was content. She and the Vatican had been shooting at each other for hundreds of years now, she had no intention of retreating this time. Not with the end within her grasp. All she needed was a little more time. If they could just hold them off long enough for Harmony to come online she could throw the switch and be damned for whatever happened afterwards.

Robert, was a different matter. As soon as the first explosion had gone off she was truly terrified of what might happen to him. He had done his part. He had given her the tools she needed to see this through. Even if he was not going to help her, it would be enough she told herself. Now she had to get him out of here before it was too late.

"Jay, get the car!" she yelled reaching the bay floor just as the old man emerged from a nearby stack of crates. "Jay?"

His back to them, Jay grabbed the corner of the nearby crate with a bloody hand to steady himself. He twisted towards them, his back hitting the stack of wooden boxes, and quickly slid to the ground. It was only then they saw his other hand clutching at his stomach in attempt to keep more blood from spilling out.

"Hello Angel," smiled Sebastian as he emerged after Jay. In his hand was a bloody knife that he slowly rotated one way and then the other as a twisted smile full of sinister pleasure crossed his face.

With a scream of unbridled rage Amber hurled herself at him.

"Bring it on bitch!" he roared and his smile transformed into a sneer of equal hatred aimed at her.

Amber was on him an instant later. He swung his knife, but she ducked under the swipe, then drove upward into his gut. Thrown off balance from the impact, momentum carried them into a pile of neatly stacked boxes and crates where they disappeared in an avalanche of cardboard, wood, and mutual curses.

Robert rushed over to Jay's side and began checking his wound. It did not look like a large cut, but a good deal of blood had already soaked through Jay's shirt and the old man was noticeable pale. "Stay still Jay," Robert instructed and pulled his own shirt off so he could use it to apply pressure over the cut.

"No worries there," Jay smiled.

"Where's the emergency kits?" Robert demanded, but Jay shook his head.

"There's no time Robert."

Nearby Amber was thrown backwards from the debris but rolled off the impact. Even as Sebastian was staggering to his feet she was leaping at him again. They both had cuts and scrapes over their faces, but neither one of them seemed to notice. They began trading punches, blocks, and counter attacks relentlessly. Sebastian had mass that clearly staggering Amber when he landed a hit, but Amber had speed and could strike twice for every one of Sebastian's attacks against her. Seemingly oblivious to anyone else but each other, the two disappeared behind a row of equipment.

"You need to get out of here," Jay urged pushing something into Robert's hand. "She's buying you time."

"She's being a fool," Robert muttered looking at the blood covered car keys Jay had pressed into his hand.

"We usually are when it comes to the people we love," Jay answered, smiling. "She's a fighter. It's what she's done her entire life."

"I can't just leave..."

283

"You have to Robert. If you stick around she'll be too busy trying to protect you instead of saving herself," Jay pushed as he struggled to breathe. "There's an emergency exit behind you. The car is in the lot just outside. She'll find you when this is over. Now get the hell out of here."

Glancing one last time in Amber's direction Robert let out a growl then turned and ran. He used the narrow aisles created within the web of machinery and pipework to make his escape. All the while squeezing the car keys until the metal cut into his palm and began to hurt. He hated himself a little more the further away he got, but Jay was right that Amber was a fighter and the unspoken implication that Robert was not. He should have been thankful that he had a way out, that the insane plan that Amber was going to enact was at an end, but he was not.

Maybe he was not a fighter, but he was not a quitter either. Given time he was certain he could have swung her opinion and bought some time to figure out another route. Time, and now the events getting carried along with it, were moving way too fast to afford him the luxury of that debate now. *It's always about time,* he thought as he barreled out the emergency exit and a wave of humid hot summer air and industrial stench swept over him. The alarm on the door began to blare, but with all the other sirens going off he did not think one more meant anything as he ran into the parking lot.

Just like Jay said, their stolen car was just outside. It came to life with a quick turn of the key and Robert yanked the shifter into gear and slammed on the gas making the tires squeal a little as he gunned the engine. He exited the lot, jammed his seat belt on just to silence the annoying warning alarm, and made a left onto one of the avenues that circumvented the plant. When they first arrived, they had come in on the opposite side of where he was now so he had an idea where the main exit was. He caught a few glimpses of the chain link fence surrounding the complex and wondered if there might be another way out. He was sure that there had to be, but where was the question. He was looking for the next turn he could take when his back window shattered. The headrest on the passenger seat exploded sending fragments of foam in all directions and caused Robert to almost lose complete control of the car. Keeping his head down he glanced in the side view mirror to see the headlight of an SUV just before it slammed into his rear end. He barely had a second to brace himself before the vehicle made contact and sent a bone jarring jolt through the car and his body.

The car fishtailed from the impact, but he managed to regain control before he slammed into a steel guardrail running along the side of the road. He pressed down hard on the gas petal just as Amber had done when the motorcycle riders attacked them on the highway and the distance between himself and his pursuer grew, but by no means was he going to be able to out run them. Suddenly, the turn he had been looking for was there under a glaring street light and he twisted the steering wheel, desperate for the car to make it. The rear tires screamed against the pavement as the backend swung wide. Robert fought for control but raked another guardrail in the process. A shower of sparks flew up alongside the window and he gunned the engine to keep the car from stopping. His pursuers were right behind him using Robert's near accident to close what little distance he had gained on them.

Straight ahead he could see the end of the plant complex and the front gate just beyond. There was a black military style Humvee, complete with a machine gun turret on its roof, blocking the burning remains of the gate entrance. A gold phoenix symbol on its door glowed in the firelight and Robert thought there was just enough room behind it that he might be able to manage an escape. Wishing he could push the gas pedal even further down he committed himself to whatever was about to happen.

Another jarring hit from behind let him know that his pursuers were not done with him yet, but, when Robert saw the turret of the Humvee swinging towards him, he no longer cared who was after him. Out of good options, he chose the best of the bad ones left to him when he spotted a small alleyway and cranked the steering wheel hard to the left and slammed on the brakes. The car responded for an instant before momentum took over and sent it rolling through the air. His world became a blur of colors and thunderous sound of crunching metal as the car did a twisting summersault down the road. Inside, he felt like the rolling was going on for a long long time, but before he could finish a complete thought it was over and he was miraculously still alive.

The pain hit him a second later. It was the type of pain where you wished you were dead but were not. He thought his head was going to explode and if he moved his neck it was like his spine was on fire. His left leg was throbbing and he could not feel his right which probably would have worried him more if his head was not in agony. Even though it was painful, he could move his arms so he knew they were not broken at least. Thankful to be alive, he really wanted to close his eyes and let himself drift into oblivion, but a voice inside his head was yelling at him to stay awake. He had to stay awake. He had to stay away from the darkness that was threatening him or he was not going to wake up ever again.

He tried to collect his jumbled thoughts. He knew he was sitting in the car. Broken glass and deflated air bags surrounded him along with a burning smell. His mind was having a hard time connecting anything together. He could see smoke leaking out of the sides of the crumbled engine hood and slowly swirling upward until a breeze caught it and sent it spinning away. In his confused state Robert thought it was kind of elegant, almost like watching a ballroom dance.

The cry of metal peeling apart broke through the fog Robert's mind was experiencing and was followed by his door suddenly opening allowing a wave of fresh air to circle around him. His mind cleared a little more making him wonder what it was he had been breathing if the outside industrial air felt so good. An angry, weathered face, whose dark skin was glistening with sweat appeared and he began cutting Robert's seatbelt away. When he was done he pulled Robert roughly from the car and more or less dropped him onto the unforgiving ground.

"Careful," someone warned beyond Robert's sight. "His Grace wants him alive."

"He's alive," the tall dark-skinned man replied and then kicked Robert in the side bringing forth an anguished gurgle.

"Alex!"

"Alright, alright," Alex said holding up his hands in surrender.

Robert was helpless as Alex and one of his other nameless comrades hoisted him to his feet. He thought he might have some cracked ribs, it was hard to breath without grimacing in pain, and probably a concussion to go along with the countless number of cuts and scrapes. As he was half dragged, half carried, towards his pursuer's vehicle he saw what looked like a smoking metal tube laying on the ground. It hurt, a lot, but he managed to turn his head just enough to get a look at the front gate to see the Humvee that had been stationed there sheathed in flames and Robert realized his injuries were probably the least of the problems he was going to have to face in the near future.

CHAPTER TWENTY-NINE

"His Grace wants to talk to him before we move out," the leader of Robert's escort announced when they arrived back at the entrance to Harmony. His name was Trevor but Robert was not sure if it was his first or last name. "Use the conference room we cleared earlier."

They dragged Robert through the same entrance he had walked through on his own only a few hours earlier and passed the security desk now manned by a dead man before venturing into a series of small hallways. Alex had Robert's right arm and a masked man name Pietro had his left. The two men used Robert's body, seemingly much to their own sadistic delight, to open any doors that they came to. Which included a few extra where they wanted to double check that the room on the other side was clear. Robert was thankful there were not very many of these side treks and a few doors later, with fresh blood slowly flowing from various parts of his face, they entered the large conference room that his guards had been bringing him to.

The center of the room was dominated by a large, gray rectangular table surrounded by a dozen or so basic, rolling office chairs. Alex kicked the closest chair sending it spinning and an even faster shove sent Robert falling into it. The force of the impact was too much to counter the effects of gravity and he and the chair were sent crashing to the floor. Before he even had a chance to push himself up they were hauling him back to his feet and slamming him down into another chair. This time the wall kept him from falling over backwards, but the impact to the back of his skull threatened to knock him out. Alex produced a pair of handcuffs and dangled them in front of Robert's face. Wearing a smirk, he grabbed Robert's right hand, deftly secured one of the cuffs to his wrist, and then yanked Robert over to lock the other cuff around his left ankle.

"Now you look respectful," Alex laughed and smacked Robert's head. "Let's go."

"We're gonna leave him alone?" Pietro questioned, clearly not happy about it.

"He's not going anywhere," Alex answered and led them out the door.

Robert was not alone for long. According to the clock over the conference room door it had only been six minutes when the door was opened and an elderly man entered. Robert's initial impression was that he had to be in his seventies, maybe early eighties, and frail in the way that all people became when they grew old. Even so, he moved with determined steps, and his eyes were alert as they regarded Robert. He wore a simple priest's outfit, black pants and a gray long sleeved shirt with a white collar.

John David stopped a half-dozen steps away from Robert and made the sign of the cross over himself and in the air towards Robert before coming any closer. He did not say anything. He only surveyed the remaining empty chairs until he found one he thought was suitable, pulled it in front of Robert, and sat down.

"Afraid I might bite you Father?" Robert asked with a bit of a slur when he realized how much room there was between the two of them. The disorientation he felt earlier from his car crash had lessened, but his faced had swollen, and he wanted to aim his growing anger at someone who deserved it. The man sitting in front of him appeared to fall into that category quite nicely.

"Oh, I'm very much afraid of you Mr. Kariot," John David answered in a clear, precise tone. "Wouldn't you be if you were in my situation?"

"That depends on who you are I suppose."

"My name is John David, Mr. Kariot. I'm the..."

"The Pope," Robert cut in. "I've heard of you."

"Yes Mr. Kariot. I am the Pope."

"You're a long way from the Vatican. You look a lot different without your white robes on. Did the airline lose your bag or something?"

"Very humorous Mr. Kariot," John David replied with a small forced laughed that made it clear he was not amused in the least. "Let's not pretend we don't know why we are here. May I call you Robert?"

Robert did his best imitation of a shrug that he could. His left shoulder raised an inch while his right shoulder barely moved at all, but John David seemed to understand the gesture nonetheless.

"The church has been preparing for your arrival for a very long time."

"Yea, I've been told. Guess I'm special," Robert countered as he tried his best to shift his body in the chair. His comfort had not been a priority to the guys who had brought him here.

"You are indeed special Robert, but I'm afraid not in a good way."

"Do tell."

"As I said before Robert, let's not pretend we don't know why we're here. If you've come this far then you must be aware that you are a child of Judas. *She* must have told you that much at least."

"Actually John," Robert answered enjoying a small victory in seeing John David's annoyed reaction at being called by his first name. "Do you mind if I call you John? Anyway, *she* told me a lot of things."

"I expected nothing less from the father of lies."

"You lost me there, John."

"I'm speaking about Mary, Robert. Or at least, that was her name before she changed it to Amber."

"Amber..." Robert began to respond but stopped himself when he remembered the business card Amber had given him on the plane. *Amber Magdalene.* "Mary? Mary Magdalene?"

"You've heard of her?"

"I've read the story. Let ye without sin cast the first stone."

"There's so much more to it than that Robert. Mary Magdalene was mentioned many times in the bible and it's only an assumption that that particular verse deals with her at all. "

"She said she is Jesus' sister."

"What that creature says is irrelevant Robert," John David proclaimed with venom.

"Creature?" Robert demanded fixing John David with an intent stare.

"You mean you haven't figured it out yet Robert?" John David asked appearing genuinely surprised. "Come now Robert, we're talking about the end of the world. The ultimate battle for mankind's salvation and you haven't stopped to ask yourself who you are dealing with? The father

292

of lies. The deceiver of men. The destroyer. The angel that rebelled against God. Lucifer."

In a suddenly eye opening, and haunting way, what John David said made sense. *Could it be possible?* Robert wondered. Amber was without a doubt cold and calculating in a very real and very horrifying way. It was not hard for him to understand others seeing her as a devil, she was seductive and cruel. Yet as Robert thought back to his conversations with her he knew she was so much more. She cared about those around her and what mattered to them was important to her. She was the proverbial damsel in distress, albeit with a murderous side, tortured by her dedication to a duty she believed in with every cell of her being and the personal cost she had to pay in achieving it.

"Some believe there are two sides to every story Robert, but I argue that there are always three sides to the truth," John David interjected into Robert's thoughts. "In this case, there is her side, the church's side, and then the gray area where both our stories mix. I'm sure she's told you less then glowing details about the church. It's no great secret that the church has undertaken some reprehensible actions in its history."

"In its history? My neighbor, who worked for you, tried to stab me in the back only a few days ago."

"You misunderstand Robert," John David held up his hands before him in innocence. "No one's been trying to kill you. On the contrary, we've been trying to save you. Justin was there to protect you. Why would he have moved in otherwise? We knew sooner or later she was going to reveal herself and we wanted to get you away from her and somewhere safe before that happened. Somewhere even out

293

of her reach, but I'm afraid we were not fast enough in that respect. Perhaps the church has done things in its more recent history that I am not proud to admit to, but attempting to kill you was not one of them."

"But you think I'm the antichrist. Why wouldn't you be trying to kill me? I'm supposed to bring on the Rapture!" Robert could feel his temper rising. He was starting to feel like a pawn in a much bigger game where neither side trusted him.

"Did she put that absurd notion in your head?" John David asked with a heavy sigh. "Robert, only God can bring on the Rapture. Right now, you and I are talking about the destruction of the world as we know it, which is not the same thing."

"But you think I'm the antichrist?"

"Honestly, were you willingly going to help her bring about the deaths of billions of innocent people?" John David countered. "Was that how you envisioned Harmony was going to be used?"

"How do you know about Harmony?" Robert demanded. He felt affronted that the Pope would even know about his research.

"I know a great many things about you, about your research, and the events that have brought us together. The church has been in a constant struggle with the Devil since its inception so don't believe that Amber is the only one who keeps historical information. But you still haven't answered my question. Is this your vision of Harmony?"

"No," Robert grudgingly admitted.

"Well, there's your answer. Just because the blood of Judas flows through your veins doesn't mean you yourself are a betrayer, but your science is dangerous. Even you have to admit that. Look at how your idea has been twisted and warped. Which is exactly why we must stop this before it goes any further."

"It was never supposed to be used like this."

"Leave it to the Devil to alter a man's good intentions," John David consoled. "And you are a good man Robert."

"So now what happens? What are you planning on doing with me?"

"We need to get you far away from here and her to start with. We need to know everything she's told you. Is this the only facility? Was there a contingency plan if she failed here?"

That was what John David told him, but Robert could not bring himself to believe him. There were too many lies wrapped within story after story. They might not kill him outright, but Robert believed it was still a possibility that was being considered. "There are other stations," he admitted.

"There are?" John David could not hide his surprise. He stood up and ran his finger over his lips in contemplation. The fact Mary had hidden this from them was unsettling enough. Now to hear that there were others, his felt like his victory here was falling apart. *We have Kariot now,* he reminded himself and that was a victory of its own. Once they learned what he knew they would be able to truly end this war.

"One month," Robert said stopping John David mid thought.

"One month?"

"Justin moved in next door to me a month ago."

"Yes Robert?" John David asked, confused by what Robert was saying.

Robert looked at the distance between himself and John David. Now that the Pope was standing, he really was not that far away. "If you really wanted to get me away from Amber why did Justin move in at all? Why not approach me right from the start?"

John David did not respond, but Robert could tell the old man did not like him thinking about it.

"You had ample time to," Robert continued. "So that really only leaves two possibilities. I was bait. In which case, you would have known that one guy next door wasn't going to be enough to stop Amber. Or you weren't sure I was the one she was wanted and he was just there to spy on me."

"It's true, we weren't entirely sure you were the one she was after."

"It's kind of odd that Amber would show up on the exact same day another priest shows up on my street along with some of your knights. Why didn't Justin whisk me away after your priest was murdered? He had time to. Did you know we met outside after the shooting?" From the way John David clinched his jaw, Robert felt confident this was news to him. "One thing I've learned to recognize over these last few days John, the look on someone's face that wants to kill you."

"Robert, Justin wasn't there to kill you."

"Agent Dublin talked a lot before he died," Robert declared.

John David's eyes turned cold and his soft natured expression hardened in anger. It was the reaction Robert had unfortunately expected as well as the opening he had been waiting for. In the second that followed the handcuff around his ankle fell open and Robert sprang up from his chair, using the added momentum to drive his fist into John David's stomach. The Pope lost his breath in a huge gush and crumbled to the floor gasping for air. Robert did not waste any time retrieving the handcuff shim Amber had given him on the train from the bottom of the shoe he stuffed it in and a few seconds later the second cuff around his wrist opened and the pair clattered to the floor.

Now what? Robert thought desperately. He knew what Amber would have done and it involved walking out the door and spilling a great deal of blood, but Robert was not her and John David was starting to look more composed. Before the Pope could do anything to endanger him further, Robert grabbed the old man's shirt, pulled it unceremoniously off him, and shoved it deep into John David's mouth. Then he grabbed the handcuffs off the floor and dragged him to the conference table locking his arms behind his back and around the closest table leg.

"I bet you regret not having Dublin just shoot us down back in Colorado now," Robert whispered.

He quickly surveyed the room to see what his options were. He had not had much time to look around after he had gotten his leg uncuffed before John David had entered the room. There was only the one door and no windows which was probably why they had dumped him in here to begin with. Going out the door was not a choice he could consider. He was sure that at least one of the men who brought him here was standing guard in the hall and would be armed. Even if he was at one hundred percent Robert knew walking out there was not a fight he would win. He needed an advantage. He needed another option.

He scanned the room over and over hoping to see something he had missed before but nothing changed and he hung his head back in frustration. About ten feet off the ground a drop ceiling composed of dozens of white, square foam tiles stared back at him. There was a large metal ventilation tile, blowing cool air into the room, near the door and a single sprinkler head poked through tile in the middle of the room.

If there was one thing Robert could do well, it was to think outside the box. He needed an option and he finally found one. He quickly discounted the ventilation duct. It would be too difficult to get into and even if he did, unlike in the movies, the sheet metal would make far too much noise to go undetected. First thing he needed was to get up there and get a better look at what was behind the tiles that he could work with. Grabbing the closest chair, he lifted it onto the table and climbed up after it, his body painfully protesting the whole time. Between the height of the table and him standing on the chair he was easily able to reach the ceiling tiles. He slid the tile next to the sprinkler head aside and felt a sense of relief with what he saw. A black, dust covered, cast iron pipe hung just out of reach but his greater relief came from seeing that beyond it the ceiling opened into a world of commercial crossbeams and inefficient open space. He took a deep breath, steadied himself, and leapt.

Don't break. Don't break, he caught himself praying to any deity or spirit as he grabbed the iron pipe. It flexed with his added weight but held and Robert praised the quality workmanship the installers had done. He took a measured breath and then started to pull himself up until he was able to swing a leg over the top of the pipe. His body wanted to let go the whole time and the pipe shook against his abuse, but both held together until he was able to climb onto the web of support rafters and conduits.

Dirty, dust covered, winded, and now pumped full of adrenaline that numbed his pain, Robert took in his surroundings. He was in a world few people saw or thought about when they made their way through the corridors and rooms below. *It's like a metal jungle gym,* he thought. A massive cinder block wall that dominated his view a hundred feet or so to his left made it easy to figure out which way Harmony was and where he needed to go.

Trying to find a good mix of speed with out falling, it felt like it was taking an eternity for him to get anywhere and all the while he was expecting to hear shouting followed by bright flashlights and gunfire at any moment. When he finally reached the cinder block wall he was exhausted and breathing hard. No vents or access panels presented themselves to him, it was just solid wall. He did not even see a single pipe coming through the brick which left Robert with the only option of climbing back down to the ground floor and sneaking his way inside. He started to retrace his steps to find a more appealing way down when a bright white light erupted through the section of tile he had moved in the conference room. He did not know if he had a few seconds or a minute, but either way Robert knew whoever was shining that light was going to be coming after him. If he had any hope of staying ahead of them he was going to have to do something, fast. Muttering a few self-deprecating remarks about himself, Robert cast his lot in with fate and jumped through the closest ceiling tile and into the unknown room below.

CHAPTER THIRTY

The ceiling tile shattered around Robert and particles of fiber board floated down like snowflakes in his wake. He had braced himself for the shock of jumping through the ceiling, but the bone jarring impact with the floor knocked his legs out from under him and sent him sprawling onto the cold concrete. The fact that none of his bones appeared to be broken along with the luck that he had not smashed into something, or someone else, had Robert partially believing in miracles.

He could hear the echoing sounds of his pursuers overhead and it motivated him to push himself to his hand and knees and then his feet. *Have to keep moving,* he kept telling himself.

The room he unceremoniously landed in was nearly pitch black and had a musty, unused smell to it. The low hum of nearby machines and the soft glow of red and green LEDs on the surrounding walls led him to believe he had landed in some sort of utility room. The only light came from the panels he could not identify and the outline of a single door that was illuminated by a bright white light leaking in around the frame.

It was not going to be long before the Pope had even more people after him in force and Robert could feel the gap in time growing smaller with each passing second. He did his best to listen at the door to determine if anyone was on the other side, but it was a fruitless effort. He found the light switch on the wall, hesitated for a second with his hand on it, and then decided to leave it off. He did not see the lights from any flashlights overhead, but he was confident that at least one knight was up there and he was not about to turn on a beacon for him to follow. Which left Robert with only one option, so with a heavy sigh he did the only thing he could and cracked the door open.

He squinted against the light. The sliver of a view before him did not offer up very much to see, but what he could was going to have to be enough to figure out his next move. He would have said that he had gotten lucky making it all the way to this point, but considering how much luck was involved in that he was starting to believe that Amber might have been on to something about mathematical probability. Peering out from his hiding spot he could see Harmony's spider like control room suspended on its steel legs a couple hundred feet away from where he was. Just outside the door there was a wide aisle and on the other side of that a network of pipes and conduits connecting to dozens of dull steel refrigerator sized boxes that could provide enough cover to keep his pursuers guessing. Or so Robert hoped.

He still did not know what had happened to everyone else. It was a dark thought filled with ugly possibilities that he had refused to think about up to this point. He was hoping anyone following him would be expecting him to flee out one of the exits and through the parking lots outside. By staying inside the plant Robert had an almost infinite number of hiding places to choose from and if he could find a good one he could at least start to try and figure out some sort of plan.

He opened the door a little bit more and took a quick survey of the immediate area. From what he could tell it looked clear at that moment, but would it be when he stepped out? He took a deep breath to calm himself and opened the door the rest of the way. He was committed to crossing the open aisle now, the no man's land, and reaching the industrial jungle beyond.

No one challenged him as he limped from the room. There were no shouts or gunfire when he disappeared behind the dull steel boxes and started snaking his way over and around not only pipes, but drums of oil and the occasional box of supplies or a tool cart. Along the way, he picked up a box cutter someone had left sitting on top of a locked rolling tool chest. It was not much of a weapon, but it was better than nothing and he knew from a personal, and painful, experience at his lab that the blade was wickedly sharp. If he could get close enough with it he would be able to do some serious damage to the person on the receiving end.

As he neared Harmony he thought he heard someone but in the dull hum of all the surrounding equipment the obscure sound was muddled. Not quite sure if what he heard was real or not he cautiously pressed on. He struggled with the urge to toss caution aside. *What if that was Jay? Or Amber,* he considered and desperately wanted to charge ahead and find out. The stress of this cat and mouse game was nearing a breaking point and it was only sheer willpower that kept him from a complete commitment to doing something suicidal.

"Any sign of Kariot?" a deep, static laced voice demanded over the sound of machinery. Robert froze. The question had come from a radio speaker very close to where he was standing.

"Negative," another voice replied. *"Emergency exit to the east and hallway access to the west are clear."*

"Alpha team, secure the office areas," a third, angrier, voice ordered. "Charlie team, if he made it outside again make sure he doesn't leave the compound alive."

"Understood," came two replies one on top of the other.

"Bravo team, sweep the plant."

"Understood."

"Unit one, have you secured surveillance yet?"

"Negative."

"You've got sixty seconds Paul or I swear I'll shoot you myself. The police are starting to show up. We need those eyes!" the deep voice threatened and then the radio chatter fell silent again.

"Seems like your boyfriend has some fight in him."

Robert froze. The man who said it was on the other side of the large stack of crates to his right. As quietly as he could he slowly edged himself to the corner and peered around. He fought to stop himself from gagging aloud at the scene that greeted him.

Amber dangled from a black nylon rope secured from Harmony's bridge. Her forearms were scraped and bloodied from where she had struggled against the bindings. Her feet swayed back and forth only a few inches off the ground and torn blood-stained clothes framed deep lacerations that crisscrossed her back. A slow, steady stream of crimson blood was falling into an ever-growing pool on the concrete floor beneath her.

Sebastian stood behind her, his back toward Robert, and had an open worker's tool chest nearby. A bloody hammer and various hand tools littered the floor at his feet. He held a battery-operated saber saw idly in his left hand,

303

the white blade covered in blood, and he clenched and unclenched his right hand into a fist. "Repent Mary," Sebastian growled looking every bit the modern-day inquisitor in his tactical gear as he tightened his fist and drove it into the torn flesh of her back. Robert watched in horror as the strike broke open her shredded skin and sprayed blood in all directions. "And after you watch me saw the flesh off Robert's body, I'll kill you quickly."

Amber howled her defiance through gritted teeth. She knew it was a vain effort, but it was all she could do. She would never give Sebastian the satisfaction of seeing her break even if she knew she already had. All she wanted was for her life to end now. For all of Sebastian's talk about killing her, which she knew he desperately wanted to do, the Pope was never going to let her go. She was going to be locked up in some underground Vatican vault, forever, but at least Robert had escaped. If nothing else she could be happy about that and dream that they would never catch him, even if it was just a lie she kept telling herself.

Robert circled back around the crates as quickly as he could to get closer to where Amber struggled to keep from sobbing. He still had no real idea what he was going to do as he emerged almost directly behind Sebastian, but the one thing he knew he was not going to do was leave her. A box cutter and a moment of surprise were the only two things he had going for him as he slowly started to advance. Surprise was going to be the key if anything else was going to work out and it was a gamble that surprise would be enough to give Robert any sort of advantage against a trained, psychopath knight of the Vatican. As Amber often pointed out to him though, it was all in the math.

He was so focused on Amber and Sebastian as he crept forward that he almost stumbled over Jay's leg. Robert could only afford a momentary glance towards the old man. He was still sitting where Robert had left him. It looked like he had lost a great deal of blood, but the slow almost imperceptible rising and falling his chest showed he was unconscious but still alive. Knowing there was little he could do to help him, Robert pushed the sorrow from his mind and focused on Sebastian's back. If he was going to have any hope at all of surviving this ordeal, then Sebastian had to be his focus. *No more time,* Robert kept repeating over and over to himself. He had heard the radio transmissions less than a minute ago. The other knights were already searching everywhere inside and out. It was no longer a matter of if they were going to find him, but when were they going to find him. *No one's backing down tonight,* he thought. *Including me.*

Sebastian focused solely on Amber's back. He could not see her closed eyes, but he heard the soft whimpering she was trying so hard to conceal. Those soft sobs were like a sweet wine to him and more intoxicating than any scream he had ever heard. She was breaking, along with everything else she had worked so hard for. All he had to do was push her over the edge and making her watch Robert Kariot die would do just that. All those months lying to him and believing she was covering up who she really was. Hiding what she was really trying to accomplish. He knew it had always been about Kariot. She had attempted to manipulate him to see the fruition of this day, a notion he found laughable.

He was so lost to the fantasy of her agony and his endless torment of her behind the Vatican's walls that he was

305

completely unaware of Robert approaching from behind until the very real, burning pain erupted as the back of his right leg was cut open. The shock was so overwhelming it threatened to buckle his legs from underneath him, but years of military training instinctively took over and guided him to retaliate. He twisted himself, shifting his weight to his good leg and allowed his momentum to lead his rage as he spun towards his assailant.

Robert was shocked at how quickly Sebastian reacted to the knife wound. He barely managed to raise his arm fast enough to block the blade of the saber saw from sinking into his neck, but the desperate move instead caused the serrated edges to sink into the top of his forearm. It was a feeling that Robert was never going to forget. It was like being stabbed and electrocuted at the same time and he unconsciously jerked his arm backwards to get away from the pain. He instantly realized his mistake as the blade cut even deeper into his arm as he tore himself free. Even the adrenaline pouring through his veins could not keep the agony at bay.

Sebastian attempted to follow up his counter attack with a left-handed jab but his injured leg refused to support him and he crashed into Robert sending the two men spiraling to the floor in a twisted heap. Entangled and off balance, it became a true struggle for self-survival as they clawed at one another.

Sebastian let go of the saber saw and hammered his forearm across Robert's face. He tried to get a hand on his throat, but Robert deflected him with an elbow across his jaw. He landed another pair of punches and still Robert fought him like a wild man. Sebastian's could feel himself growing weaker with each punch he threw. His leg wound had to be deeper than he first thought. He was losing blood fast and was going to have to end this fight quickly if he wanted to stay alive.

He's faster than me, Sebastian thought, *I've got to contain him.* He made a feint attack by pulling his arm way back for another punch and when Robert went to dodge he used his other hand to grab Robert's throat. Quickly, he sunk his fingers in the soft flesh around the man's Adam's apple with a vice like grip and then drove his good leg between Robert's knees, hard, and brought the struggle to an end.

Robert lost his breath all at once and moaned as he tried to suck it back in. Tears dripped from his eyes and all he wanted to do was curl into a ball to shield himself from the agony in his groin.

Sebastian threw his full weight on top of Robert, searing pain shooting down his spine which he pushed aside so he could wrap both of his hands around the man's throat. Leaning his weight into the hold he thrust his arms toward the floor trying to crush the life out of him. It was not how he wanted to kill him, and Amber would not see it, but he needed to end this fight now. After he took care of his leg he would drag Kariot's carcass in front of her and cut off his head.

The pressure was building behind Robert's eyes and he could feel unconsciousness approaching. His vision was tunneling into blackness and panic was setting in as he desperately tried to get Sebastian to release his hold on him. He tried to claw the man's steel like grip away from his throat and when that failed he pounded against his chest, but the pain in his groin and his light headiness both aligned against him. In those final seconds, even though he knew he was going to die, he kept pawing at Sebastian like a child clinging to the hope of a miracle. He even begged God to save him.

"Hey Sebastian," Jay weakly shouted with all the strength he had left to muster. "Remember what I told you when you started torturing Amber?"

Sebastian, basking in the euphoria of watching Robert die in his hands, turned his wicked smile of triumph towards Jay. "Yea. You were going to enjoy watching me die. Sorry to disappoint you Jay."

"You didn't," Jay murmured as blood trickled from the corner of his mouth and his lifeless head fell sideways.

CHAPTER THIRTY-ONE

Sebastian only had a moment to contemplate what Jay had said before Robert plunged the knife that had been attached to the front of Sebastian's body armor into the exposed area under his arm pit and into his chest cavity beyond. Sebastian released his strangle hold and tried to get away, yet his desperate move only caused the knife to twist even more. Through the gray haze of his blurry vision Robert thought he saw genuine surprise on Sebastian's face in the instant before he died and slid sideways off of him, as if, Sebastian had discovered some great revelation in that final moment. Grunting and gasping for air Robert curled into a fetal position and rolled away from Sebastian's corpse. He knew he needed to move, that he had to do something, but all he could think of was how much he just wanted the pain to stop.

"Amber," he called hoarsely and started dragging himself towards her. "Amber!"

Amber's eyes slowly slid open at the sound of Robert's voice. She was able to turn her head just enough to see him drag himself into her view. "I'm *so* sorry Robert. Run. If Sebastian finds you he'll kill you."

"Let's not get carried away," he replied. The sorrow in her eyes made Robert's heart ache. "He's dead after all."

Amber's eyes grew alarmed suddenly and she tried to move, but pain caused her to stop as new tears sprung from her eyes. "Sebastian's..."

"Dead," Robert finished, but it still did not seem to sink in right away.

"Dead." she whispered as the realization hit her.

"Yea," Robert answered looking at where Sebastian's lifeless body was. "Give me a minute."

He did his best to push the pain aside so he could stand and stagger over to where Sebastian was. He fell to his knees, pulled the knife free, and tried to ignore the sucking sound it made as it came out. He could hear calls coming over the radio for Sebastian and knowing that they would be rushing here when he did not respond helped Robert shake off some of the pain, but his exhaustion left room for little else. It was a struggle to stand back up and he half stumbled back to Amber. She tried to hold onto him when he cut her bonds but the two of them collapsed onto the ground together.

"Can you walk?" Robert asked her.

"Sebastian cut my spine," she answered trying to hold back the tears and conceal the pain in her voice. "Just run Robert. Get out while you can and keep running."

Seeing what Sebastian had done to her, he felt nothing but defiant rage. "I'm not going anywhere."

She was pale and loosing blood fast. How she was even still conscious Robert could not understand. Then he remembered Colorado and all the gunshot wounds she had taken. She was half dead then and was still able to walk. She was still able to point a gun at him and tell him what had to be done. *How can anyone stop a force like that*, he wondered.

"You have to," Amber pleaded. "Just go and don't stop running...ever."

Robert quickly looked around trying to figure out which way Sebastian's backup was going to come from. It

310

was a pointless attempt, they could be coming from anywhere, and if he did not figure out something fast they were going to find the two of them looking like fools. He had to admit that running sounded like a great idea. He could try to escape like she wanted but, at some point during this hell, he had decided that no matter what was about to happen to him, he was not going to leave her behind again.

His eyes came to rest on the bridge leading to the control room. He scooped Amber in his arms, growled against the pain as he stood, and started walking toward Harmony. Carrying her was going to slow him down, but if they could reach the control room in time it might offer them the only chance at salvation they were going to get.

He knew Amber did not leave much to chance, so he was gambling that there was more to that room than it appeared. He remembered that the bridge was motorized. When they had first arrived, it had been retracted against the control's room body and had to be lowered from the inside so they could go in. If the Pope had not had the systems turned off or destroyed already, then maybe he could cut power to the bridge once they were inside and buy them even more time. That was not a cure for their current crisis, but if it bought enough time for Amber to heal maybe they could still escape. So many unknowns and possibilities raced through his mind.

The attack had happened suddenly, but Robert remembered hearing gunfire after they had captured him. The knights had not been able to take over the surveillance room and the police were outside too. Although it was a tossup whose side they would be on. The news crews would be right behind the police and he was pretty sure that was something the Pope wanted to avoid. He would have to leave before the cameras got there, taking some of his men with him. It might only be a couple of them, but every fewer of them there was, the better Robert liked their odds. So much was riding on this decision. On his decision.

"Sorry," he apologized when he realized Amber was trying to say something to him, but he ignored her anyway and she stopped trying to talk to him. He hoped he was not making her wounds worse. His arms and upper body were covered in her blood and he wanted to stop, or at least slow down, to make it easier for her but he did not dare to. Time was biting at his heels. He could not afford to stop now as he stumbled his way up the outer staircase and onto the bridge. "What did you say?"

"Why?" Amber gritted her teeth and hissed through the waves of pain that washed over her every time he took a step.

"What?"

"Why ... aren't ... you ... running ... away?" she demanded, sucking in a sharp breath between words.

"Because," he answered and looked down into her pale blue eyes, eyes he could lose himself in, and smiled. "I'll always come for you."

They were only a few steps from the control room when Robert heard the murderous shouts behind him and he threw himself those few final feet along the bridge. He slammed his elbow down on the bridge control just as a burst of sub machine gun fire peppered the ceiling above him. He instinctively dropped down, nearly letting go of Amber in the process which earned him another painful gasp from her lips. He peered back over his shoulder and saw a spider web of cracks covering the closed glass door where he had just been standing and sighed in relief.

"Is there a way to shut power off to the bridge?" he asked as he laid her on the floor. If he could shut off the bridge's control system from this side, he was certain they would not be able to lower it from the other side again if there was an emergency override. Considering all the extra safety measures his lab had at the university he was confident there was something like that here as well. Amber raised her arm and pointed towards a circuit breaker panel hanging on the nearby wall. It took Robert two strides to cross the distance and throw the door open. Two rows of breakers stared back at him, each with a dozen switches, set in various states of on or off.

"Right side," she wheezed. "Near the bottom."

Robert scanned the handwritten labels, only one said anything about the bridge so he shoved the lever to off. He felt exhausted and relieved, even if it was only a momentary comfort. More bullets futilely struck the glass just as the bridge locked into place. He grabbed a first aid box off the wall and knelt next to Amber. He wrapped his bleeding arm the best he could and swallowed a handful of pain killers. He knew they were not going to have long but he was happy they were together. It was strange how his feelings for her had changed so quickly and in such a short time.

"Nice trick with the bullet proof glass," he remarked treating her smaller wounds the best he could. There was not much he could do for her so he turned and poked his head up over the control console next to the entranceway to see what was going on. Another burst of machine gun fire dotted itself along the glass.

313

Amber struggled to nod. "Double layer. At first, I wasn't going to have it installed, but my paranoia got the better of me. Guess that was a good thing," she weakly smiled up at him but it quickly disappeared as her face turned serious. "The control room has its own generator and battery backup system above us too if they cut the power. You turned off the hydraulic controls for the bridge but it's only a matter of time before they get in. Once they figure out where the hydraulic line is and cut it they'll be able to pull the bridge down."

Robert nodded and looked at the heads up displays. The system had completed its calibration cycle and was waiting to connect to the three other stations around the world. On the computer screen where Sara had sat only a short while ago he could see a single line of text: *Proceed with system link? Y/N*. A blinking cursor sat patiently at the end of the line of text, without a care in the world, waiting for someone to enter a response.

If the operator pressed 'Y', then a system wide link would be established and the operator could unify the efforts of all the drill platforms into a single purpose. If the operator pushed 'N', then the station would work independently from all the others. Theoretical, there was no limit to the number of drilling platforms that could work in unison. How powerful the operating network was dictated what could or could not be done. Looking around at all of the state-of-art equipment surrounding him, Robert had no doubt that Amber could control all the drill heads throughout the world as single working entity.

"Thank you, by the way," she said bringing his attention back towards her.

"For what?" he asked before peering over the console to see why they were no longer being shot at. Two knights stood at the top of the stairs, their light machine guns staring in Robert's direction. They did not fire at him, there was no point with him sitting behind bullet proof glass, and it looked like they were just finding out that the bridge was out.

"Coming back for me. It was pretty stupid on your part, but...but it still means a lot. I wish you had run though. You know that, don't you? You would have at least stood a chance of getting away if you did."

"Yea I know. Guess I'm just not the running type anymore." *And at least I'm not going to die alone,* he told himself. It was not that Robert was afraid of dying, but when the time came he did hope it would happen quickly. His body hurt all over. It was hard to breathe and he was more tired than he had ever felt in his life. "So, are you?"

"Am I what?" Amber grimaced as a spasm of pain shot through her as her muscles began knitting themselves back together.

"Lucifer," he said in a calm off handed manner. He figured he was dead either way so he did not really see a point in getting upset over whatever the truth really was at this stage.

"What?" she shouted with more strength than Robert thought she was capable of. "Who told you *that*?"

"John David. We met after I was captured. Apparently, he didn't want to miss the party either."

"He's here? John David is here?" The pain in her eyes was quickly replaced with rage and hate. She stared at Robert, but she was not really seeing him in front of her. She was thinking about the night she met John David and was now regretting not killing him. "What did he tell you?"

"That you're Mary Magdalene from the bible and the devil." Robert answered expecting Amber to say something to deny it, but it looked like she was thinking about what he said. "Is it true?"

"I was named Mary after my mother," Amber told him and raised her head a little showing him the pride in her eyes. "Magdala was the name of my husband's village and where I became Mary of Magdala. It was only later that history changed it to Mary Magdalene."

"So, is he telling the truth? That all this time you've been using me as a means to an end?" Robert questioned, clearly disappointed. "The truth Mary, if you please. It's not like what you say now will change what's going to happen once they get their hands on us."

"I told you I would never lie to you Robert and everything, *everything*, I've told you was the truth!" she managed to say, using her growing rage to help keep her voice steady against the pain. "Jesus *was* my brother. And after his death it was the Disciples, my brother's closest followers, that twisted the story of Mary Magdalene.

"You wanted to know where I got the scars across my back from. It was from my husband. A lashing for any wrong I did. For every time I looked him in the eye. For every time he thought I needed to know my place. And when I escaped, when I found out where Jesus was, the Disciples were the ones holding the rocks Robert. That was how his *friends* greeted me when I arrived. With curses and stones for the disrespectful wife. Jesus came to see what all the commotion was and when he saw what was about to happen he walked by them without saying a word and took me in his arms. He looked at me and spoke the famous tale about guilt, but any fool could tell he was talking directly to them. They dropped their rocks and apologized, but you could see the hate still in their eyes and they never forgot. When Jesus died, they turned against me that very day. As revenge, they tried to paint me as a whore and the devil's servant.

"But then I stopped aging and could heal any wound. On top of that I was Jesus's sister and so I became a living miracle and a symbol for the church in the beginning. During the crusades I gained influence with the Templars and later became their de facto leader. I had money, power, influence. I had an army. Until King Philip and Pope Clement turned on me and that's when I became Amber, on the very day the Templar's fell, and I have been at war with the Vatican ever since."

"Robert. Can you hear me?" John David's crisp voice interrupted her story over the intercom system.

Robert broke his gaze with her and glanced over the console to see what was going on now. John David was standing at the bridge's steps, looking up at him. One of his knights stood nearby while the rest seemed to have spread out to circle the control room. Robert could see lights being turned off across the plant, probably someone attempting to shut down power to Harmony. It was a futile effort on their part which he found oddly reassuring for reasons he could not explain.

"Is that John David?" Amber demanded and when Robert did not respond quickly enough she grabbed his hand and squeezed hard. "Is it?"

Robert ducked back down beside her and removed his hand from hers. "Yes, it's him," he shook his head and blew out the breath he had been holding before he pushed the talk button. "I can hear you."

"It doesn't have to end this way," John David implored. "Drop the bridge and give us Mary. We'll lock her away and you can go home and live your life. I promise the church will leave you alone forever. Robert, we're talking about the lives of billions of innocent people."

Robert looked back at Amber, but she had turned her head away. She was leaving the choice to him. He thought about the centuries she had dedicated her life to this cause and yet she was giving him the final say. She spoke about mathematical truths and probability but he wondered he wondered if the choice had always been his from the start.

What is my destiny? he asked himself.

He could not bring himself to believe that his life was already laid out for him and he was just following the marked trail. Yet he was here now. It no longer mattered how he got here, those events were unchangeable, but what he decided to do right now was entirely up to him. He could help her or he could turn off the machine and walk out.

Maybe John David would let him go. He doubted it, considering everything they had done so far, but if they had Amber would it matter if he was free or not. Even if they did let him go he would be forever on the move. Always looking over his back. Always wondering if each day was the day they came for him. Never sleeping soundly again out of fear of hearing the door crashing in. Yes, he would be living in a world he was familiar with, but it would never be the same as it was.

The future Amber offered was far from certain. Genocide. That is what she wanted him to do. Destroy the world and murder billions of people so she could bring it all under her control. She believed in that world and that, eventually, it would be a better world than this one. With a future that would last longer than the current path humanity was walking. In that world, whether history remembered him or not, he could never forgive himself. He was not sure he could even live in it.

He stood up, without looking at either John David or Amber, and limped over to Sara's console. He sat down and stared at the patiently inquiring screen: *Proceed with system link? Y/N.* Robert tapped a single key and hit the Enter button. A series of warning lights began illuminating overhead and beyond in the plant facility as the screen's message changed: *Link Established. Proceed with Automatic or Manual Control? A/M.* Again, he tapped a single key and hit Enter. On the screen before him a virtual synthesizer window opened and he could hear the symphony of computer hard drives spinning up behind him.

"Robert? Robert!" John David yelled over the intercom. "What are you doing?"

Robert's hands rested lightly on the keyboard as he sat and stared at the screen. He looked back over his shoulder and saw that Amber was watching him again.

"It was never an equation," he explained to her.

"I didn't think it would be. I tried running automated frequencies, but the results were never close to what I needed them to be."

"You knew it wouldn't work, but you kept trying. Why?"

319

Amber did not answer him. Instead she looked toward the door. "They'll be coming soon."

"Why, Amber?" Robert pressed knowing she was dodging the question.

"Because I never wanted to put you where you are now Robert," she told him as her voice cracked with emotion. "If there was one person I could spare from having to face this, it was you, but it just wouldn't work and I couldn't make it work. I understand, believe me I do."

"You understand what?"

"Sitting there facing the reality of what will happen if you go through with this. I'd give anything to tell you that you're going to be alright, but I'd be lying. I've lost track of the number of people I've killed. I've sent armies to kill and be killed. I've lost so many friends and loved ones. It changes you Robert."

He smiled weakly and looked at her wounds. The bleeding had slowed, her body was healing, but how much emotional damage would be left behind? How much was there already? He had never thought of that before. All the wounds, the deaths, the suffering she had to survive just to reach this point and yet he never heard her complain about what she had been through.

"What keeps you going forward?" he asked. Her blood outlined her body in a stark contrast of pale flesh against a deep crimson background and Robert found himself wondering if this was what a fallen angel looked like.

"Faith," she answered.

"Faith that what I've created will actually do what you want?"

320

She smiled at him and shook her head slightly. "Faith in God, Robert. Psalm Chapter 23: Verse 1 through 6."

A Psalm of David. The Lord is my shepherd, I shall not want. He maketh me to lie down in green pastures, he leadeth me beside the still waters. He restoreth my soul, he leadeth me in the path of righteousness for his name's sake. Yea though I walk through the valley of the shadow of death, I will fear no evil for though art with me, thy rod and thy staff they comfort me. Thou preparest a table before me in the presence of mine enemies, thou annointest my head with oil, my cup runneth over. Surely goodness and mercy shall follow me all the days of my life, and I dwell in the house of the Lord forever.

Robert found no words to respond with so he turned away. He stared at his blood covered hands. It was his blood. It was Sebastian's and Amber's blood too. Two possibilities. Two possible journeys. Two possible outcomes, neither of which was going to end well, both silently awaiting his decision.

"Your Grace?"

"Yes Robert, I'm here," John David answered immediately.

"The church had its chance," Robert said as he stood to look across the divide between himself and John David. "Now it's time to see what the Devil can do."

"No!" John David roared into the intercom. "No Robert! You can't!"

As if that was a signal, machine gun fire began peppering the bullet proof glass as Robert sat back down.

321

Eventually, after enough rounds were fired, the bullets would start breaking through, but for the first time in a long time Robert felt like there was no need to rush. He watched Harmony's control monitor as information fed onto the screen. To a normal person it looked just like a large mass of swirling random colors, but to Robert it told him everything he needed to know.

He focused his concentration as he watched the swirling pattern begin to change. His fingers danced across the keyboard, tapping letters and numbers in a seemingly random pattern. It was a struggle to keep up with so many changes and tiring on his hands as he reacted to each new variation. His eyes got sore from constantly scanning the screen. Eventually, the rainbow patterns slowly began to blend together until finally only an emerald green pulsed on the screen in front of him. Robert's hands stopped, fingers resting on the keyboard, and he looked at what he had done.

All the drills had synchronized to each other. Across the globe his creations were now working in perfect unison with each other, harmony. There was nothing anyone could do to stop it now, it was self-sustaining. Even Robert could not interfere with the natural frequency affect that had occurred. It would not last long, minutes at most, before the sonic waves began to collapse and the effect started to subside, but in that time untold horrors were going to be released upon the world.

He slowly spun his chair to face Amber. His eyes found hers as he slid down and put his back against the hard console. She did not say anything while he gazed into her frosted, glacier blue eyes and he was grateful for that. The

322

gun fire, the breaking glass, it all became background noise to him.

In the plant, John David's men had had finally cut the hydraulics holding the bridge in place and were preparing to rush the room once it was lowered. The gun fire became more sporadic, but it was too late for any of them. Robert did not care if he died after what he had done today and when the sonic backlash came from one of the closer surface drills, it hit with a horrendous vengefulness.

The sound wave struck with a physical force strong enough to drive men to their knees. Their ear drums and eyeballs began rupturing and blood streamed from their ears, eyes, and noses. The damaged sound proofing of the control room protected Amber and Robert from the worst of the affects, but their bodies felt like they were vibrating uncontrollably. Robert pulled himself off the floor to stare at what was happening. This was his doing and he was going to watch the devastation he had wrought so the nightmares would always be with him.

He could see John David through the cracked glass, clinging to the handrail on the stairs leading to the bridge and holding one hand over a bloody eye. As if it was supposed to happen John David stared back at Robert and began making the sign of the cross towards him. He collapsed in death before he could finish. The Pope, the leader of the Catholic Church and one of the most influential men on the planet was dead.

Killed by a son of Judas, Robert thought to himself.

AFTERMATH

The drills died shortly thereafter. They were now buried miles below them. The fiber and electrical lifelines that kept them and all their brethren around the world operating were being severed in the wake of the destruction. It would not be long until all the drills would be lost to history. A remnant left behind for some future archeologist to discover and ponder over their significance.

Robert lost track of time as the world he had once known crumbled around him. Seconds could just as well have been minutes or even hours as far as he could tell. The power plant's super structure shattered tossing pieces of reinforced concrete and steel into an avalanche that killed anyone inside that was unlucky enough to still be alive. Harmony's control room shuddered on its independent supports and threatened to collapse on top of them, but it held. Just as Robert knew it would.

Entire cities were crumbling around the world. Once dormant volcanoes were reawakening and new ones were being born. Some mountain ranges were growing, others were collapsing, and new ones were forming as the tectonic plates shifted. The waters of the world's oceans were being pushed aside and the resulting tidal waves and tsunamis were racing to smash into the coasts where forty percent of the world's population lived. Judgment day had finally come.

Unbeknownst to Robert, from start to finish, it took him six minutes to create an unstoppable symphony to unravel all that was created and bring a literal hell to all creatures on Earth. In six more minutes, the quakes would begin to subside and in six hours it would all be over. In the book of Genesis, it was written that it took God six days to create the heavens and the world with all things on it and then on the seventh day he rested. Robert thought about that as he sat there. He thought about how he destroyed all that god created in mere minutes. Yet, tomorrow, there would be no rest for him. Perhaps he would never rest again.

"We need to get moving Robert," Amber stated after the worst of initial shockwaves were over, but Robert just stared blankly at her. "It won't take long for the tidal waves to reach us."

He nodded but did not say anything. What he was looking at now was just the beginning of the horrors to come. Harmony had managed to crack the Earth's crust, dislodge the tectonic plates, and generate a multitude of other natural disasters. *Yes, the devastation has only just gotten started,* he thought. He was not sure what he was feeling at that moment; cold, numb, maybe it was shock. Whatever it was, Amber's calm demeanor was a beacon for him to latch onto.

"How are we going to get out of here?" he asked. He thought that he might prefer dying here as he pressed the button to open the door. Crushed by a wall of water seemed infinitely better than going out into the world and seeing what his hands had wrought. He was disappointed the system still worked and that the door opened letting the sounds of the outside pandemonium into the relative quiet of the control room.

"When Harmony was activated an automatic transmission should have been sent to a rescue helicopter to get airborne," she told him while he bent down to pick her up again. Her back was still broken, but the worst parts of her bleeding appeared to have stopped except for where the wounds were deepest.

The sounds of the surrounding destruction were deafening to Robert when he stepped onto the mangled bridge. Inside the control room he had only heard the surrounding plant falling apart, but now the death knell of the world crept in through the gaping holes in the building. Deep black smoke painted the backdrop for the wisps of gray smoke that danced through the air around them. There was an overpowering aroma of gas and chemical fumes in the air. The heat from the fires of broken pipes around the plant were uncomfortable against his skin and the constant thunderous din of distant explosions assaulted him like punches to the gut.

Although he could not see John David's body, the bodies of his knights were strewn throughout the rubble and told of the horrible deaths still to come to billions of more people. Each of Robert's senses kept adding a new level to the realism he had not been anticipating and the weight of his actions caught up to him when he was halfway across the twisted metal structure. He stopped in the chaos, unable to take another step. Denial slamming into his mind that any of this was real. It was all a nightmare. He just had to wake up. It had to be a nightmare. He really did not cause all of this.

Amber looked up at him and found his eyes pressed tightly closed, tears streaming down his face, and he began to tremble. She raised her hand and gently placed it on his cheek. There was nothing she could say to him that would help relieve the shock and the pain, or the guilt, that was going to come with this. Silently, she promised him that she

326

would always be with him and hold him when the nightmares forced him to wake up screaming in the middle of the night.

It took some time, but finally her soft touch calmed him enough for the trembling to subside and he opened his eyes again.

"What do we do now?" he whispered so softly that if she had not been so close to him she probably would have been unable to hear what he had asked.

She wrapped her arms around his neck, pulled herself up, and softly kissed his lips. "Now, we figure out a way to talk to God."

Made in the USA
Columbia, SC
12 July 2020

13714410R00180